THANE

The Fæ Prince
Of
Fir Manach

Copyright © 2012 K. R. Flanagan
All rights reserved.

Cover photo
Robert Taylor: "The Castle is on Fire in Woodford County, Kentucky on May 10, 2004"

ISBN:-10: 146795778X
ISBN-13: 978-1467957786

DEDICATION

For my dear friend Suzy Stegmaier.
If not for your encouragement,
Nathaniel would still be curled up behind the tomb.
Thanks for being my muse.

CONTENTS

1	The Siege	1
2	Lost then Found	15
3	Four Years Later...	33
4	Pointy-Eared Freak	43
5	The Battle of Flodden Field	54
6	The Raid	63
7	Hot Trod	76
8	Writtle	86
9	Taliesin the Bard	96
10	Whyte Wyndmyl Inn & Tavern	108
11	A new Life	117
12	the Nightmares Are Real	135
13	Tally's Tale	153
14	Sword Practice	162
15	Nock, Mark, Draw, Loose	177
16	Fæ Powers	188
17	Playing with Fire	195
18	Betrayed	206
19	Orphan's Secret	226
20	On the Beach with Embarr	241
21	Tír inna n-Oc	257
22	A Royal Feast	276
23	A Stranger's Aid	288

"Follow your fate, you must else,
Follow you, your fate will."

Muirghein
Fæ Goddess of the Sea

Chapter One

The Siege

Nathaniel lay awake listening to the sounds of the wind whistling through the big oak tree outside his bedroom window. Its skeletal branches whipped about wildly casting eerie shadows that stretched along his walls and crept around the corners of his bedroom to tickle the furniture with its long, dark fingers.

He snuggled deeper into the warmth of his bed and pulled the covers over his head. He wished he could go running for the comfort of his mother's arms, but he was determined not to give his best friend, Damien, yet another reason to tease him. He was trying desperately to convince himself that, at seven, he was really too old to seek the comfort of his mama's bed.

His stomach grumbled noisily.

He groaned and rolled over restlessly under the bedclothes. Now, all he could think about was how hungry he felt. He thought longingly of the pastries he'd filled full of fruit preserves and honey that morning with Martha, the castle's head cook. He had managed to eat just as much of the sweet mix as he'd scooped into the dough. When they were done, she had only let him have three of the warm, sticky treats before she shooed him out of the bakery and hid the rest. He knew exactly where she stored them; he could go get more!

Before he could change his mind, he threw the heavy blue covers off of his legs and hopped out of the bed. He stopped just long enough to grab a small yellow blanket off of the end of a chair, tossed it haphazardly across his shoulders to ward off the chilly air, then stepped out into the dark and quiet hallway. The rough stone floor felt ice cold under his feet making him regret not stopping to put on some shoes, but as he was already halfway down the stairs, he didn't want to take the time to go back.

As he snuck past the closed door to his father's library, he noticed a little crack of light just visible between the floor and the base of the door. He thought briefly of stopping to see what his father was doing, but hunger won out over curiosity. If his father saw him up, he would take him back to bed. He tiptoed toward the back of the castle and slipped silently through the heavy wooden door into the kitchens.

Nathaniel looked around to make sure he was alone before he moved further into the large room. An immense stone fireplace stood at its center. He'd seen the cooks prepare as many as three boar at one time in that fireplace, but not tonight. Tonight it was cold and empty. He knew it was going to stay that way for the next few days as most of the men had left to intercept a group of English soldiers who'd been sighted encroaching on their lands.

To his right, he could see the entrance to the dungeon and just beyond that, the door that led to his mother's gardens behind the castle. Across the room the entrances to smaller kitchens, pantries, butteries, and storerooms were dark and empty. Confident now that he was alone, Nathaniel turned left, worked his way past the fireplace, and slid eagerly through the door to the bakery with a satisfied smile. He'd made it.

Although this room was much smaller than the one he'd just walked through, all the baking for the castle was done here. Two small fireplaces were set against the far wall, and a large table dominated the center of the room. He knew it wouldn't be long before servants would be up and about warming the fireplaces and measuring out dough, so he hurried across the room.

It wasn't hard to find the pastries as Martha always put them in the same basket on the same shelf in the back of the small storeroom adjoining the bakery. Nathaniel pulled the bench away from the table, got behind it, and pushed and shoved until he had it snugged up next to the tall shelves. He climbed on the bench, reached up, and grabbed the basket that held that morning's treasures: fresh blueberry and apple pastries.

His mouth watered as he lifted the cloth cover off of the basket and the sweet, fruity smell filled his nose. He stood right there on the bench and ate his fill as honey and berry juices dribbled down his chin and onto his nightshirt. Four pastries later, he covered what was left of the treats, tossed the basket back up where it belonged, and wiped his chin with his sleeve. His sticky fingers left bits of fruit all over the wooden bench as he pushed and shoved at it until it was tucked under the table where it belonged.

Stuffed full of pastries and confident that he wouldn't be caught, he tightened the blanket around his shoulders, slipped out the door, and started down the narrow dark hall. Now that his belly was full, he was eager to climb back into his warm bed. He wound his way through the corridors toward the stairs. As he neared the library he could see that the door was open; a long, shaft of light was now spilling out into the hall. He paused to listen to the loud, angry voices. His father was arguing with someone.

Nathaniel frowned. How was he going to get past the open door without being seen by them?

He peeked around the door frame and could just see his father standing in front of the fireplace facing Zavior, a Færie like his mother. There was something different about Zavior, something that felt almost evil. Nathaniel had been happy he not been seen at the castle in the past year, as he had never liked the Færie. Zavior had always made him uneasy; now, as he stood there listening to them argue, Nathaniel got scared. Something was dreadfully wrong.

"I want the Key to the Gateways, Cianán," Zavior demanded angrily.

"It would do you no good. As you were told by the Council, the Gateways have been locked against you and those of your bloodline. You cannot wield the power of the Key," his father argued. Cianán's mane of shoulder length, black hair framed his handsome face; his keen black eyes were focused intently on Zavior.

"The years of waiting are over. I will use your son, and he will use the Key. He will open the Gateways under my direction," said Zavior.

"No!" His father drew his sword from the scabbard at his side. "As long as I draw breath, you will not harm my son," he vowed as he advanced on Zavior.

"You can do nothing to stop me. Most of your trusted warriors have been lured away to fight in your petty human quarrel over lands that will not be yours for long. They are too far away to aid you now, and they cannot be recalled in time for what is in store for you. Your castle is surrounded by my army. You are defenseless, Cianán Mag Uidhir." Zavior was tall, thin, and pale. His light hair hung loosely around his shoulders and a double braided beard dangled from his chin to rest on his chest. Dark robes swirled around his legs as if an evil breeze teased at the folds of cloth.

"You will die tonight," he promised, the braids on his chin quivering with every word, "and I will raise your son as my own. Have no fear, my righteous Lord. I will take great care of him."

"You will not get away with this." His father approached him with his sword raised threateningly in front of him.

"Who could challenge me, Cianán? Who would dare?" As Zavior spoke, he raised his right palm toward the fireplace. Red flames erupted from the cold dark hearth, and sparks flew high in the air.

"Time to introduce my latest creations to your world…meet my Roki. I think you will find them quite horrific and very effective." Zavior's eyes glittered with an unnatural red light.

The flames crackled and parted. Nathaniel gasped as one of Zavior's gruesome Roki stepped out of the fire, then another, and yet another until five unearthly beasts stood between Zavior and Cianán. Zavior stood back and watched as the snarling beasts surged forward, his arms folded nonchalantly across his chest, a satisfied sneer pasted on his pale face.

The Roki were even taller than his father; their long, hairy arms ended in vicious clawed hands. Long, snout-like mouths, lined with a ragged row of black rotting teeth; lips fixed in a snarl. Small black eyes gleamed below their thick hairy foreheads. Alive, angry, and vengeful, they attacked Cianán with nothing more than their claws and snapping jaws.

The blade of his father's sword arched high and low, again and again. Through the smoky red haze, the beasts; massive, hungry, ferocious creatures, advanced on him. Taking fear from the very air, they fed on it, seemed to grow larger and even more vicious as they fought.

A Roki slipped under the arc of Cianán's sword and swiped a large clawed hand across his father's left thigh driving Cainán to his knees. Cianán stumbled awkwardly to his feet as he drove his sword down low to take the legs out from under the attacker, before lurching around to plunge the weapon deep into the chest of another. His father staggered back in shock as the beast burst into flames and exploded into dust.

Wiping the grit out of his eyes, Cianán swung his sword in a mighty arc. Nathaniel gagged on fear and revulsion as he watched another Roki disintegrate as it was beheaded.

Despite receiving wound after wound, Cianán battled with every ounce of strength and cunning he possessed. No sooner would Cianán kill one Roki, than another would step out of the swirling fire to join the fray. It was becoming obvious to Nathaniel that his father was losing to the evil permeating the room.

If he was going to be a warrior like his father, he needed to help, to fight, but fear held Nathaniel immobilized. His arms and legs felt like lead, and he felt as if the air was being squeezed out of his chest. He couldn't move; he couldn't find his voice to call for help. All he could do was stand and watch.

"Arrrrrghhh…."

Someone grabbed his shoulder, placed a soft hand over his mouth, and pulled him away from the open door. He looked up to find his mother standing next to him, her face deathly pale.

"Shhh…" her breath whispered in his ear. "I want you to run Nathaniel…run away…hide in the catacombs below the crypt…"

Nathaniel looked into her eyes, beautiful blue eyes filled with tears, and his whole body began to tremble.

"No! I won't leave," he shook his head, mumbling through her fingers in protest.

Instead of fighting Roki, he found himself fighting his mother. She pulled him along behind her, back down the corridor, back through the quiet kitchen he had happily left just moments ago. They stopped at the door that led directly to the gardens behind the kitchens.

His mother pulled out a large pendant from inside the neck of her gown, and drew it up over her golden hair. She slipped it over his head and gently tucked the luminous pendant into his nightshirt. The weight of it lay warm and heavy against his chest. Her long fingers pushed a lock of his black hair out of his eyes, and tucked it behind his small pointed ear while she quickly pressed her lips to his forehead.

"Go. Please, Nathaniel. You can do nothing here," she whispered to him before pushing him away from her into the night. "Run now. Hide behind Monpier," she beseeched, "I will find you."

She shut the door abruptly between them.

Nathaniel stood there staring at the dark wood in front of him, torn between wanting to run away in fear and wanting to rush back into the castle to fight. Making up his mind to go back into the castle, he tugged furiously at the iron latch only to find the door locked solidly against his reentry. Panicked, he alternately pounded on it with his fists and kicked at it with his bare feet but to no avail. It wouldn't budge. She'd locked him out. He dropped his forehead against the cold door and gave up.

To his left, he heard the unmistakable sound of steel against steel and the loud angry shouts of a sword fight. He lifted his head and squinted into the darkness. The castle was under siege. He couldn't stay where he was or he would be caught in the middle of a fight, so he turned and fled into the gardens.

He threw himself under the nearest hedge of yews, shivering in the cold wind that pulled at his thin blanket. Sharp needles pricked at his fingers as he parted the thick branches of the shrub to look back at the castle. Through the skeletal limbs of the oak tree, he saw a candle flicker on in his bedroom window and the shadowy figure of his mother appear. He could see her moving around next to his bed, the bed where he should have been peacefully sleeping. What was she doing? Why didn't she run and hide? Where was his father?

A tall shadow entered the room and as the figure came into the light, Nathaniel could see that it was Zavior. The darkly cloaked figure waved her away from the bed then ripped back Nathaniel's blankets. It was obvious that he hadn't found what he had been searching for as he spun quickly back around to confront Nathaniel's mother. She tried to fight her way past the Færie but didn't even make it around the bed. Zavior threw his arms forward as if he were pushing something heavy away from himself. In a flash of blinding red light, Nathaniel's mother was gone.

Zavior spun around to the window and threw it open. A furious howl rent the air and his terrible voice bellowed magically magnified into the night, "The Prince has escaped! Find him! Bring him to me...alive!"

The sound of feet pounding on cobblestones close by jerked his attention back to the precariousness of his hiding place. Nathaniel pressed his hands to his mouth and swallowed the scream that had been rising in his throat. He held his breath as the footsteps rushed past him and around the far corner of the castle. The moment he was sure he was alone, he crawled from underneath the bushes and ran out of the garden towards the familiar outline of the stone church that stood near the edge of the old forest. He was so intent on escape that he hardly noticed the sharp stones that tore at the soles of his bare feet.

Nathaniel hesitated beside the front of the church and turned to look back. Preternatural red lightening flashed and struck the roof of the castle. It caught fire, and before long, smoke and brilliant orange flames began to pour from the upper windows. In the eerie glow of the flames, he could see hundreds of warriors and dozens of Zavior's monstrous Roki attacking the castle. Some were battering the doors with thick wooden beams, while others were scrambling over the walls like enormous black spiders.

The few guards who had been left behind to defend the castle were fighting desperately to stave off the attack, but Nathaniel could see that they were woefully outnumbered and rapidly losing ground. The noise of the battle, even from this distance, was deafening. His stomach, so recently warm and full, clenched into a painful knot as he fought to keep down the pastries he had so blissfully eaten just a short time ago.

The sharp scent of burning wood and hay reached him. The stables on the other side of the castle were most likely on fire as well. He hoped desperately that the animals had found a way to escape and that someone had been able to save his horse.

Tears were streaking down Nathaniel's face as he turned away from the fight, and snuck toward the massive burial crypt where the catacombs and Monpier's tomb lay. Nathaniel had explored it many times in the past with Damien and was usually not afraid to go there, but tonight was different. Tonight he was alone.

He hesitated when he saw two huge, misshapen, ugly soldiers guarding the front door to the tomb. A third burst out of the door behind them waving his enormous arms and shaking his head "no." He must have been searching the inside of the building.

The guards began pushing and shoving at each other, vying for the most comfortable position against the wall, as they settled back to wait. Nathaniel had to find another way in. He remembered the bolt hole, the crypt's secret escape tunnel that he and Damien had discovered last summer. He could get in through there!

He snuck around the side of the church and circled the far edge of the graveyard until he was able to approach the stone crypt from the backside of the building. He stumbled, tripped and fell forward onto his hands and knees at the base of the wall.

Nathaniel tore at the vines and leaves that were twined across the opening, and dug around in the dirt with his fingers until he felt the outline of the small trap door. The rusty handle creaked as he pulled at it with all his might. He heard his blanket tear on a jagged section of rotting wood as the heavy door swung back but he didn't care. He pushed his way through the opening and just managed to pull the door shut behind him without loosing his fingers.

Nathaniel sat in the dark for a moment panting, crying, and trying hard to catch his breath. He was so scared; he couldn't stop shaking. Leaning forward on his hands and knees, he started to crawl. He made his way through the narrow tunnel that led into the catacombs by feel alone because there was absolutely no light in the passageway. The cold packed earth beneath him sloped sharply downward. He slipped and fell on the slimy muck that layered the ground and walls around him. A burning pain seared his chin.

The putrid stench of damp and rotting plant and animal bits assaulted his nose and he gagged. The pastries weren't going to stay down any longer. He twisted around and threw up a bittersweet mess in the tunnel behind him. Gasping for breath, he wiped his mouth on his sleeve and continued to pull himself forward.

At the end of the tunnel, he sat back and used his feet to kick at the heavy wooden barrel that blocked the entrance to the tombs. It took a few good blows before the barrel rolled far enough to the side.

He pushed his body forward and crawled through the narrow hole. Rats scattered before him as he crept over small bones and detritus and tumbled headfirst into the dimly lit, dank catacombs.

Nathaniel knew exactly where he was. He was on the bottommost floor of the crypt near Monpier's tomb. Monpier had been his father's advisor, his most trusted knight, and his life long friend. He was a fierce warrior who had been killed in The Battle of Lough Erne not long after Nathaniel was born. Although his body was never found, Lord Cianán insisted on having a tomb erected in his image to honor him. Eternal Fæ flames burned from two brass torches mounted on the wall on either side of his monument. Nathaniel crawled unsteadily towards the marble slab.

He thought briefly about all the exciting times he and Damien had spent inside these musty burial chambers exploring and playing at war. They'd spent hours sitting across from Monpier's enormous tomb gazing down at the pale, still image of the fierce warrior. He was tall, or long if you consider the fact that he was laying down. His hair was parted down the middle and rested neatly on his shoulders. A sharp, slightly hooked nose protruded from below his closed eyes; eyes that, Nathaniel knew from the portrait in his father's library, had been blue. Monpier's hands were wrapped around the pummel of a long marble sword and he was dressed in a splendid marble suit of armor.

Nathaniel's knees, hands and feet were bleeding and there was a long shallow cut across his right jaw. His white nightshirt was covered in a strange mix of mud, blood and pastry fillings and what was left of his blanket was now clutched tightly around his head and shoulders.

He curled up in a tight ball on his side behind Monpier's tomb, and threw his arms over his head for protection or maybe for concealment. If he couldn't see them, maybe they wouldn't see him! His face was pressed into the cold, dirty stone floor, and he was quaking in fear.

Nathaniel's heart skipped a beat as he heard scuffling and grunting coming from across the room. He peeked out from under the dirty blanket and watched as a Roki the size of a small child appeared in the entrance of the bolt hole. It was holding a torn piece of his yellow blanket in its hand and breathing heavily. Nathaniel crawled around the back of the stone monument and peered from the other side as the beast stood up.

The creature began to swell and grow until it reached its full, gruesome size. It seemed to fill the room with malevolence. Nathaniel, eyes wide with horror, watched as it flexed its hairy arms over its head and let out a terrifying bellow, spit flying from its open mouth to spray across the room. The small piece of Nathaniel's blanket was still clutched in its filthy hand, and with its teeth bared, the beast looked fearsome and terrifying.

The beast began sniffing the air as if it was trying to discern Nathaniel's scent, swinging its head back and forth, like some horrifying travesty of a dog. That's when Nathaniel caught the stench emanating from the Roki's body and, for the third time, he gagged and struggled to swallow the bile that rose in his throat.

Frozen in fear, and certain that he was about to die, Nathaniel was startled when, in his mind, his mother's voice spoke softly,

"Nathaniel, my son, remember I love you. Know that I will always be with you."

Pieces of stone and dust rained down from the ceiling as the walls of the catacombs shook around him. Monpier's tomb started to hum and vibrate; falling dust began to swirl around Nathaniel and the tomb.

The beast lifted his ugly head and growled. It looked in Nathaniel's direction, inhaled sharply through its long hairy nose, and rushed forward, stomping toward the tomb. It was so close; he could feel its fetid breath blow across his face.

Nathaniel felt the ground beneath him rumble; the whole room shook violently. The Roki paused just inches away from him and looked up as a huge stone block broke free from the ceiling. It fell onto Monpier's tomb, splitting it down the middle. Nathaniel's insides began to burn. A blinding white and blue light exploded up and outwards from the broken tomb. In a flash, Nathaniel was gone.

Chapter Two

Lost Then Found

He opened his eyes to find his face wedged between the hard, dirt floor and a cold stone wall, his eyes inches from a fat spider who was painstakingly working the tiny threads of a cobweb. The yellow blanket tore from his shoulders as he bolted upright and scuttled away from the spider with a startled cry of surprise. It took a moment for his heart to stop pounding in his chest, and he chastised himself for being frightened by such a small creature. He stretched his arms and legs, relieved to find that although they felt sore, they were unbroken and still exactly where they should be. A long cut on his jaw dripped blood onto his filthy nightshirt. He wiped his chin with a sleeve that was covered with a strange, sweet smelling, sticky goo.

Turning so his back was against the wall, he looked around the room. He had no idea where he was. He was crouched behind a great dirty tomb in a burial chamber. The tomb had been broken in two halves, and the wooden ceiling above ripped open. Moonlight streamed in through the enormous hole, bathing the walls and the solitary tomb with an eerie silver glow. He wrinkled his nose. The room smelled like dirty old boots that had been left out in the rain too long and had never really dried out completely.

He didn't know why he was here all alone. He found he couldn't remember anything about himself. It was like he hadn't existed before he'd awoken here. He squeezed his eyes closed and tried desperately to remember something…anything. He had a vague recollection of being called "Thane" by someone, but he didn't know who. The name didn't seem quite right either, but it was all he could remember.

'Thane' wasn't sure how long he sat there leaning against the cold stone wall trying to decide what to do. Should he stay here in the relative safety of the crypt or leave to find some help? There had to be people around here somewhere; hadn't there? He finally decided that trying to find help would be preferable to sitting on the chilly ground in the dirt with the spiders.

He dragged himself out from behind the wrecked tomb on his hands and knees and cautiously crawled across the dusty floor toward the only door he could see. Scared and confused, he pressed his ear against the wood to see if he could hear anything on the other side, listening for something familiar in the night's sounds. He heard nothing but the chatter and hum of bugs so he stood up on shaking legs and struggled to ease open the heavy door. Sticking his head through the crack between the wooden door and the stone frame, he peered out into the night.

Unfortunately, it was as quiet outside as it was in the crypt. An ancient graveyard was just discernible in the moonlight between him and the dilapidated remains of a small, ancient, stone church. A thick knot of trees spread out behind the church and disappeared into the darkness beyond.

Thane slipped through the door, stepped down, and silently picked his way through the broken, moss covered headstones toward the front of the church. There were no other buildings in sight. The stone steps crumbled a bit beneath his bare feet. He stumbled forward, raised his arms to stop himself from falling and knocked his elbow on the door frame. Pain radiated up his arm. He steadied himself against the door for a moment before pulling it open and walking through.

The long, narrow room was as dreadful on the inside as it was on the outside. Cobwebs and dust layered everything. A stone alter of sorts was positioned in an alcove across from the door, and a few benches lined the side walls. He made his way to one of the unbroken benches in the far corner behind the altar and sat down. From there he had a good view of both the front and the back doors.

Thane wrapped his arms around his legs, leaned his head back, and listened to the wind whistling through the cracks in the walls and the steady hum of the bugs outside. He was so scared and cold he couldn't stop shaking. Eventually, exhaustion took its toll on his little body. He laid down and curled into a tight ball on the dirty bench. He slept sporadically for what was left of the night, jerking awake with the slightest noise only to find himself still alone in the dark and still unable to remember who he was.

卌

The first rays of dawn filtered through the broken windows. Soft, yellow sunlight pierced through the air highlighting the dust making it look like there were millions of tiny diamonds swirling in the room around him. He lay there on the hard bench and struggled to remember what had happened to him, but his memory wasn't any better this morning than it had been the night before. He still had no real idea of what he should do or where he should go and he was beginning to get hungry. He stood up and crept silently out of the church.

The building and the surrounding graveyard looked just as frightening in the soft morning sunlight as it had in the moonlight the previous night. Huge blocks of the dark stone from the church were scattered across the ground. Most of the glass in the small windows was either shattered or missing. The graveyard was overgrown with weeds, and Thane couldn't see one undamaged headstone in the fenced in yard.

Thane sat at the top of the crumbling stairs and watched the orange sun rise above the trees. He decided to look for his family. If there was a church here, surely there would be a village nearby. Maybe someone there would be able to tell him who he was and where he belonged. Thane picked a direction and began to walk.

Without the cover of trees, the sun quickly warmed him as he slowly picked his way up the grassy slope beside the church to the crest of the hill to look over the other side. He studied the countryside laid out below him. He could see for miles in every direction, but the view didn't give him much hope. There was nothing but the church behind him; below him was a forest interrupted here and there by open expanses of land. A wide ribbon of water cut through the landscape below him. He decided to head toward the water.

Thane made his way down the hill and meandered through the forest under a tall canopy of trees until he stumbled upon a narrow deer trail. The path was a bit flatter and easier on his sore, bare feet.

The sun was directly over head by the time Thane found the river. It was too wide and deep for him to cross. After taking a long drink of the cool clear water, he trudged along the river bank. He stopped many times to rest, and just as many times to cry. He was discouraged, tired, and hungry.

As evening approached, Thane walked through a large clearing and followed the trail through the trees to a quiet spot on the riverbank. His feet were scratched, cut, and bloody. As his knees and elbows had taken the brunt of more than one fall, those too were bruised and bleeding. His face was filthy and sticky with dirt and dried tears. He was exhausted. He dropped wearily to his knees in the mud next to the river.

Cupping his hands together, he bent forward to scoop up some water. His reflection stared back at him, and he wasn't surprised to see that he looked just as scared as he felt. He paused and stared down at himself. His long somewhat plump face was surrounded by shoulder length, dirty, black hair. The pointy tips of his ears were just barely visible under the matted tangle. The cut on his jaw had left blood streaked across his pale round cheeks and down his pointy chin. His black eyes stared back at him as he lent forward to drink out of his hands.

A small gold medallion, dangling from a strip of thin intricately woven leather, slipped out from under his shirt and swung back and forth from his neck. Startled, he jerked sharply back only to get it snagged on a stick in the riverbank. The medallion tore from his neck and plunked down into the mud. He scrambled to catch it before it slid further into the river but only managed to shove it and himself even deeper into the muddy river bank.

With a frustrated grunt, he reached forward again. He had to use his fingers to dig it free of the slippery muck. A thick layer of slimy mud now covered his hands, his chest and the medallion. As Thane stared down at the lumpy mess, he felt it warm in his hands. The medallion began to vibrate and glow with a silvery blue light. Startled, he dropped it again...right back into the mud.

The medallion fell dark and quiet.

Thane grabbed a long stick and poked at it. It slid a bit further away from him, but that was all. He poked it again with the stick, but it continued to lay there still and quiet. After another few pokes, he picked up the ends of the leather string between his thumb and forefinger. He held it away from his body like it might come alive and bite him.

The medallion swung innocently from his fingers...back and forth and back and forth. The mud had hardened around the medallion so that it now looked like nothing more than a dirty brown stone hanging from a thin strip of delicate leather.

Thane tried to wash the mud off it. No matter how hard he scrubbed, and scraped, the mud wouldn't come off. He even tried to bang it against another stone to break it apart, but not one piece of the mud came loose. Shrugging his shoulders, he gave up. He was too tired to care so he clumsily tied the leather around his neck and tucked the hard lump into his shirt. He wasn't sure why he didn't just leave it behind.

He walked up the bank and leaned back against a Hawthorn tree to watch the river. The water flowed swiftly past the muddy bank; tumbling over rocks and tossing about broken branches. He had walked for what seemed like forever, and he hadn't come across any people. He thought briefly that he should be grateful he hadn't come across any wild angry animals, but that just reminded him of how vulnerable he was. He started to shake again because he wasn't sure he could walk any farther and it was beginning to get dark.

Eventually, he sought refuge under the low hanging branches of a nearby bush. The moon had risen over the treetops, and, as much as it provided some light for Thane to see with, it also created eerie shadows that frightened him. He heard the same steady hum of the insects from the night before, but now he could also hear the cry of strange wild animals calling to each other and the rustling and snapping of leaves and branches as animals moved past his hiding place.

He lay awake long into the night staring through the undergrowth looking for threats. He was too afraid to close his eyes for fear that something would sneak up on him and too afraid to keep them open for fear that he would *see* what was going to sneak up on him. Somewhere close to the rushing water, he could hear the loud, rhythmic chirping of a frog. It was almost dawn before he finally fell into an exhausted sleep.

††††

The thunderous pounding of horses, the clanking and clattering of metal, and the shouts of many men's voices jolted him out of a deep sleep. His eyes flew open to find the sun hanging over the same tree tops it had set over the night before. He must have slept through the entire day!

Eager to see who was making all the noise, he rolled over and edged slowly toward the source of the commotion. He crawled on his hands and knees behind the underbrush and trees that separated the river and the clearing. He hid under a bush; his backside sticking up behind him. Parting the branches, he was shocked to see at least a hundred men setting up camp in the late afternoon light. They looked like warriors.

They were all dressed in different types of clothing. Thane saw that a few wore odd green and red patterned skirts that fell in soft folds around their knees. How peculiar he thought to himself. If the men wore skirts, what did the women wear? Many of them were dressed in simple breeches and shirts while others wore no shirts at all despite the chill in the air. Almost everyone wore the same bulky, short quilted vests above their breeches or skirts.

They all carried weapons…a lot of weapons. Some he recognized as swords, knives and lances, but others he couldn't even begin to identify. He was sure they were all very sharp.

The men were all tall and broad. Their long hair and light eyes were just visible under pointed steel helmets. They looked very different from Thane with his almost black hair and eyes. He found he had to pay close attention to understand them. They were speaking the same language he spoke, it just sounded very different to him.

Small, sturdy horses were tied to trees on the other side of the clearing and were being rubbed down and cared for by a couple of the younger men. A stooped old man leaned against a wagon barking instructions to someone just out of Thane's view. Beyond the wagon, Thane could see a large herd of cattle and sheep. What were these people doing with all that livestock in the middle of the woods? Why were there no women or children?

A handful of the men were setting up small cooking fires, while others dragged freshly killed game into the clearing and were beginning to skin and dress the meat. Bags filled with breads and cheeses were opened and wine skins were being passed around. They were laughing and talking loudly amongst themselves as they settled in around the fire to roast their kill.

As the smell of cooking meat began to fill the air, Thane's stomach started to cramp and rumble. He sat crouched in the bushes with his arms wrapped tightly around his stomach to deaden the noise; he was afraid the loud sounds would give him away. Surely they couldn't eat all that food! They didn't look like the type of people who would willingly share their meal with anyone let alone a small grubby boy. He could just hide here in the bushes until they fell asleep. Then, when it was safe, he would sneak over to the fire and take just a little bit of meat and bread. They wouldn't miss the little bit of food it would take to fill up his small belly.

It seemed like hours, before the men finally settled down and stopped talking, eating, drinking, and moving about the camp. Thane saw a tall man with long, blond hair and a dark cloak order a few men out of camp to act as sentries while the rest of the group settled around the fire. Most of them wrapped themselves up in cloaks and lay down around the fires to sleep. The old man he had noticed earlier was curled up alone next to the small wagon. Eventually, he heard grunts and snores as, one by one, they began to fall asleep.

Peeking out through the thick leaves, he watched as the guards moved to the other side of the camp. Thane figured now was as good a time as any since he wasn't sure that his stomach was going to hold out much longer. Parting the branches, he slowly moved forward on his tummy. He slunk and slithered out of the bushes, cringing as the branches shivered and snapped closed behind him. His mouth was watering and he could almost taste the bread. He crept toward the nearest fire…just a bit further…

"Urrggghhh…" Thane screamed.

He was hauled up by the back of his shirt and was flying through the air. He was held over the same fire he had been crawling toward. Dreams of lying under the bushes stuffed with meat, cheese, and bread were quickly replaced by nightmarish visions of being toasted over the fire like the game he had just watched them roast.

"What da ya think ya're doin'?" growled an angry voice from above.

Fear charged through Thane.

"Nothing," Thane answered as he twisted his small body in the air and struggled to get loose. He stopped abruptly when he looked down and realized getting loose meant dropping right into the fire below him. The heat was already burning his face, chest and arms.

"Ya was stealin' me food!" the man bellowed as he shook him over the fire again.

"No. No. I wasn't." Thane lied.

"Yeah, ya were too!" he barked.

The men who had been falling asleep around the fire started to wake. They began to grumble and squint into the darkness to see what all the fuss was about.

"Awe, Frammel, what are you grousing about?" one man said.

"Where'd ya get that boy? Le'm go and be quiet." Thane looked back to see the old man from the wagon sitting up and glaring at them. "Canna ya no see we're sleepin'?"

"I willna!" the angry voice bellowed back.

"Well then, tie 'im up till morning if ya so set on tormenting 'im. Just be quiet ya big oaf. You're keeping us awake with all ya blubbering," someone else yelled out from the dark camp.

"He was stealin' our food!" bellowed Frammel again.

"You heard Avril, put him down!" said a quiet, calm voice.

After a short pause, Frammel replied, "Yes, Cessford."

"Tie him up and give him something to eat. It has been a long day for all of us and we need our rest. We will deal with him in the morning," the disembodied voice ordered. "He is obviously no great threat."

Frammel gave Thane another shake, glared at him and tossed him to the ground. Thane landed next to a tree with a hard thump. A small piece of stale bread and an even smaller chunk of cheese were dumped in his lap. Frammel roughly tied a length of leather to his ankle. The other end was tied loosely to the tree. Thane was tethered just outside the warmth of the fire and out of reach of the leftover food.

"Don't think ya've gotten away with anythin'! I got me eyes on ya," Frammel sneered displaying a row of misshapen, crooked brown teeth. He stumped away to lie down on the other side of the fire and glare at Thane.

Defeated, Thane folded himself up as small as he could and tucked his shaking legs under his nightshirt. He devoured the food because, as awful as it tasted and as little as it was, he hadn't eaten in two days and he was starving. Shivering in the cold air, Thane huddled on the ground with his back against the rough bark of the tree and his arms wrapped around his folded knees pressing them to his chest. He rested his head against the tree and watched warily as the men slowly settled back down around the fires.

The sun had long ago sunk below the line of the trees on the other side of the camp and it was almost completely dark. The moon was hiding behind a thick layer of clouds tonight, so the only light they had was coming from the dying cooking fires. The night was full of the sound of snoring and the high pitched hum of bugs. The smell of cooked meat still hung in the air teasing Thane with its mouthwatering aroma. Last night's frog began his cheerful solo, blissfully unconcerned with Thane's plight.

This was not good. Not good at all. This strange band of rough men were holding him captive and it looked like they were going to make his life hell.

The next thing Thane knew he was being untied and roughly hauled to his feet by the man they called Frammel. Thane shook his head and blinked the sleep out of his eyes. The soft, blue-gray light of dawn was just beginning to color the campsite, and fat gray clouds were misting the air, threatening rain. The strangers had gathered their sleeping gear and were beginning to pack up. Horses were being cared for by the same men who had the chore last night, while others began to put supplies back on a rickety old wagon. The very old, wrinkled man was still ordering folks around in his low gruff voice; his arms were waving wildly and his gnarled hands were gesturing vigorously to add emphasis to each of his commands.

Frammel closed a beefy hand around Thane's upper arm and dragged him over to the fire. Thane got his first good look at the man who had been holding him captive. He was close to six feet tall with a stocky build. His hair was parted in the middle not because he appeared to be well groomed but because it seemed his thin graying hair was so dirty it was just matted down that way. Thane couldn't tell what color his eyes were as they were bloodshot and swollen half closed. His face was red and blotchy and his clothing was stained and worn. Thane wrinkled his nose in disgust at the smell of sweat, unwashed body and stale ale that wafted from Frammel's body.

"Cessford said ya was ta work off ya meal! He wants a word wi' ya first," Frammel snarled at him as he pulled him toward the largest fire in the camp.

The man everyone addressed as "Cessford" was standing next to the fire, his hands folded behind his back, staring down into the dying embers. He was even taller than Frammel, leaner and definitely better groomed. His blond hair was shoulder length and tied back from his long, sharply angled face with a black piece of cloth. He wore a long, dark cloak over one of the strange vests Thane had noticed last night. This was the man who had posted the sentries the night before.

Cessford looked up as they approached. His pale blue eyes looked Thane over with curiosity and speculation. His eyes lingered on the damp, fine linen nightgown that hung torn and filthy around Thane's body. He raised his gaze to Thane's wavy, black hair which was matted with mud and muck and tangled about his face. His brows drew down in a frown as he took in the little points of Thane's ears just visible through the dark, dirty mess of his hair. Thane's black eyes were full of fear and yet a spark of defiance flared in them as he met their leader's stare.

"What is your name?" Cessford asked.

Thane continued to meet his gaze but didn't answer.

"Who are your parents?" Cessford questioned him again. "Where are they?"

No answer from Thane. He didn't know himself so how was he going to give the man an answer?

Frammel picked him up with a beefy hand on each arm. He found himself held over the dwindling flames yet again. "The Kerr of Cessford asked ya a question! Answer him!" Frammel growled at him.

"Frammel! Enough!" Cessford commanded. "Put him down."

Frammel dropped him to the ground, but kept a firm hold on one of Thane's arms.

Cessford said, "I'm going to ask you one last time. What's your name, boy?"

"Thane?" he finally replied. It was just as much as question as an answer. He was still not at all certain that it was really his name, but it was all he had.

"So you fancy yourself a clan chief as well?" their leader replied. He was staring into Thane's eyes as if he could see right through his skull, and probe Thane's memories for the truth.

Thane just stood there, gazing blankly back at him. Clan chief? What was he talking about? Was this man their clan chief?

"And your parents…'Thane'…who are they? Where are they?" prodded Cessford again.

Another shake from Frammel and Thane mumbled, "Ah…I don't know…dead…I think." It seemed liked the right answer but why would he think they were dead when he couldn't remember anything about them.

Thane tried once again to shake himself loose from Frammel's biting hand but with little success. It was hard to think with this giant man looming over him.

"Well, Thane of the dead parents, looks like you belong to me now." The Kerr of Cessford dismissed him with a wave of his left hand and turned his attention to Thane's tormentor.

"Frammel, get him out of those nasty rags and into some clean clothes. Feed him properly and take him to Old Man Jennings. He is to ride with him. Once we get back to the village, he will be put to work in my stables. We break camp soon."

Frammel began to tug Thane away when Cessford grabbed at Frammel's dirty sleeve. "I assume responsibility for him. He is mine. Understand Frammel?" He waited until Frammel grudgingly acknowledged his orders with a grunt before he let him go, then turned and left without a backward glance.

Thane realized that Cessford was making it known to the men, specifically Frammel, that he was Cessford's property. He figured out rather quickly that it did not necessarily mean The Kerr would take any steps to ensure his safety or his wellbeing.

Thane was dragged over to the wagon and thrown on the ground next to its giant wheels. He was getting really tired of being manhandled by Frammel but didn't have the strength to fight him, so he just remained where he was. The old man hobbled out from around the front of the wagon. After a brief exchange of angry words with the old man, Frammel stumped away without a word to Thane and worse, without giving him anything to eat.

Thane looked over his newest guard. Old Man Jennings was old. There was just no other word for it. He was so stooped that he was perpetually looking down at the ground. His hair was white and so thin that you could see clear through to his scalp and the root of each individual hair, and he had tiny tufts of hair coming out of his ears. His white eyebrows were long, scraggly and sticking up in crazy directions over his faded blue eyes. He was one of the few men wearing the strange green and red skirts that Thane had seen last night.

The old man stared down at Thane in silence for so long that Thane was beginning to wonder if he had fallen asleep on his feet. Thane was just leaning forward to see if his eyes were open under those bushy white brows when Old Man Jennings looked up and grumbled "Well, 'oo in the 'ell are ya? And what 'm I s'posed ta do wi' ya?"

Old Man Jennings told him that as long as he didn't try to escape, he would be left free to move about the campsite. One wrong move on his part and he would be tied to the wagon for the remainder of the trip back to the village. Thane didn't try to leave. Where would he go?

They left the forest and followed a trail that led steadily up and down many hills and in and out of many forests of tall pine trees. It was slow going. The livestock had to be driven ahead of them as the trail was narrow and steep in some places. The beasts were not always willing to move, and it was often difficult to maneuver the wagon through tricky sections of the trail.

Thane spent that night in the wagon and woke the next morning, groggy and confused with the strange expectation that someone was going to bring him a tasty meal and help him get dressed. Instead, he was gravely disappointed to realize he would have to scrounge around the fires himself if he wanted to eat. He didn't need to worry about having anyone help him get dressed because he had only been given one set of clothes and he was already wearing them.

The trip back to the village passed in a blur for Thane. He traveled next to Old Man Jennings on the front seat of the wagon during the day. Under Old Man Jennings' animated orders, he helped pack up the camp in the morning and unpacked whatever they needed in the evening.

Thane was always hungry. By the time he was done with the work Old Man Jennings gave him, there wasn't much food left. There were only scraps and pieces of meat that none of the other men would eat. The clothing Frammel had eventually tossed him that first day was ill fitting and Frammel had given him neither boots nor a cloak. As the days progressed, he found that he was weak from hunger and exposure to the cold wet air. He could barely summon the energy to leave his makeshift bed in the cart to fight for food or a warm place at the fires.

By the time they finally arrived at the village, Thane had a fever and was too weak to leave the cart. Avril carried him to the back corner of the stables and gently laid him on a pile of horse blankets. Thane watched through half closed eyes as he turned quietly and walked away. No one had made a move to make sure that he was fed or safe on the trip back, and he was too young and small to fend for himself. It seemed to the gravely ill Thane that no one cared if he lived or died.

Chapter Three

Four Years Later...

"Thane, ya good for nothin' slug...Whe're ya...?"

A harsh voice jolted Thane out of his nightmare. His eyes popped open. Looking around, he realized he was outside under his favorite Hawthorn tree by the lake...not lying next to a dusty broken tomb in a crypt. There were no huge hairy monsters breathing their fetid breath in his face.

His nightmares were becoming more frequent, and he was finding it harder to pull himself out of the vivid dreams. He wished he could remember them, but once he woke up, he was left with only a jumble of images and intense feelings. Images would come into focus for only a moment, before slipping away to disappear into the foggy shadows of his mind. The pictures were there, just beyond his memory; barely visible through a translucent screen.

Sitting up abruptly, Thane rubbed the side of his head. He felt confused and disoriented. He shook his head again trying to clear the frightening images from his mind and rubbed the tight knot of fear from his chest with the heal of his hand. He berated himself for falling asleep. He had only meant to close his eyes for a moment, but he had not been sleeping well at night.

"Thaaaane!"

Frammel was calling his name again, but his grating voice sounded like it was getting further away. Maybe he had time to sneak back into the stables before Frammel found him. He would be in trouble again. Frammel had ordered him to clean out the horse stalls this afternoon and he would be really angry to find Thane missing and the work not done.

He scrambled up from the grass, ran up the hill, past the fenced in paddock, and around to the back door of the long wooden building. Stopping just long enough to make sure Frammel was nowhere to be seen, he slowly cracked open the door to the stables and slid inside.

He reached for the handle of the pitch fork just as Frammel slammed through the door and came into the stables behind him. The large angry man cuffed Thane in the back of his head with his beefy hand and started yelling.

"I told ya I'd tie ya up to the wall with no food if I found ya missin' again. Put ya in the back stall with them beasts ya love so much with nothin' ta eat for the night. See if that don't stop ya lazin' 'round here like some prince," Frammel bellowed in his face. Thane had to look away when he saw spit gathering in tiny white bubbles in the corners of Frammel's mouth. It was disgusting.

"Get ta work!" With one more slap to the side of Thane's head, he stormed out mumbling to himself. "I'll be back to fix ya to the stall meself!"

The pain in his head made his ears ring. A silvery light flickered briefly in Thane's dark eye's. He tightened his grip on the pitch fork, turned away from the door, and furiously began to muck out the stall. Resentment and anger at Frammel quickly replaced the fear and confusion he had felt after waking from his dream.

Thane had spent the last four years living and working as a stableboy for The Kerr Clan. They made their living as Reivers, raiding rival Scottish clans and English towns across the Borderlands. Most of the men were indifferent to Thane, often leaving him to his own devices unless they needed something from him. Frammel, on the other hand, had no compulsion against using his fists to bully, to show his displeasure, or to take his bad mood out on Thane. He saved the hardest and nastiest chores for him. Of all the men in the clan, he was the only one Thane truly hated. It had been like that between the two of them for as long as he could remember.

Thane sighed, steeling himself to be tied yet again to the back stall of the stable tonight and with no evening meal. By the time he cleaned his way through half the stables, he was feeling a bit calmer.

That evening, Frammel returned just as Thane was shutting the gate to one of the stalls. He ordered him to the back of the stables and true to his word, tied one end of a long thin leather rope to Thane's ankle and the other end to the back of the stall near his bed of horse blankets. The leather was soft and pliable, so Thane could have untied it, but it wasn't worth the bother or the beating he would get if Frammel came back and caught him loose. It was now more for show than anything else; to prove that Frammel still had some semblance of control over him.

As luck would have it, Frammel and Old Man Jennings were headed out for the evening. Many of the Reivers went to nearby towns to spend their evenings drinking in the taverns. Tonight was no exception. They would be leaving on their first major raid of the season in the morning, so several of the men were heading to the village for a last night of revelry. Thane was grateful to be left alone.

Not long after the Reivers left, Thane heard the rear stable door squeak. He looked up and smiled as Natty, the castle baker, came around the corner of the stall carrying a large covered basket in her arms. She was a big box of a woman with bright blue eyes. Her long thick graying hair was tied back with, of all things, a pretty pink ribbon. Her ample bosom and thick waist were wrapped in a greasy brown cloth that she had tied around her as an apron. She wore it as if it were armor.

"Went and got yourself in trouble with Frammel again didn't you?" she scolded him. "I knew you were in a fix when you didn't come back to the kitchen after supper. What'd you do this time?"

"I fell asleep next to the Hawthorn tree this afternoon. It's not my fault. I was going to come back and finish my chores in the stables but Frammel caught me. He's crazy. I swear!"

He scooted his body across his pile of blankets to make room for Natty to sit down. With a grunt and a sigh, she eased herself down to sit next to him. Once she was settled, she began to pull food and drinks out of the basket. "I know why I hate him, but what have I ever done to him to make him hate me so much?" Thane grumbled.

Natty looked over at him and shrugged her shoulders. "I don't know. I don't think even he knows. Eat up. You have a long trip ahead of you tomorrow, and I won't be there to make sure you get enough to eat!" she ordered as she shoved a piece of pie in his mouth.

The basket was stuffed full of meat pies, smoked fish, scones dripping in honey, and spiced cider. Once he had eaten almost everything, he put the bowls and towels in the basket and leaned contentedly back against the wall with his hands folded neatly across his stomach.

"Frammel is just an unhappy man, Thane. He has made it his life's mission to make everyone around him as miserable as he is. Unfortunately, the only one he has any influence or control over is you," Natty continued their conversation. "I heard Avril fussing at him this morning for complaining about you in the taverns again. Frammel resents that a 'black haired, black eyed outlander brat' has been taken under the protection of our clan and will grumble about you to just about anyone who will listen."

"Avril told him that clan matters need to stay within our clan and ordered him not to be talking about you outside of the village and especially not in the taverns," she huffed. "The fool! I think that was why Frammel was especially angry with you today. He doesn't like being told what to do."

"Natty? You're not part of the Kerr Clan. Doesn't Frammel resent you too? Why do you suppose Cessford's father let you stay in the village with his clan?" Thane said. "Why does The Kerr let me stay?"

"Trent Kerr had a good heart. He was a Warden of the Scottish Middle March and unlike many other wardens, he tried really hard to be fair to those clans around him. I think he felt a bit responsible for what happened to me and my village. Even though his clan didn't do it, he was still part of a society that considers reiving a respectable way of life." Natty paused for a moment then continued. "Asiag Kerr is very much his father's son. He saw something in you Thane."

"I know you feel abandoned here, but he knows everything that happens in this clan, and he will not let anything happen to you." She got awkwardly to her feet and dusted off the back of her dress. "I would be very surprised if he didn't know about our evening meetings. Now stop fussing and get some sleep."

Natty put a hand on the top of his head for a moment then bent to scoop up the basket. "Come to the bakery in the morning before you leave. I will gather some treats for you to take on the raid. Good night to you, Thane," she said before she turned and slid quietly out the back door.

Thane lay awake late into the night thinking about what she had said. Did Cessford really know that Natty had been sneaking into the stables for as long as Thane could remember?

Some nights they would sit together and talk for hours. She would tell him tales she had heard from a traveling storyteller who used to come to the village many years ago. They were fantastic fables about Færies, Kings and Queens, magical lands, enchanted gateways, dragons and horrific monsters. Those were the only times Thane felt safe and content. His belly was full, he was warm, and for just a little while, he felt the comfort of friendship. As he couldn't remember his parents, she was the closest thing to family he had.

Natty also liked to tell him about the evening he arrived at the castle. She described, in great detail, how she had been laying food out on the long table in the Great Hall, when Avril came in to make a report to The Kerr. Cessford briefly looked over at Natty standing by the table and asked Avril rather loudly about the small boy they brought back to the village. He told Cessford that the boy had been left in the stables with Old Man Jennings, and he was gravely ill. Avril wasn't confident that the boy would make it through the night. With a sideways glance at Natty, Avril left the room. Cessford caught and held her stare. She stepped forward and daringly asked to be allowed to care for the sick boy in the stables. He had raised an eyebrow at her boldness but instantly gave her his permission.

Natty left the castle and ran directly to the stables to search for Thane. She had found him lying under a dirty horse blanket in the back of a stall. He had a raging fever and wasn't conscious. She had been appalled and angry at his condition and had spent many days and nights nursing him back to health; often holding him when he cried out from horrific nightmares in his sleep.

Those first few months at the village had been the hardest on Thane. Once he recovered from his illness, he was given chores to do in the stables. Because there had been no calluses on Thane's feet and hands when he arrived, they had blistered and bled continuously. Natty had secretly cleaned and cared for the blisters as well as the many other cuts and bruises he had received. She was also the one who went to Cessford begging him to find Thane some proper boots, better fitting clothes and a warm cloak. He had agreed but made it understood that once Thane was well enough to work, he was to be left to fend for himself.

Cessford made Natty promise that she would not be seen caring for Thane. She knew the men would make things more difficult for him if they felt that an outsider was being treated in a special way. She would bring him leftover stew, bread, cheese and treats, but only late in the evening to ensure that she would not be seen.

Thane was sure that Natty was the only reason he was still alive.

Thane rolled over on his back and stared at the dark wooden rafters. He knew very little about her life before the Reivers. She had only spoken of her family to him once.

She had been married to a baker named Sam Wynn and had a small son named Isam. They lived down in Cocklaw, one of the border towns in the Scottish Middle March. She and her husband had both worked at the bakery in the small town. Isam was full of smiles and mischief and was the light of their lives. He would come to the bakery with Natty and Sam every morning. His job was to measure the flour, while Natty rolled and kneaded the dough, and Sam would work the ovens. Often, women from the village would bring their children to play with Isam while Sam baked their dough in the massive stone ovens. They were happy and content with their lives.

Late one night, Reivers from Otterburn, a rival town across the southern side of the English Border, attacked Cocklaw. The villagers fought for their little town but the raiders were fierce and well armed and they had no qualms about killing. Her husband and son died trying to defend their home. Their small house had been looted and set on fire. Natty escaped the inferno with small burns on her back and legs.

The raiders returned a number of times that fall and continued to terrorize the villagers. The Reivers carried off all of the village's winter stores leaving the locals to scrounge for whatever they could find to feed themselves and their families.

Natty had no desire to stay in a town full of memories of her husband, their son, and their horrible deaths. She begged Trent Kerr to let her stay in the village of Cessford. He agreed. She had worked in the castle kitchens and in the village bakery ever since.

Natty had told Thane that he reminded her of her son Isam and she wasn't going to let anything happen to him. She had reached out and taken his chin in her palm and rubbed his small nose with her thumb. Her sad blue eyes looked into his as she combed her fingers through his thick, dark hair, tucking it deliberately behind his pointy ear.

"Isam was full of happiness and light," she sighed. "You, on the other hand, have so much sadness in you. You have secrets Thane; secrets that I know terrify and confuse you. I remember your nightmares and how you cried out when you first came here. I know that evil Færies and monsters still haunt your dreams. Always remember that I will be here for you and I will protect you where I can."

She never spoke about her life or his nightmares again, but it helped to know that he wasn't truly alone. She was looking out for him and maybe The Kerr was too.

Thane rolled over and felt the mud medallion roll across his chest. He reached his hand into his shirt and pulled it out. It was unnaturally warm in his hand despite the coolness of the night air. He was surprised that it hadn't been seized by one of the bigger kids, but he supposed that they thought it was just a worthless rock. Thane could not recall what it looked like before it fell into the mud, but he knew that the mud covered something important.

He fell asleep clutching the lump in his hand; his dreams again full of raging fires and vicious monsters.

Chapter Four

Pointy-eared Freak

A sharp pain in his shin jolted Thane. His eyes flew open to find it was just after dawn. Frammel must have kicked him. He was looming over Thane with a scowl on his ruddy face. Was he in trouble again? It was hard to tell with Frammel as he always looked angry.

"Get up boy. Get them water skins filled and the food packs loaded on the cart," Frammel groused. He bent down, and untied Thane's leg. He kicked him again for good measure then stumped out of the stables grumbling to himself about "lazy, good for nothin's."

Thane sat up rubbing his eyes. With a sigh, he drew his feet up under him and stood. It took him a moment to fold his bedding and tuck it away in the corner next to the wall in the back of the stall. He changed into clean clothes, pulled on boots, checked to make sure his hair was covering his ears, and headed out of the stables to make his morning visit to the outhouse.

When he was done, he headed toward the main castle. He didn't sleep well last night and was having a hard time waking up. He stretched his arms to the sky and shook his head to clear the cobwebs from his fuzzy brain. He yawned as he watched the flurry of activity outside the stables. Men were rushing about completing last minute preparations for the raid. They looked just like ants did when someone stepped on their anthill. There seemed to be no rhyme or reason to their scurrying, but Thane knew everyone had a job to do or someplace to be. The Reivers were leaving the village as soon as they were packed.

The autumn nights were getting longer and colder; perfect conditions for raiding. The cows and sheep would be fat and lazy after a summer of feeding and grazing. The villagers and farmers along the Marches would be nestled into their homes much earlier in the day. They would spend the evenings in front of their fires where they felt safe and warm.

The Reivers would attack villages across the Border, into towns like Wark and down into Harbottle, stealing their livestock and plundering anything they could get their hands on that was light enough to carry on their horses. If the villagers resisted, they would fight them. If they didn't resist, the Reivers would either let them run away or just gather them up and guard them until the Reivers had rounded up the livestock and looted the homes. Unlike the Reivers that attacked Natty's village, the Kerrs tried not to kill anyone unless they were attacked and had to defend themselves. It was one of Cessford's strictest rules and no one dared to defy it.

When they were finished raiding, the livestock would be driven northwest, back across the border and up through a convoluted series of trails and passes to the Reiver's village. Once the livestock was settled in Cessford and the stolen goods were divided and distributed, they would head across the border and do it again. The Reivers would make the trip to the Border Lands at least a dozen times each season.

Thane usually accompanied the Reivers on the longer overnight raids. For the most part, his duties were simple; fetch water, care for the horses, clean the Reivers' riding equipment, and load or unload the small supply wagon. Since he had no family to claim him, he was put to work by anyone and everyone. If there was something nasty that needed doing and no one else willing to do it, Frammel would make sure Thane was given the job.

When they were not out raiding, Thane worked in the stables at the castle or in the bakery with Natty. Most days he got his chores from Old Man Jennings. Jennings had no family either, so he slept in a small room in the front of the stables when he wasn't visiting the taverns in other towns. He was not unkind to Thane as much as indifferent to him. As long as Thane did his chores in the stables and the horses were fed and well groomed, Old Man Jennings left him alone.

Thane enjoyed working in the stables. The hobby horses trusted him. He had an innate ability to know what they needed. He was always able to settle them down and get them to do what he asked. Old Man Jennings began to rely on him, even as young as he was, to train the ponies and work with the horses that were difficult.

He reached the bakery to find it empty of everyone except Natty. She was bent over a long wooden table rolling out dough. Thane rushed in and grabbed a piece of bread and cheese before it was either all packed up or devoured by the other Reivers. Natty, nodded to him without looking up from her baking. She tilted her head toward the rear of the kitchen where a little package was wrapped up. Thane nodded and sat on a low three-legged stool next to the massive stone fireplace. He chewed and watched as Natty worked the dough. Her body swayed back and forth with the motion of the rolling pin.

"Boy! Don't you go getting all kinds of comfortable! You have work to do." Natty grumbled at him without breaking her rolling rhythm. He knew better than to take her gruff attitude to heart.

Thane had been with the Reivers for more than a year when Natty went to The Kerr with a request for help in the kitchens. She pointed out that the boy, Thane, was old enough to fetch water, scrub pots and run errands for her. He agreed as long as Thane's work in the kitchens didn't interfere with his duties at the stables. Thane was very careful not to appear too friendly with her. He did not want to raise anyone's suspicion and get her into trouble.

She was able to keep a closer eye on him after that. It was easier to sneak him extra food when he had a valid reason to be around the kitchens. Thane's health improved and it wasn't long before he began to grow stronger and taller. In fact, he was now almost as tall as Natty.

Thane hopped off the bench. He dusted his hands on his breeches just as Natty looked at him.

"Don't you be wiping those dirty hands on your clothes! Don't you think they are dirty enough?" she scolded him. "Make sure you get down to the lake and wash up before you leave," she beseeched him. She nagged Thane occasionally to bathe and to keep his clothes clean.

He did as she asked. He figured it was the least he could do since she was taking a great risk sneaking him extra food.

He wrinkled his nose at her and mumbled a promise to get down to the lake before he left. She raised one eyebrow at him to let him know she understood that he hadn't promised to wash...just go down to the lake.

He stuffed the sack of cheese and pastries under his tunic and grabbed another piece of bread. With a wave and a quiet grunt of thanks, he opened the door and hurried outside.

Thane ate the bread as he walked. A group of children were playing in the center of town. Watching them always reminded him of his one disastrous attempt to join in their games.

Not long after he had started to help Natty in the kitchens, he had been sent to the village square to get a package from the apothecary. Kids were running around the square playing 'Reiver and Trod.' One of the boys held a wooden stick up in the air. It had bright green turf on the top and he was running as fast as he could. The rest of the children were running after him to steal it. Whoever caught him would lead the next Hot Trod and they would start the game over again.

Thane had stopped on his way back from the apothecary. He leaned against the well in the center of town and watched the game. A tall boy named Donny had the stick and was running toward the well. They rushed past Thane in a tangle of arms and legs. Thane put the package on the ground next to the stone wall and joined in the chase, laughing and yelling. With a sudden almost unnatural burst of speed, he pulled ahead of the group and caught the Trod. Everyone stopped.

It fell quiet. They all stared at him with wide angry blue and brown eyes that were so different from his obsidian ones.

"Get out of here…you…pointy eared freak," Donny shouted breaking the silence.

"You're ugly," another yelled.

All around him kids started to taunt and tease him.

"You smell like horse poo," a girl cried out.

A couple of older boys rushed forward and pushed him down into the dirt next to the well. They piled on top of him and began to hit him with their fists. The rest of the kids encircled them and cheered on the bullies.

"Hit him, Donny!"

"Get him," another screamed.

"Yeah!" a small girl in the back of the pack cried.

Thane struggled to get out from under the pile of boys. His already threadbare, dirty clothes were getting torn and covered in mud. His lip was bleeding and he was angry.

Just as Donny, the oldest boy in the group, swung his fist back for another punch, Thane's eyes flashed silver. A pulse of blue light shot from his body. The boys nearest Thane screamed in agony as their bodies lit up like they had been hit with a bolt of lightening. They flew away from him as if blown by a giant gust of wind.

Several of the boys were lying on the ground crying. Most of the other kids ran from the fight screaming. The adults nearest the well came rushing over to help. A small crowd gathered around Thane and the wailing boys.

Cessford and Avril watched the mayhem from a distance but didn't interfere. It wasn't long before Frammel shoved his way through the crowd. Without a word he grabbed Thane by the scruff of the neck and dragged him back to the stables.

Once there, Frammel beat him and tied him to the back stall. Frammel left orders that Thane was to be left there and given no food for three days.

Thane huddled on his horse blankets in the corner of the stables that night. He was in pain from the many cuts and bruises he had received from both the boys and Frammel and he was shaking in fear and confusion. He had no idea what had happened at the well. He was being pummeled by the bullies one minute, and the next minute all the boys were scattered on the ground around him crying.

What was that blue light?

Where did it come from?

It was all so unfair! They were the ones beating him so why was he the only one being punished? He hadn't done anything but try to join their stupid game.

Late that night, after everyone was asleep, Natty had snuck in through the backdoor of the stables. She carried a small basket with some sweet rolls, cheese and warm honeyed milk. She found Thane curled up in a tight ball on the dirty floor. Both arms were wrapped around his bruised and shaking body and his head was tucked into his knees. She sat on the floor next to him and pulled him up in her lap. Natty rocked him as he pressed the side of his face onto her ample bosom and sobbed his heart out. She gently stroked his dark hair while he cried; the basket of food lay on the floor forgotten.

After that day, he made sure that his ears were always covered by his hair and he never tried to talk or play with the village children again. The children, for their part, stayed as far away from him as they could. If they couldn't avoid him, they pretended he didn't exist; like he was invisible to them.

Thane finished up the last piece of bread as he walked past the laughing children with a sigh. He just stopped himself from wiping his hands on his breeches again. He went back into the stables to gather the few belongings he was going to take with him. He looked around to make sure no one else was in the long, dark room before he headed into the last stall. He dropped to his knees, glanced around the stables again, and pried out a large loose stone from the back wall to reveal a rectangular hole. He used the space to hide the extra food Natty snuck him as well as the other small things that he had collected over the last few years.

After spreading out his cloak on the dirt floor, he turned back to the hole and pulled out a leather sporran Natty gave him a couple years ago. It had been her husband's. It was now filled with Thane's little collection of treasures. He tied it around his waist over his loose breeches. He reached back in the hole and withdrew a couple of oilcloth wrapped packages filled with cheese and bread. He laid the bundles in the center of the woolen cloak.

Thane replaced the stone across the hole and turned to open a wooden chest next to his bedding, and pulled out the only other set of breeches and shirt he owned. He added them to his small pile and folded the cloak around his meager belongings.

He reached under his bed of horse blankets and ran his hand along the blade of the wooden practice sword that Cessford had given him when they were returning to the village after a raid last spring.

The Reivers had been camped for the night when he was ordered to report to The Kerr. Thane had found him standing next to a fire holding the wooden practice sword in his left hand and slicing it back and forth through the air as if to test its balance. Cessford glanced up as Thane joined him in front of the fire and tossed the sword casually to him. Thane fumbled and caught it just before it landed in the dirt at his feet.

"Do you recognize this?

Thane shook his head and said, "I've never seen it before."

Cessford told him he had found it in one of the cottages during the raid. Thane had been shocked when Cessford said it was his to keep and that now that Thane had his own weapon, he was officially a Reiver.

The men standing on the other side of their Chief laughed uproariously at his comment. Thane had noticed that Cessford was still staring intently at him and that he hadn't been laughing along with his men. He watched, with a strange expression on his face, as Thane clutched the sword in both hands.

Thane stammered a sincere thank you and ran away with it before Cessford could change his mind and take it back. Since The Kerr had given it to him in front of so many witnesses, no one dared to challenge Thane for it.

Thane treasured the wooden sword. It was a little longer than his arm and had strange intertwining circular designs carved into the blade. It must have been made as a practice sword for someone's child. He decided to leave it here under his blankets where it was safe. Reivers didn't steal; they raided. The punishments were severe for stealing and as everyone knew the wooden sword was Thane's, no one would dare risk a hand to take it. Nevertheless, Thane left it hidden under the blankets; no need to tempt anyone. With one last look to make sure things appeared just the way he had found them, he grabbed the wrapped bundle and went outside.

Since he still rode behind the men with Jennings and the supplies, he headed toward the small cart first. He tossed his cloak under the bench then ran back to the kitchens to help gather the provisions they would need to take on the raid.

He found Old Man Jennings already standing in the kitchens directing some of the older boys. The extra weapons had been stacked in the cart last night and the only other supplies they would be taking were wine skins, bags full of baked breads, strips of dried beef, dried fruits, nuts, and cheeses. Anything else they would need they could get on the trail.

It didn't take them long to finish packing the cart. Old Man Jennings walked slowly back toward the stables grumbling about how much time everyone wasted these days yammering instead of working. It looked like he was headed to his room to take a short nap before they headed out.

Thane had some time to himself since his part of the packing was done, so he headed down to the lake. Natty wanted him to bathe but he didn't see why he should bother. The water was very cold and he was just going to get dirty again. He decided to rinse off the visible parts and knelt down by the side of the lake to wash his face and hands.

He paused for a moment to gaze down at his reflection. He took some notice of the changes he'd begun to see in his face. His cheekbones were more angular and his chin and jaw were becoming more prominent. Thane pulled his long black hair away from the side of his head and examined his ears. The tips were pointier and more defined than they had been just last year. He was beginning to worry about how much longer he would be able to keep them hidden under his hair.

He splashed water on his face, around the back of his neck and over his hair. When he was done he stood and shook the water off his head like a dog. That should be good enough until he got back. He sat back against the Hawthorn tree and watched the orange and yellow leaves fall from the surrounding trees and float across the lake. He was not looking forward to leaving. It was going to be a long, boring, and cold trip.

Chapter Five

The Battle of Flodden Field

The late afternoon sun was a molten ball of flames pressing on the horizon when the call to ride was finally sounded by The Kerr. Thane rushed up from the lake, around the backside of the men, and hopped up on the narrow bench of the supply wagon. He had to hold on to the back of the seat as the wagon tipped and rocked when Old Man Jennings, garbed in his old green and red kilt, climbed up and settled on the bench next to him.

Although Old Man Jennings hobbled and limped as he walked, he was still agile enough to climb up on the supply wagon and strong enough to drive it, but he was very slow now and he tired easily. He was also hard of hearing, so there was never a lot of conversation when Thane rode with him. Once in a while, when he was in a particularly good mood, he would tell Thane stories of battles he had fought in and raids he had been on when he was a younger man.

As the group started forward Thane glanced back and caught sight of Natty standing in the door to the bakery. She was clutching her greasy smock in her hands and watching them as they rode away. Thane raised his hand in a little wave. He was thinking he would have to find something special on this trip to bring back for her. He sometimes brought her little things he found on the trail, around the villages, or in the towns that they raided. It was always something small: like a pretty handkerchief, silver spoon, or shiny stone that he could easily tuck in his boot or in his stockings without drawing unwanted attention.

They rode at a steady pace out of the village and down a narrow pass. Avril led the large group through a forest of tall evergreens. By the time it was completely dark, they emerged into a large open field and were headed toward the hills.

Just after midnight, the Reivers made one stop. A small river provided water for the horses, and everyone took turns relieving themselves.

Not long after they got back on the trail, Old Man Jennings leaned over to Thane and handed him the reins. "Time ya did some of the work on these trips instead of just sittin' there like some prince enjoyin' a ride in the countryside," he grumbled.

Thane preferred driving the wagon to just riding. He knew it was beginning to be difficult for Old Man Jennings to make these long trips without a break, and it gave him a chance to do something besides sit on the bench and count pine trees. The horses responded to his commands as if he had been driving wagons his whole life.

"Uh, sir? Can you tell me a story about one of the great battles you were in?" Thane hesitantly asked. "It might help pass the time."

"What'd ya say?" Old Man Jennings mumbled.

"Could you tell me a story?" Thane asked much louder this time.

"Do I look like some foppish court poet to ya boy?" Jennings growled at him.

"No, sir!" Thane quickly replied. He fell silent and waited patiently for the old man to start. He knew Jennings would bluster and complain because he didn't want to appear to be enjoying himself. The more Jennings blustered, the better the story would be. Thane had to hide his grin behind his hand as Jennings continued to grumble just under his breath.

"I ain't akin ta that tall traveler what used ta visit up ta the castle some years back," he insisted. "He'd tell all kinds a' strange tales; ya know that silly drivel 'bout monsters and Fæ folk?"

He didn't give Thane a chance to answer the question before he rambled on. "Never did know what everyone found was so interestin' about them tales because meself never took a likin' ta them stories."

"Now, our Cessford, well, he was just a young man then. He and Avril used ta follow him around askin' him all manner of stupid questions 'til I thought their tongues would fall out of their heads from all the waggin'. Fair drove the traveler mad I 'magine."

Old Man Jennings looked ahead to where The Kerr and Avril led the group and frowned at them as they rode close together. "Funny, we ain't seen hide or hair of the man in many a year. Humpf. Well then, I ain't no story teller just so's you understand," he said again.

Old Man Jennings settled back against the seat and stretched out his legs. "Did I ever tell ya 'bout the Battle of Flodden Field?" he questioned Thane.

"Ah, no, I don't think so," Thane eagerly lied. He adjusted his bottom to sit up straighter on the hard bench and grasped the reins tighter in his hands. He loved to listen to Old Man Jennings tell stories of the battles and raids he fought in. Although some stories, like the Battle of Flodden Field, were difficult to listen to as they did not end well for the Scotsmen or the Kerr Clan.

"Well, now le' me see. It started many years ago, just a few years before the big battle, when John Heron, that blighted Englishman, went and murdered our Robert Kerr. Robert was the Clan Chief and the Warden of the Scottish Middle March. There was a mighty uproar against them English that done it. We demanded vengeance for our Chief's death. That vengeance took five years in comin'." The old man began his tale.

"Now English King Henry, well, he had his greedy eyes on our bonny Scotland. He was awantin' ta call heself our Overlord. Well, I don't be needin' ta tell you that our King James wanted none of it. So King James used the murder of The Kerr as a reason ta plan an attack against England and King Henry."

Old Man Jennings took a deep breath and continued. "Our King James, he was clever he was. He went and made a deal with the French you see." Old Man Jennings squinted sideways to watch Thane maneuver the cart around some rocks in the path. When he was satisfied that they were safe, he continued. "The Scots promised ta keep the English busy fightin' on the Borderlands. Then the French could attack England and have a better chance at defeatin' them. In return for our help the French promised ta provide King James with arms and money for the fight against King Henry." Jennings paused and asked. "You followin' me boy?"

Thane nodded that he understood and waited for Old Man Jennings to continue.

Old Man Jennings paused and sighed; just as he always did at this point in the story. "It was a dreary, drizzly mornin' in early September back in 1513. Me and my boys, Jamie and Angus, well, we was gathered around a fire at the camp at the top of Flodden Hill when the call came that the English were sighted. We burned everythin' we could put our hands on ta make smoke ta hide behind. The smokescreen was so thick we could hardly see our own hands in front of our faces." He paused to spit over the side of the wagon.

Thane had heard this tale many times before but he had never heard him mention his boys. Jennings continued, "Well, them English were right surprised when the smoke cleared let me tell you. There were thousands of us ferocious Scotsman lining the rise between Flodden Hill and all the way across ta Branxton Hill. You should have seen the terror in their eyes. I think they done 'bout wet themselves ta see so many mighty Scots."

Old Man Jennings leaned in closer to Thane and whispered, "There was many a Scott that was bent over and showin' them English just what was under the back side of their kilts." He snickered as he remembered the strange sight, "and it weren't no tail!" He cackled out loud at his own joke.

"Jamie, Angus, and me, we was dug in next ta a huge cannon at the crest of the hill. Them big artillery guns was bulky and hard ta move 'round so's once we got 'em set up, that was where they was a goin' ta stay. The artillery fire was so loud we couldna heard each other curse if we wanted. Boy, I tell ya, we fought wildly."

Thane listened as he described the battle; the sounds of an artillery fight, the smell of blood, and gun powder and the screams and cries of the men as they were hit with the returning artillery fire and arrows.

"Angus was the first ta go down. He didna even see it comin'. One minute he was next ta me loadin' the gun and the next he was cut down where he stood. Me boy, he was lyin' on the ground in pieces." Old Man Jennings voice was little more than a whisper now.

"There werena nothin' left of him ta take back ta me wife. He done gone and took the low road home."

Thane had heard the Scots talk about the low road; the underground Færie paths that men who died in foreign lands took to get back to their place of birth. He wondered to himself, if he died out here, where would the Færie paths take him? Do you have to know your place of birth or would a path be chosen for you?

"One by one our cannons were destroyed," Old Man Jennings continued a bit louder, "so me and me Jamie, we grabbed our pikes and swords and joined the rest of our countrymen in a charge down the hill."

"What we didna know was there was a bog at the bottom of that hill. We couldn't maneuver ta fight and our pikes were ment ta fight horsemen not arrows and cannons. Them pikes were blasted inta kindlin' and we was strugglin' and sloggin' through bogs of peat and moss. The Scottish Army was mowed down." Old Man Jennings cleared his throat and paused as he replayed the nightmare in his mind.

"Even a mighty Scot is no match for the death cannons them English brought ta the battle. King James died on that field just like my Jamie and thousands of good Scotsmen." He said softly. He cleared his throat loudly then leaned over the side of the cart and spit on the trail again.

"It was a much smaller and much sadder group that returned ta Cessford that next day. We'd lost almost every clansman what went ta fight and our Chief, Cessford's grandfather, ta boot. Those of us that returned, why if we werena missin' a part of we body we was pretty close ta it. Me, I almost lost me own leg there." Old Man Jennings reached down and rubbed his left thigh then leaned back and stared at the dark moonless sky.

"I heard tales of some clans of Reivers from both English and Scottish Marches strippin' the dead of spoils and raidin' right inta camps and plunderin' the baggage of the armies durin' and after the battle. Them that had no pride!" he barked.

"I am proud ta tell ya, us Kerrs, we fought with loyalty ta King James and with honor for our Clan." They fell silent then; each lost in his own thoughts.

Thane had always known that Old Man Jennings had no family. He had heard clansmen say that his wife had died many years ago leaving him alone but he had always believed that the old man had never had children. He never would have guessed that his sons died in a battle. He understood now why Jennings was always so grumpy and forlorn.

Thane looked ahead at the men on the trail and for the first time he became aware of how relatively young they all were. Not one of them was older than thirty-five or forty. These men would all have been just children when that battle took place. He thought back to the older folks in the village and realized that almost all of them were women. Old Man Jennings was one of the few men his age and the only one who was still in one piece and still able to reive. It became painfully apparent to Thane that the clan was missing a whole generation of men. These people led a difficult existence in which violent unexpected death was just part of life in the Borderlands.

After a while, Old Man Jennings glanced sideways at Thane and asked, "Ya sure ya can handle me wagon?"

"Yes Sir. I think can manage," Thane replied.

"Well then, I'm a goin' ta just sit here and rest me eyes for a bit. I gots me some thinkin' ta do," the old man mumbled.

"I'll be sure to wake you, ah, I mean let you know, if I have any trouble." Thane assured him with a grin.

Old Man Jennings harrumphed a reply deep in his throat and closed his eyes. He snuggled his back into the seat as if it were lined in cushions and wiggled his legs around to make himself more comfortable. The back of the bench was no taller than shoulder high to the old man and the side of the seat turned up in a short armrest that would at least prevent him from sliding off the bench in his sleep. It didn't look all that comfortable but before long, the old man was sound asleep.

As hard as Thane tried, he couldn't avoid all the ruts and rocks on the path. Each time the wheels hit a bump; the jolt rattled and shook the cart. Old Man Jennings wobbled around but managed to remain upright and sound asleep for well through the night. Thane wrapped his woolen cloak tighter about his shoulders and concentrated on following the shadowy trail of Reivers ahead of him.

Chapter Six

The Raid

Early morning gray light was filtering through the trees by the time the Reivers stopped for the day. They would be setting up camp beside one of the many secluded rivers that were scattered about the Scottish countryside. Thane placed a hand on Old Man Jennings' shoulder and gently shook him awake. The old man snorted, slowly opened his eyes and looked around. He was a bit disoriented but quickly got his bearings. He grumbled and slowly climbed down from the cart and limped away into the bushes for some privacy.

Thane jumped off behind him. He put his hands on his lower back and stretched the kinks out of it. He was glad to be standing for a change. His backside was beginning to get numb. It took him a little time to unhitch the horses. He gathered up their reins and led them to the riverside where they eagerly bent their heads to drink the cold water. Thane glanced around and watched the Reivers rushing about the clearing; each one eager to finish his chores so he could relax.

As the sun rose above the trees, he could see that many fires were lit, and food was already passed around by those whose jobs were done. Dozens of men were gathered around the fires in loose circles eating, drinking, swapping battle stories and singing ballads about some of Scotland's great heroes.

It was at times like these that Thane felt the loneliest. No other children were ever allowed to be taken on raids. Even if there were other children around, Thane would not have been welcome among them. He was too young to be included in the men's circles so more often than not he was left to entertain himself. Raids with the Reivers were just plain boring.

After the meal was finished, the Reivers paired up to train and spar. Sometimes they used swords, sometimes knives, and sometimes just fists. Thane sat on an enormous rock just outside of the circle of men and watched them drill. He laughed as Avril took a swing with his sword at his cousin, William. He hit him in the upper arm with the flat side of the blade. Frammel was fighting young Angus and winning, not because he was greatly skilled but because he was twice the size of the younger man. The Kerr was walking among the men making suggestions or comments.

Thane scrutinized every detail of every move the men made so he could reenact them with his wooden sword. Some evenings, back in the village, he would sneak out and pretend to fight with his favorite Hawthorn tree at the edge of the river behind the stables. He would close his eyes and envision himself to be over six feet tall, broad shouldered, muscular and fierce. He would swing his sword back and forth, slashing and jabbing at his imaginary foe. He would pretend it was Frammel. He could almost hear the steel of his blade striking Frammel's sword. He could picture Frammel's defeat and hear the grunts and groans of the older man as he begged for mercy.

Thane wished that he had brought his wooden sword so he could practice too. He looked over to where Cessford was standing and realized that the man was staring at him. He wasn't doing anything wrong but decided it was time to leave before someone found something unpleasant for him to do.

The training was breaking up anyway. They were beginning to gather their swords and knives. The Reivers would not be leaving again until the cover of darkness. The men who were not on patrol were taking advantage of the long wait to catch up on their sleep and were curling up next to the warmth of the fires.

Thane jumped off the rock and headed back to the wagon. It had been a long night and he too was tired. The sun was directly overhead but it was barely visible through a thick layer of clouds. It was very cold. He wrapped his wool cloak tightly around himself for warmth and lay down near the fire Old Man Jennings had made. He stretched out on his back and gazed at the yellow and orange leaves swaying on the trees above him. It wasn't long before his eyes began to droop. He was lulled to sleep by the snores and grunts of the men around him.

††††

Old Man Jennings shook Thane awake just before sunset. It took Thane a moment to remember where he was and why he was sleeping on the hard, cold ground.

"Go get somethin' to eat. We're heading out within the hour." Old Man Jennings grunted at him as he limped toward the supply cart.

Thane mumbled his assent, then headed into the bushes to take care of his full bladder. It was going to be a long hard ride and they weren't going to be making any stops. After the sun set, they would be traveling to an even more secluded clearing where they would set up a base camp on the Scottish side of the Border. Once there, a large contingent of Reivers would be assigned to defend the site while others would be sent out to raid. Thane always stayed with Old Man Jennings. They would wait for the stolen cattle and sheep to be driven to them by the raiders. The wait was always dark, cold, and even more boring than the ride out since they couldn't light a fire for fear of being discovered.

Thane returned to the wagon to find that the old man had wandered away. He dug under the bench and pulled out the packages of food Natty had put together for him. Leaning back against the side of the cart, he munched on some of the dark bread and cheese. He was just rewrapping the leftovers when Cessford walked over to the supply cart and stopped next to him.

Thane swallowed quickly and shoved the package under the seat. He straightened up and said, "Sir?"

The Kerr leaned an arm against the side of the cart and asked Thane, "Are you busy?"

"Ahhh, no Sir. I mean yes Sir. I'm supposed to be fetching the horses for the cart," Thane stammered. He was sure he was going to be reprimanded for sneaking food or for lazing about when he should have been working. "I was just headed over to the river," he assured him and turned to walk away.

"Just a moment longer if you will. I wanted to speak to you alone." Cessford put a hand on Thane's shoulder to stop him from scurrying away. He looked around the camp to make sure no one was listening or watching them. Satisfied that they were unobserved; he looked into Thane's eyes and continued, "Thane, I want you to tell me the truth. Do you remember anything, anything at all from before we found you?"

Thane relaxed a little when he realized he wasn't in trouble and thought hard about the question. "Not much really," he could honestly say. "I only remember waking up in some kind of old crypt. I crept across a graveyard and spent the night in an old crumbling church. From there, I just remember walking for hours until you captured me…I mean took me in," he amended nervously.

Cessford frowned at his interpretation of their first meeting but didn't say anything. He dropped his hand from Thane's shoulder and folded his arms across his chest.

"Really, Sir that's all I remember" Thane insisted. He shifted his weight from one foot to the other. He was not used to speaking with the leader of the clan.

"I believe you," Cessford glanced around again before continuing, "I may have some knowledge concerning your past. I have heard tales of a people from across the seas that have your…features." Cessford paused as his eyes flickered to the hair covering Thane's ears. "I will tell you all I know upon our return to the castle. There is not time now and we may be overheard. What I don't understand is how you could have made your way from there to here all alone," he said almost to himself.

Thane stood there and gaped at him. He didn't have the faintest idea what he was talking about. As far as he knew, he'd never been near the sea. If The Kerr knew something about his past, why did he wait so long to tell him?

"Why are you telling me this now, Sir?" Thane asked.

Cessford shrugged his shoulders and said, "I have an uneasy feeling about...leaving you behind at the camp tonight. I want you to accompany me on the raid. You are more than old enough now to learn to fight. You must learn how to defend yourself."

Thane noted that he didn't really answer his question.

He was sure he was joking until Cessford unfolded his arms and pulled a small sheathed dirk from inside the folds of his cloak. He held it out to him. Thane took it and pulled the knife from the sheath. The blade was slightly angled and blunt along one side and straight and lethally sharp on the other. Both the blade and its casing were etched with an intricate drawing of circles and ribbons. Thane was surprised by the design; it was the same as his practice sword.

"I don't understand. This looks just like the sword you gave me in the spring," Thane blurted out in surprise.

"We'll discuss that upon our return to the castle as well. There is not sufficient time to explain and right now you must be protected. Be ready. We leave within the hour. You will ride with me and assist me as needed." He paused as if he wanted to say something else but apparently changed his mind as he turned on his heel and walked away without another word.

Thane stood there with his mouth hanging open. Before he could think through the implications of what The Kerr had said, Old Man Jennings was ambling back and barking at him to hitch the horses to the supply cart.

The Reivers were packed and on their way within the hour. They wound their way through hidden trails and dense forests. After a couple uneventful hours of hard riding, they burst through the forest to find themselves at the edge of a large meadow. They were surrounded on three sides by trees and a tall rocky hill rose sharply up from the remaining side of the clearing. A burn cut through the rock face providing a much needed supply of fresh water.

No time was wasted in assigning duties. Everyone was scurrying around making preparations for the night's activities. Cessford was standing over a drawing on the ground finalizing his plans. He would be leading a raiding party across the Border to a small English village that was an hour's ride from the base camp. Avril was leaning over a similar drawing organizing a simultaneous attack on a handful of farms in a secluded English valley.

Thane was summoned to The Kerr's side. The men were already assembled around him and were receiving final instructions. Every Reiver had a sword hanging from a wide belt at their waist and an assortment of knives and weapons strapped to their arms, legs, back and other parts of their bodies they could quickly reach. They were all wearing pointed steel bonnets on their heads and thick quilted vests lined with plates of steel for protection over their usual myriad styles of clothing.

Cessford paused to toss Thane a helmet and a steel lined vest. "Here, put these on," he ordered Thane. "You will be riding Bandy. Take care not to fall off." Thane felt his face heat up as some of the men chuckled.

"Yes, Sir," Thane replied. He quickly donned the strange items. He felt awkward and ungainly as they were very heavy and much too big for him.

He was not given a sword so he took a length of leather and tied the sheath of the knife to his belt so he could get to it quickly. He caught the eye of more than one Reiver as they snickered at him and whispered amongst themselves. He obviously looked as ridiculous as he felt. He was still wondering why he was being included. Thane looked at the fierce warriors around him; he felt unprepared and ill-suited for the upcoming raid. He was beginning to get a sick feeling in the pit of his stomach. It was one thing to wait at a boring campsite for the returning Reivers and quite another to actually be expected to participate in a raid.

"We ride." The Kerr passed the word quietly to the gathered men.

They mounted the surefooted and swift hobby horses and split into two groups. One group gathered around The Kerr and the other around Avril. Dozens of Reivers charged out of the camp, and despite the frightening speed they were traveling, they were relatively soundless.

In the past, Thane had only ridden a hobby horse around the gated paddocks back at the castle where it hadn't really been able to gather much speed. It was an entirely different experience riding among the Reivers. He hoped he would be able to stay astride his small horse because at the pace they were riding, he would be lucky not to be thrown off and left behind in some bush in the middle of the English March.

The Kerr led them through narrow passes, wide fields and up and down countless hills. Thane was hopelessly turned around. He hoped that his horse knew where it was going, because it was so dark he could barely make out the man in front of him let alone see any kind of trail. His hair under the wobbly steel bonnet was whipping around his face as he desperately gripped the reins and held on tightly to the horse. The wild ride seemed as if it would last forever. They finally came to an abrupt stop in a dense copse of trees just outside the main road to a small village.

Thane knew that their greatest advantage would be surprise, speed and cover of the complete darkness of the moonless night. Two Reivers were sent ahead to investigate the village while the remaining men hid in the forest. Cessford signaled to Thane to join him. It wasn't long before the scouts returned to report to The Kerr that the villagers were all settled in for the night.

Thane stayed behind the tall Clan Chief and listened as the scouts described the layout of the intended mark. Eleven buildings encircled a large town square. Almost half had enclosures for livestock. The one road led into the middle of the town. No guards were posted and all the homes were dark.

Thane could feel the tension and excitement in the Reivers as The Kerr split them up into smaller details and gave them their final orders. Frammel was sent with the group that would be removing the villagers from their homes. His size and nasty demeanor were perfectly suited to terrorizing the villagers into quick submission and rousting them out of their homes with little resistance. Thane was ordered to wait at the end of the road with the Reivers who would be driving the livestock out of the town.

The Kerr sat on his horse with his sword in his left hand. He raised it high in the air. All eyes were on him. In one swift motion, he lowered it to point at the village and with a terrifying roar; he led the charge into the town.

The assault was deafening. The Reivers were making as much noise as possible to scare and confuse the townsfolk. Thane's heart was pounding in his throat as the Reivers hopped off of their horses and forced their way through homes and shops. The English villagers and their families were seized and forced into the town square and guarded. Though they offered little resistance, Thane saw that a few managed to escape into the forest. The Reivers stuffed bags full of silver pieces, wheat, honey, bolts of material, and anything else they could carry that they thought might be valuable.

Thane felt a sick pain in the pit of his stomach as he watched the villagers. They were huddled together as they watched the looting of their homes. Their expressions varied from anger and fear to resignation and surrender. It was obviously not the first time the village had been raided and Thane was sure the villagers believed it wouldn't be the last.

Cattle, sheep, and a couple horses were gathered up and driven from their fields and out of their stables. They were chased and prodded until they were clustered together at the end of the road where Thane and a half dozen other Reivers waited.

Thane jumped off his horse to help herd the animals and get them all pointed and moving in the right direction. He swung ropes over the heads of the two stolen horses and began to croon to them to try to settle the terrified animals. He had been ordered to keep hold of the ropes and would be responsible for leading them back to camp.

Before long, The Kerr was back and leading the retreat from the town. It was slow going as they had to continually drive the livestock ahead of them. The Reivers who were guarding the villagers had orders to stay behind for a short while to allow the rest of the group to escape with the slower animals. The guards would be retreating from the village in a different direction. They would lead anyone who might follow them away from the slow moving group, then they would double back to the camp.

Thane thought they would never get back to the campsite as they too often doubled back and headed in the opposite direction. A number of times, he heard The Kerr signal to men who were hidden along the trail. Thane couldn't see them, but he knew that Reivers were set up at intervals along the path to attack any English Hot Trod that might try to follow them.

It was just after dawn when the Reivers rode back into the camp driving cattle and sheep through the mist. Avril's group was already there. They were in an exceptionally good mood. In fact, the Reivers were jubilant that they had not been followed. Thane was tired. The excitement had waned half way back to camp and the retreat was not yet over. They needed to put as much distance between the villages they had raided and themselves as quickly as possible. They would not be stopping at the campsite for long.

Spoils that were too large to carry on the backs of the horses were quickly loaded onto the supply cart. The rest of the stolen items were divided up and stuffed into saddlebags. The returning Reivers devoured a quick meal of bread, cheese and ale. When the excited group was finally ready, the call to ride was sounded.

Once again, The Kerr plotted a route that was convoluted and nothing like the path they had taken to get to the Border. The new trail twisted and turned and often doubled back on itself in an attempt to confuse anyone who might be following them. They didn't want to lead anyone back to their village.

The Reivers traveled as fast as they were able while driving the livestock ahead of them. Thane led the two stolen horses and although the horses would have been able to travel swiftly; the livestock couldn't. The slow pace had him on edge and repeatedly looking over his shoulder for the English.

Thane couldn't see Old Man Jennings but he knew he was driving the cart alone near the back of the group. Thane would have liked to have ridden nearer to him. He desperately wanted to talk to someone about the raid.

When they finally stopped for the night, everyone was too exhausted to do much more than eat. Guards were posted around the camp and everyone else settled around fires for some well earned rest.

The Reivers never shared their spoils with Thane even though he worked just as hard as everyone else during the raids. He was sure that this raid wouldn't be any different regardless of the fact that he had actually participated in the raid. Sometimes, on nights like tonight when the men were tired and busy talking around the fires, he would help himself to something small from the things the Reivers had lifted from the village. He never pocketed anything that hadn't been taken from a raid and it was almost always something for Natty.

Thane easily moved about the camp unnoticed. He walked among the pile of saddlebags that were stuffed full of stolen goods. Glancing around to make sure no one was watching him; he slipped his hand into the nearest bag. It just happened to belong to Frammel. He ran his fingers through the property the Reiver had stolen. After all these years, he was pretty good at guessing what the objects were that he was touching without having to actually pull them out. He felt his way through packets of food, some cups, a dull knife and a ribbon.

Weaving his fingers through the ribbon, he slid it out of the bag. It was bright blue with little yellow embroidered flowers, and it was as long as his body. What on earth would Frammel want with such a pretty ribbon? It wasn't like he had anyone to give it to, and Natty would love it. She would fuss and grumble and complain but he knew she would love it. He glanced around again to make sure no one was watching, stuffed it in his boot then casually sauntered away to lay down next to the supply cart with a satisfied smile.

Chapter Seven

Hot Trod

The Reivers were up and about before sunrise the next morning. Some men were passing around dried beef and bread; others removed their whiskers with the edge of a knife blade, while a few more were gathered around in groups talking quietly amongst themselves. Thane gathered his few belongings, including the steel bonnet and vest. He tied them to the back of one of the horses they had taken from the English. Old Man Jennings would be riding in the cart by himself again. When everyone was done eating, they began to pack up camp once again. It wasn't long before they got back on their horses.

They were beginning the second most dangerous part of the journey. The journey back to the Reiver village was always harder and took much longer than the trip out, and this trip was no exception. The livestock, normally slow, lumbering beasts, were even more so now as they were scared and tired. They stopped often and were difficult to get moving again. Everyone took turns riding behind the animals making noise and shooing them in the right direction. They were driven up and around to the Northwest, then along a path that led east toward their village.

Once they reached the Cheviot Hills, it became even harder to manage the livestock on the constricted trails that weaved through the rolling hills. Their defenses were spread out along the long line of men and beasts and it was much harder to protect the large vulnerable group.

Surprisingly, there was no trouble on the return trip. Just three days after the raid, and they were almost back to the village. The Reivers were anxious to get home, and they began to get a bit careless. Even Thane had stopped looking over his shoulder. The rear guards pulled in closer to the main body of men and were making preparations for entering the village along with the rest of the Reivers.

Many of them were telling jokes and making plans to go to the village tavern that evening. Everyone was eager to see their families, have a decent warm meal, and spend the night in a warm comfortable bed. Thane was no exception. He was secretly hoping that Natty would bring him some stew and some sweet milk and sit for a while to listen to his adventure. He was looking forward to spending the night tucked into his warm horse blanket bed in the back of the stable.

Thane came out of his daydream to see that they were already at the entrance to the village. The livestock were driven in through the gates to the fields along the Northwest side of the village. Thane rode one of the stolen horses behind the supply cart. He noticed that Old Man Jennings was hunched over his reins quite a bit more than usual this afternoon. Thane had offered to switch places with him but he was gruffly told by the old man to mind his own business. The trips were much harder on Old Man Jennings than they used to be, but he adamantly refused to be left behind. "I'd 'ave plenty o' time to be left behind when I'm dead!" He growled at anyone who had the nerve to suggest he stay back.

Thane and Old Man Jennings parted from the main group of Reivers, turned left, and crossed through the side of the village. They had to weave their way through hundreds of villagers who were milling around looking for their loved ones. They headed toward the castle with a dozen Reivers who were tasked with unloading the cart of stolen goods.

"Get those beasts into the stables and back out 'ere to help unload this cart," ordered Old Man Jennings in his gravely voice. "Don't be taken all day boy; me bed awaits me!" He grumbled.

As they approached the yard in front of the stables, he saw the door to the bakery open and Natty step out. She nodded and waved to him as she headed toward the center of the village to join the women gossiping at the well.

From behind the cart, Thane heard a wild whoop and the sound of horses thundering into the village. Arrows began to fly over head. Women and children started to run; screaming in fear and confusion. His horse whinnied in terror and bolted; carrying him straight toward the stables as if it sensed that safety would be found in the long wooden building.

Thane jumped off of the frightened animal, rolled in the dirt and scrambled awkwardly to his feet. He followed the horse into the stables desperately searching for something to use as a weapon. It was very dark inside after the brightness of the daylight and it took a few seconds for his eyes to adjust. Those few seconds seemed to last forever as the screams and cries from the battle outside filled him with terror.

Thane rushed through the stables to the last stall where he kept his things. He was thankful he knew every inch of the place so he was able to move swiftly and easily through the dark building. He quickly unearthed his practice sword from beneath his pile of horse blankets, grabbed it by the hilt and stumbled back outside to join the fight. Not once did he remember that he had a sharp dirk strapped to his side.

Thane found himself in a maelstrom of death and destruction. The Reivers who were still mounted when the attack began, had come about to meet the advancing soldiers head on, while those on foot were confronting the invaders with any kind of weapon they could lay their hands on. They were all fighting fiercely to defend their village. Thane watched the surrounding battle unsure of what to do.

That's when he spotted Old Man Jennings. He was struggling to control the wagon as the horses were bolting away from the noise in fear. He just didn't have the strength he needed to reign in the runaway horses. Thane watched in horror as the wagon tipped over scattering wine skins, bags, stolen goods, and the old man leaving a long trail of wreckage strewn across the ground from the stables to the forest. The old man lay twisted and unmoving, half buried among the spilled supplies.

The horses continued to drag the remains of the wagon away from the fight in a panicked frenzy. They headed straight into a little copse of trees behind the stables. They tangled themselves and their reins in the branches and brambles of the bushes. The horses were desperately struggling to break free; their frightened panicked screams were almost lost in the noise of the surrounding fight.

One of the soldiers rode into the middle of the fight carrying a piece of burning turf held high on a pike, proudly displaying it like a standard. It was the Border Marches' symbol of a Hot Trod, of legal retaliation against Reivers. Thane remembered it meant that the soldiers pursuing the Reivers had right of entry into the village with unlimited license to murder and destroy for as long as the turf burned. That was why they had had such an easy time in the Marches; they had been set up. What was worse was that they had become complacent with their easy victory and had lowered their guard. They had easily been followed back to the village by the heavily armed soldiers of the English Middle March.

Thane looked across the village square and realized that he couldn't see Natty. She had been standing just beside the well with a small group of women and children. He ran toward the place where he had last seen her and as he rounded the side of the well, his stomach clenched in fear. She was lying face down on the ground behind the well with a pool of blood spreading out from under her.

With a cry of denial, he threw down his wooden sword, dropped to his knees at her side and rolled her gently over onto her back. He could see the broken shaft of an arrow jutting out of her greasy apron; the fletching lying in the dirt next to her. Blood was covering the grease stains and dripping onto the ground around her. Natty's blue eyes fluttered opened. She stared into Thane's frightened eyes.

"You need to leave. It is not safe here for you any more. You've been found. We know what you are Thane, and you don't belong here. You need to leave." She coughed and blood trickled from the corner of her lips.

"What? Thane shook his head. "I won't leave you. I can get you to the stables. You'll be safe there. I can take care of you." He gathered her up in his lap just as she had done for him so many times before.

"No! No! You must leave me and go. You can do nothing here," Natty whispered.

Thane's eyes widened in shock, as cold flushed through his veins paralyzing him.

"No! Not again!" he thought as visions of himself being pulled through dark stone halls momentarily blinded him.

Natty reached up and clutched his tunic and gave him a surprisingly hard shake. He looked down into her eyes as she pulled him closer.

"Thane...run," she whispered. "The Kerr will hold them here long enough for you to get away." She coughed up more blood. He was unwilling to leave her. "Please...hide, Thane."

Thane's eyes flashed bright with silver light and he shook his head in pain and denial.

"I don't understand."

She didn't answer. Her hand clutched his tunic tightly once more, then it fell to her side. Her sweet blue eyes were wide and empty.

"I WILL NOT HIDE!" he yelled to the sky.

On the ground next to her hand was the bright blue ribbon he had taken for her. It must have slipped out of his boot when he knelt down. It lay there looking happy and cheerful, absurdly out of place with death surrounding them.

"NATTY!" Fear and pain exploded in his chest; pressing down on him; he couldn't breathe.

"No! No! No!" he cried, as he held her tightly, his face pressed to her head as he struggled to catch his breath. He held her and rocked her lifeless body. Tears ran unchecked down his face and dripped into her soft gray hair. The battle raged around him unheard and unseen. His whole world had collapsed in on him and all he was aware of was Natty; the battle was just a buzz of noise ringing in his ears.

He finally looked up and was almost shocked to see the soldiers and Reivers still fighting fiercely all around him. Sheep were scattered among the fighting men bleating. Most of the cattle had lumbered away to find safety in the fields outside the village.

Through his tears, he watched as Frammel turned to fight an attacking soldier. As mean and as fierce a fighter as Frammel was, his moves looked lumbering and slow compared to the seasoned practiced moves of the English soldier he fought. He was no match for a fully armed and trained warrior.

In one clean lunge, the soldier ran his sword through Frammel's thick middle. Frammel stood still for just a heart beat then slid from the sword and fell slowly back. His heavy lidded eyes widened in shocked surprise as he went down. Thane could finally see the color of his eyes. They were pale blue.

Avril was swinging his sword left and right, right and left, but he couldn't break through the advancing soldier's attack long enough to strike a solid blow against him. His sword was knocked out of his hand. Thane watched as Avril pulled a knife out of his boot and charged at the man. Before Avril could use the knife, he was hit hard on the side of the head with the hilt of the soldier's sword. He fell to the ground as the Englishman turned to attack another Reiver.

Everywhere Thane looked, Reivers were being attacked. Though they were fighting desperately; they were still losing. There were too many English soldiers and he was afraid they were too badly outnumbered to survive. He watched, in shock as forces of the English March began to ride through the village setting the buildings on fire, setting livestock free, and looting the houses.

A number of women and children began fleeing the village square while others remained huddled against buildings holding on to each other in fear and confusion. Countless more were scattered within the mêlée cradling wounded loved ones in their arms or kneeling over the dead wailing in grief.

Thane didn't know what to do. He knew he wasn't strong enough to carry Natty, but he couldn't just leave her alone. He looked around for help and spotted The Kerr.

The Clan Chief was one of the few Reivers still astride his horse. He held his sword tightly in his left hand and he gripped a knife in his right. He was fighting against two soldiers at once. He knocked one down with a kick to the chest, while he sliced across another's stomach. He looked up and scanned the carnage as if searching for someone. His gaze met Thane's from across the square, and time seemed to slow down. Cessford's eyes widened when he saw Natty in Thane's arms.

"Run!" he mouthed to Thane before he turned his attention back to the battle.

The Kerr was assaulted from the other side of his horse by two more soldiers. He slashed and jabbed and blocked but only managed to take down one man when a third soldier joined the fight. Thane watched in terror as the last soldier managed to drag Cessford from his horse and out of sight.

Thane shivered in fear as he continued to watch the square from the well. Amidst the chaos, noise, and confusion of the fight, he spotted a man who stood out from the rest. He was tall, thin, and pale; with light hair, and a beard that was parted into two long braids. Dark robes billowed eerily behind him as he sat leisurely and fearlessly upon his black horse in the middle of the battle. His pale, cold eyes were flashing with an eerie red light as he scanned the village as if he were searching for something or someone. Thane recognized him but couldn't quite remember where he'd seen him.

The man turned and looked directly at Thane as if he could sense his stare. His eyes locked with Thane's and the corner of his lip lifted in a sneer. He turned his horse toward the well and charged. Thane could feel the ground shake with the pounding of the horse's hooves. In a moment of clarity, he realized that this was the evil man from his nightmares.

Thane quickly ducked back down behind the stone well. He gently eased Natty down off of his lap and onto the ground. He picked up his wooden sword in one hand and the blue ribbon in the other and stood to defend himself in any way he could.

The ground began to shake more violently. Thane could hear a bellow of anger from the charging man as his insides began to burn. Water shot up from the center of the well and began to swirl faster and faster around him. A white and blue light exploded upwards and outwards from the well.

In a flash, Thane was gone.

Chapter Eight

Writtle

Thane gradually became aware of the warmth of the sun beating down on his face. His eyes flew open in panic as he recalled the Reivers and the Hot Trod. Squinting up into the sunshine, he twisted his head frantically trying to get his bearings. He was lying on his back in the dirt, his arms flung over his head. His knees were bent and jammed up against a short stone wall. Quickly pulling his arms down to his sides, he rolled over, and pushed his body up, and sat back on his heels. He rubbed the side of his head and looked around.

Nothing looked familiar.

Where was everyone? Where was he? Where was the village, the people, the horses, the soldiers, The Kerr, the man with the black cloak…Natty…?

Thane pulled his legs around, sat on the ground, and leaned his sore body against the sun warmed stone. He put his head back, closed his eyes and let his shaking body absorb some of the heat. The battle replayed in his head. The cries of the terrified villagers and Natty's empty blue eyes would be forever imprinted in his mind. Never in his years with the Reivers had he witnessed anything as brutal as that attack.

A clear image of the man in the dark robes popped into his head. How could a man from a nightmare appear in the village? Who could he be? Why was he so intent on reaching Thane? Thane's fear of the stranger and the strong metallic smell of Natty's blood were making his stomach clench painfully. He wrapped his arms tightly around his middle, put his head on his knees and struggled not to vomit.

He was shaking uncontrollably. Tears streamed down his cheeks and he was finding it hard to breathe past the lump in his throat. The pain was so intense he was sure that his chest must be torn apart. He reached inside his shirt to look for a wound but there was nothing there; no blood, not even a bruise.

Natty's blue ribbon and his wooden sword were lying on the ground next to him. He put his hand under his cloak and closed his fingers tightly around the sporran full of his treasures. He felt for his mud medallion inside his shirt with the other hand. It was still there. The casing was warm. Mud crumbled off of it onto his hand. He pulled it out of his shirt and examined it. Gold and a strange blue stone were now shining through the cracks in the mud and the stone was glowing with eerie silver light.

He felt around his head, arms and legs for any injuries and found that although he was bruised and sore, he was relatively unharmed. His hands brushed over the dirk at his hip. In the terror of the moment he'd completely forgotten that he had it. What an idiot he was!

Taking a deep breath, and wiping the back of his trembling hand across his cheeks and eyes, Thane finally stood up. His legs were shaking so hard he wasn't sure they would support his weight so he leaned back on the waist high stone wall.

He looked down and realized the wall was actually the side of a very large well much like the well he had been taken from. It was next to a row of small wooden buildings and surrounded on two sides by a sparse forest of trees. He took another shaky breath and closed his eyes for a moment to steady himself.

When he opened them again, he began to really look around. He was near a thoroughfare. People were rushing past him; going about their business as if a boy had not just fallen out of thin air into their midst. They were traveling on a wide dirt road that looked as if it headed straight into a large busy town.

He wiped his eyes and nose again on the sleeve of his shirt and took another deep breath. He picked up Natty's ribbon and stuffed it into the sporran before bending slowly to retrieve the wooden sword from the ground. He was confused and unsure of what he should do next, but he knew he couldn't stay at the well. He decided to join the crowd heading into the town. Maybe someone there could tell him where he was and how he could get back to the Reivers.

The road was fairly wide on the outskirts of the town, but narrowed significantly as he walked toward what he hoped was the center of the town. He passed tall narrow buildings that held shops with painted wooden signs. Images denoted the services that were offered: a baker, an apothecary, a noisy open air blacksmith's shop, a leather shop, a cobbler, a weaver, a butcher and a fishmonger. He had never seen so many buildings or people in one place.

People passed on foot and on horses, scattering pigs and dogs as they rushed by in their haste. They were dressed in a wide variety of clothing from ornate rich fabrics to dirty rags. Shoes seemed to be optional. He wondered how they avoided stepping in all the shite and garbage that littered the streets. He tried halfheartedly to stop a few villagers to ask about the Reivers but his tentative inquiries were easily brushed aside.

After a while, he came to a crossroads at what appeared to be the busiest part of the town. He was standing in front of one of the biggest buildings he'd seen in the village so far. It appeared to be an inn with three floors and many small windows and was the only building he had seen in the village with any appreciable land around it. People were going in and out of the large wooden front door. This looked like as good a place as any to get some answers.

Thane walked to the tavern and sat down on a long, rough wooden bench under a small window in front of the building. He leaned his wooden sword against the wall next to him. A sign swinging over the door had a painted image of a large white windmill with the letters: *The Whyte Wyndmyl Inn and Tavern.*

Each time the heavy door swung open, Thane could hear the loud drone of conversation coming from within. The smell of cooking onions and meat mixed with the nasty smell of the sewage on the streets. He pressed a hand to his stomach again as it grumbled in protest.

The sun was still high in the sky so Thane figured it must be somewhere around noon. He gathered his cloak tighter around his shoulders and leaned his head back against the wall of the inn and closed his eyes. He had no idea what he was going to do next.

Thane remembered the mud medallion. He pulled it out from inside of his shirt to look at it. The mud was crumbling from it in large chunks now. He picked at it until he'd pulled all of the big pieces from it and then blew on it until most of the mud dust was gone.

Embedded in the center of an oval gold pendant was a strangely iridescent blue stone a little larger than the size and shape of a robin's egg. He was not sure but he thought he could see something swirling around inside of the stone. The longer he stared at it the more convinced he was that he could discern movement. The designs of the gold casing had tiny sculpted figures of a dragon, a dog and a horse. The animals were entwined amid an elaborate design of interwoven ribbons. The hoofs, paws and claws of the animals were clutching the stone at even intervals securing it to the center of the medallion.

A loud crash and an angry shout jerked him out of his reverie. The sounds of scuffling and fighting were coming from somewhere down the narrow alley between the inn and the building next to it. He got up quickly and followed the noise toward what appeared to be a back courtyard of the inn. He peered around the rear corner of the building.

A large man was kicking and cursing at a young boy who was sprawled out on the ground in front of him. Thane crept slowly around the outer wall toward the fight. Anger was quickly replacing his feelings of melancholy. He knew what it felt like to be beaten and abused, and the man was too big to be hitting the small boy so hard. Thane watched the boy kicking and yelling at the top of his lungs while trying to scramble back away from the man's swinging fists and feet.

Fury surged through Thane. Looking around, he spotted a large wooden bucket of kitchen slop outside the back door of the inn. Without thinking about the consequences, he grabbed it and ran toward the struggling pair. Thane lifted the heavy bucket shoulder high and flung the contents into the big man's face. The man howled and stumbled back away from the boy.

His head was covered in a layer of thick smelly muck. Carrot and onion peelings were sticking to his hair and shoulders and a gooey slush was dripping from his face and chin. He was bellowing at the top of his lungs and stumping about blindly trying to wipe his face and eyes with his dirty fists but he only managed to rub the filth further into his eyes. Thane grabbed the boy by the back of the shirt before the man could clear the muck from his eyes. He pulled the boy up to his feet and shoved him away from the angry man.

"Come with me…RUN!" he yelled.

Together they ran around the other side of the inn and into the confusion of the main street dodging people, large and small animals and wagons; down side paths and around the backs of a half dozen buildings. Out of breath and clutching at the stitches in their sides they finally flung themselves down behind a long wooden building on the edge of town. Both of their heads were cocked as they listened intently for the sound of the man's pursuing footsteps. They didn't hear any. It didn't look like they'd been followed.

Thane looked across at the boy and thought he couldn't have been that much younger than Thane was; he was just small and skinny. He had a thin long face, pointy chin and bright green eyes. His shoulder length dark red hair was covered in mud and was tangled about his face as if it had never seen a comb. His life appeared to be just as hard as Thane's.

The boy suddenly jumped up and kicked Thane hard in the leg.

"What did you do that for? I'll be in even more trouble now!" he shouted. His small hands were clenched at his side and his eyes filled with angry tears. "What are we going to do if they kick us out?"

Thane rose slowly keeping his eyes on the boy's fists and backed away from him.

"You're welcome! I just wanted to help. Next time I will leave you there to have the snot beaten out of you!" Thane threw back at him.

"I had him right where I wanted him. Another minute and I would have gotten away," the boy screamed looking down at Thane without an ounce of fear.

"Yeah, you wouldn't have gotten far after he'd knocked you out cold!" Thane shouted back. He wondered if the boy wasn't just a little bit crazy.

An angry tear ran down the boy's face. Thane stared at the tear, fascinated by the clean trail it was leaving through the dirt as it ran down his cheek. He continued to watch it as it dripped off his chin and onto his shirt. The boy took a shuddering breath, stomped his foot, and dropped back down on the ground with a mighty huff.

"I would have gotten away," he muttered as he wiped the tears from his filthy face with an equally filthy hand.

Thane stood there for another minute just staring down at the boy. With a sigh, he slowly sank down next to him. They sat in silence for a bit, each one lost in his own thoughts.

Thane was the first to speak. "Who was he?"

The boy looked Thane over and finally answered. "Markus, he's the brother of Marsden, the owner of the tavern. I work there, and Marsden gives me and Tally a place to stay and food to eat."

"Why was he beating you?" Thane asked.

"I knocked a mug of ale on a drunk," he replied with a smirk.

"Why would he beat you if it was an accident?" Thane questioned him.

"It wasn't an accident," the boy said. Defiance and anger returned to his voice as he stared back at Thane.

Thane raised an eyebrow and said, "Oh."

The boy crossed his arms over his knees and dropped his head down on them.

Thane picked up a stick from the ground next to him and started to draw intertwining circles in the dirt.

"Can I ask you a strange question?" Thane asked softly.

"What?" came a muffled reply.

Thane hesitated.

"Where are we?" he eventually asked. He was so scared and confused he thought he would risk the anger and scorn of the boy for a little bit of information.

The boy lifted his head slowly and stared hard at Thane. One eyebrow rose up and disappeared under a wave of dirty red hair as he looked Thane up and down, taking in Thane's dark eyes, pale skin, and raven black hair. His dirty clothes and worn boots were splattered with blood. The boy's gaze lingered briefly on the strange medallion and circles Thane had been scratching into the dirt. He seemed to come to a decision. He stood up abruptly and held his hand out to help Thane up.

"Writtle. What's your name?" he demanded.

Thane paused and stared at the boy's hand, unsure whether or not to trust him as he had just kicked him a few moments ago. He decided to ignore the hand and stood up without any help.

"My name is Thane. What's yours?"

"They call me Orphan," he said as he dropped his hand to his side with a shrug.

"You don't have a name?" Thane asked shocked that someone would want to be called 'Orphan'.

The boy just stared intently at Thane without answering.

"Well, I'm not going to call you 'Orphan'. That's just stupid!" Thane retorted. He was beginning to get annoyed again. He had been through a lot today. He was hurt, tired, and he had no patience left. What else could go wrong?

"Fine then, don't call me anything. You can wave like an idiot when you want me," Orphan replied. He turned his back to Thane and started to walk toward the center of the village without a backward glance.

Thane stood there uncertainly. He still had no idea where he was, and after the mad dash from the inn, he wasn't even sure he would be able to find his way back to where he had left his sword. He didn't have any coins and he had nowhere to go. Even though Orphan's situation seemed to be no better than Thane's, at least the boy had food and someplace to sleep. It was painfully obvious from the bruise swelling on Thane's leg, that Orphan knew how to take care of himself.

The young boy turned around and said, "Well, are you going to just stand there all day like an idiot, or are you going to come back to the inn with me? Don't worry!" he rambled on as if he had not just kicked and insulted Thane. "I'll make up something to tell Markus about what you did. He was so drunk he'll probably just forget about it all on his own. Hey! Maybe Marsden can find a job for you to do too since it's obvious you don't have anywhere else to go."

Orphan turned around and continued to walk back toward the tavern without waiting to see if Thane would follow.

Thane stood there for a moment longer. He glanced behind him and saw that the road led down and around a long field then disappeared into a line of trees. He decided to stick with Orphan. At least he would be with someone who seemed to know his way around, and he wouldn't be alone in this strange new place. Besides, he'd left his sword at the inn. He would have to go back there anyway.

He reached up to make sure that his hair was still covering his ears. He didn't want to give this boy any reason to turn on him. Orphan's dark red head was already disappearing around a row of buildings that led into the center of town. Thane ran to catch up to him.

Chapter Nine

Taliesin the Bard

They meandered their way back through the town in silence. When they got to the front of the inn, Thane stepped over to the bench where he'd been sitting and grabbed his wooden sword. Orphan frowned down at Thane's sword but didn't comment on it.

"Just don't say anything. Let me do all the talking. Come on. Follow me." He went around the side of the inn, down the alley and around to the back of the large wooden building. They walked past the spot where Markus had been beating Orphan. The bucket was still lying where Thane had thrown it, its contents strewn on the ground around it. Markus was nowhere in sight.

"Tilda!" Orphan yelled as they entered through the back door into a warm, fragrant kitchen. "Tilda, where are you?"

Thane followed him in and looked around curiously. The kitchen was large and clean. A dark stone fireplace filled most of the wall on the right side of the room. An enormous pot was hanging from a hook in the center of the hearth and a stew of some sort was bubbling away inside it. Whatever it was, it smelled delicious.

A long wooden table dominated the center of the kitchen and was filled with plates of breads and cheeses and half dozen jugs. Low benches were pushed under the table and out of the way. To the left side were rows and rows of shelves filled with a variety of plates, bowls, mugs, and serving dishes. Thane remained standing uncertainly in the doorway next to a deep stone basin. On the other side of the basin, bright sunlight spilled through two windows that hung over a small table filled with dirty dishes.

A woman came bustling in through the doorway across the room. She was struggling a bit under the weight of the large tray she was carrying. It looked like it weighed as much as she did and was piled high with dirty mugs and plates. She was a short thin woman with mousy brown hair that was pulled away from her face and rolled into a tight bun at the back of her neck. She hurried over to the low table next to the stone basin and started to unload the tray of dishes into the basin. Her soft brown eyes were smiling out of her round, pleasant face. Her cheeks were pink from exertion. Was this little woman Tilda?

"Orphan! Where have you been? Markus stormed in here a while ago bellowing and carrying on about unruly and ungrateful wretches. He was covered in bits of food. I believe he was talking about you!" She said as she bent over the basin, stuck her hands in the water and began to scrub the dirty dishes.

"What did you do now?" she asked.

"It wasn't my fault Tilda!" Orphan cried. "Jared was drunk again and tried to hit me so I dumped a mug of ale on him. Markus saw me and dragged me out back to beat me. I just escaped with my life!"

As the boy was talking, he began to sidle over to the kitchen table. He reached his hand out and grabbed a couple rolls from the table while Tilda's back was turned.

"If you are going to take that bread, you may as well take some cheese while you are at it. Take some for your friend here too." Tilda said without turning around to look at the sneaky boy.

Thane felt a sharp stab of pain in his chest as he was unexpectedly reminded of Natty.

"Where is Marsden?" Orphan asked through a mouthful of bread and cheese.

The boy carried some food over to the corner of the table and sat down. With a wave of his cheese filled hand, he motioned for Thane to join him.

Thane glanced at Tilda and felt that, for the moment, he would be safe here. He sat down warily on the long bench next to the boy with the strange name but pushed the food away. He didn't think he would be able to swallow anything past the lump that was still lodged in his throat and his stomach was still tied in knots.

"…in the stables with the Bard. He is trying to sober him up for tonight." Tilda continued.

Thane leaned over and whispered to Orphan, "What's a bard?"

"What do you mean…'What's a bard?' Where've you been living…in a cave?" Orphan snorted. "A bard is a storyteller…a poet…

someone who knows all the old tales and songs." He finished shoving the bread and cheese into his mouth and stood up.

"The Bard is teaching me to read and write," Orphan continued through a mouthful of food. He swallowed, wiped the back of his hand across his lips and said, "Come with me... I'll introduce you to him. I bet he wouldn't mind teaching you too," he said as he grabbed Thane's hand, pulled him to his feet, and dragged him toward the kitchen door.

Thane mumbled a quick, "Thanks," to Tilda as he passed her, and stumbled along after Orphan.

"Watch out for Markus. He is still looking for you," Tilda called out after them. "Don't forget to come right back. I need help serving."

The stables were tucked behind the inn across a small dirt courtyard. It was a long wooden building with tall wide double doors and a thatched roof. There were many small windows along the side that were propped open with various sized sticks.

As they entered the stables, Thane breathed in the smell of horse, leather, and dirty hay. He found some comfort in the familiar odors. There were only three horses in the stalls: an old mare, a young stallion, and a beautiful white palfrey.

Thane's first sight of the Bard was a little alarming. He was expecting someone well dressed and clean; someone who looked educated and refined. The Bard looked like none of those things. It was hard to imagine that this man could teach Orphan anything. His thick white hair was sticking out in all directions as was his scraggly white beard. His thin body was wrapped in an old brown cloak. He was slouched over, folded up upon himself and sound asleep... or...passed out. A large man was standing over him with his hands on his hips muttering and cursing.

"Tally, you better be up and about within the hour. I expect to hear you singing like a bird to pay for all the ale you drank last night. Come on man, get up." The large, barrel-chested man bent over and gave the Bard a vigorous shake.

"Marsden, I'll get him up for you. He'll be ready by supper. He always is, isn't he?" Orphan said.

"Orphan! Where have you been?" The big man straightened up and turned to look at the boy.

"Markus is in a rage. He said you magically covered him in onion and carrot peels and disappeared into thin air. If he hadn't been so drunk I might have believed him; then I'da beat you myself just for the bother. Vegetable peels and disappearing Orphans...humph! I sent him to Chelmsford for supplies. That aughta sober his brainless self up," Marsden grumbled; his bushy brown mustache quivered back and forth as he spoke.

"Never could trust him..." he mumbled to himself.

Marsden turned, kicked the Bard in the boot one more time and said, "Get him up and moving. He needs to be cleaned up and singing in the common room before dark." He turned to leave, and stopped short. He noticed Thane standing behind Orphan for the first time.

"Who are you?" he barked at Thane.

Thane jumped; surprised at being so rudely addressed. "Ummm…" he mumbled. "I'm…" he started again when Orphan interrupted and spoke over him.

"He's a friend and he needs someplace to stay. Weren't you saying that you needed another hand to help with the chores and with the heavy lifting around here? You know how bad your back has been feeling lately, and Thane here has a strong back and is willing to work for food and a place to sleep." Orphan spoke quickly like he was trying to get it all out before Marsden had a chance to really think it through.

"I'll just take him up to the loft and get him settled in. Tilda has already fed him so we'll just go find him a place to sleep. Don't you worry. We'll have the Bard up and moving in no time," he assured Marsden. "Come on, Thane," Orphan said.

He grabbed Thane's hand and pulled him back to a ladder at the rear of the stables. Just beyond the ladder in an open doorway, Thane saw a large orange cat, curled up, asleep in a wide shaft of sunlight.

They climbed to the top of the rickety ladder and crawled over the edge of the loft. The loft was half as wide as the stables below and ran the whole length of it. Hay was strewn about in haphazard piles here and there. Orphan peaked over the edge of the loft and watched Marsden stomp out of the stable doors.

"That was close! He's gone. Well, that went better than I expected," Orphan said with a grin as he turned to face Thane.

"Who was that? And who is that moldy old man down there?" Thane whispered, his head still spinning. He was not quite sure he understood what had just happened.

"Who are you calling a moldy old man? That is Taliesin, the Bard! The big man is your new boss, Marsden. He owns the inn and is married to Tilda, the woman you met in the kitchen," Orphan continued. He was like a little tornado; perpetual motion and noise.

"He is really all bark and no bite…well, very little bite…anyway, I have never seen him hurt a soul. His brother, on the other hand, isn't…'all bark and no bite' that is…anyway; just stay away from him and you'll be fine."

Now Thane was really confused. Who bites and who barks? Who should he stay away from? The Bard?

"Scoop up some hay and make a bed for yourself. Tilda will give you some blankets later. I sleep over there," he said as he waved his hand absentmindedly toward a burlap curtain. Thane glanced at the rough cloth hanging across the far corner of the loft.

"You can sleep anywhere but there." He peeked over the side again then said, "I'd better go back down and see if I can get Tally up and moving before Marsden comes back."

With that, Orphan scrambled down the ladder and disappeared. Thane could hear him speaking softly to the Bard. After a few minutes, a grumbling low voice was added to Orphan's soothing patient one.

Thane turned back to scrutinize the loft. It was reasonably clean. Piles of hay were stacked along the long wall. He picked a spot under the slopping roof, next to the wall, not too far from the curtain where Orphan had indicated that he slept. It didn't take him long to pull a heap of fresh smelling hay out of the pile and spread it across the floor to make a long, thick bed. He pushed his sword and his small leather sporran under the bed of hay. He checked to make sure his knife was still secured to his hip and headed down the ladder to see if he could help with the Bard.

In the short time Thane was in the loft, Orphan had managed to awaken the old man. He was holding a small metal cup to the Bard's lips and was helping him drink from it.

"Here Tally. Just sip it so you don't get sick." Orphan was talking to him in a low, soothing voice. It was obviously not the first time they had done this.

The Bard stretched out his arms above his head, shrugged his shoulders a couple times and straightened out his back. He took another tentative sip from the cup then looked up and caught sight of Thane. He choked, and sprayed a mouthful of liquid all over Orphan and himself then toppled sideways off of the bench. His cup went flying through the air, and landed with a tinkle on the other side of the room.

Thane quickly lifted his hands to make sure the tips of his ears were still covered by his hair. What the heck was wrong with the man? Maybe he was having a fit or something.

The Bard sat up, scrambled to his feet, and backed up until he was flat against the wall. His eyes widened and he looked just a bit crazed as his gaze fixed on Thane and the medallion around his neck.

He cried out…"How can it be? What are you doing here? Put that medallion away, hide it quickly! Are you insane? Anyone could see it! His spies are everywhere."

Thane looked quickly back over his shoulder to see who on earth the Bard could be yelling at but there was no one else in the stables besides himself and Orphan.

Turning back to the Bard, he said, "Me? What is who doing where? What spies?"

Orphan looked from Thane to the Bard then back to Thane again with a frown. He put an arm around the Bard's waist and led him back to the bench to sit down. The Bard didn't take his wide eyes off of Thane.

"Tally, calm down. Thane just got here. He'll be staying with us for a while since he has nowhere else to go. He will be working for Marsden and Tilda." Orphan tried to calm him in a soft soothing voice.

"Thane?" Taliesin, the Bard repeated. "No! Can't be! I want nothing to do with it. I am just a useless old Bard. I want nothing to do with it…they can't put this on me too!" He closed his eyes tightly and continued to mumble. Wringing his hands together and shaking his head he said, "Won't do any more…I can't." He looked up at Thane again.

"PUT IT AWAY!" he bellowed making both Thane and Orphan jump. His beard was trembling and his white eyebrows were drawn sharply together over his bloodshot brown eyes.

Orphan was beginning to look scared as he watched Thane hastily tuck the medallion in his shirt and tie it closed. Turning to the Bard he said, "Tally, let's go see Tilda in the kitchen. We'll get you something warm to eat. You'll feel better after you've had some food. Come on."

"What are they up to bringing him here?" The Bard persisted in his monologue without budging. "…can't trust the Divine Ones. It is not fair…no, not fair…I'm doing my part already…" he complained to Orphan as he continued to stare at Thane.

"Okay, Tally, whatever you say. Let's go see Tilda," he soothed. "Come on."

Orphan hauled the old man up by his elbow and began to lead him out of the barn. Thane started to follow but Orphan turned to him, put his hand out to stop him and said, "Not you. You'd better stay here." Orphan paused as Tally walked out of the stables alone. He looked Thane over again with a frown.

"I don't understand what's going on," he said to Thane. "Do you? Have you been here before? Do you know Tally?"

Thane shrugged his shoulders, "I don't think so."

"What do you mean, 'I don't think so?'" Orphan repeated in disbelief.

"Just what I said. I don't think so," Thane said stubbornly. "I don't remember much from when I was little so I guess I could've been here before, but I don't think so."

Thane looked at the Bard's stooped and shaking back as it disappeared through the stable door. "I certainly would have remembered meeting him. What's his problem anyway? He's weird!"

Orphan shrugged then turned around and without another word rushed out of the stables to catch up to Taliesin. Thane could hear Orphan murmuring to the Bard as they walked away.

Alone for the first time since meeting Orphan, Thane walked over to the bench the Bard had just vacated and sank down on it exhausted. He leaned back against the wall and looked around the stables again. Sunlight was streaming in through the propped open windows and was reflecting cheerily off of the dust, filling the air with millions of glittering flecks of light. Six stalls lined each side of the long building and were separated down the center by a clean stone floor.

A small square table and two stools sat between the double doors Orphan and the Bard had just hurried through and a doorway to another room. If Thane leaned forward a bit, he could just make out a narrow bed through the opening. Was that where the Bard slept?

Despite the recent commotion, the cat was still sleeping peacefully in the middle of the open doorway at the far side of the stables. Thane found the familiar sounds of the horses and the muffled noises of the village soothing.

He had absolutely no memory of this place or of any part of the large town he had been through three times already this afternoon. He was fairly certain that he had never met Tilda or Marsden. He was absolutely certain that he had never met Taliesin because that was one man who would have been hard to forget.

Thane felt totally overwhelmed. He was in pain, he was tired, and he was still grieving. He put his head back against the wall of the stall and closed his eyes. He thought again of Natty and the Reivers. His chest tightened painfully and he had to fight back the tears that threatened to spill out of his eyes. He wanted to go back up the ladder and lie down in a corner of the loft and just sleep forever.

After awhile, he stood up and stretched. Every part of his body hurt. The white horse that had been standing quietly in the stall right behind him leaned over the rail and whinnied loudly at him. Thane turned toward him. He reached his hand up and rubbed the horse across his nose, along his jaw, and behind his ear. He trailed his fingers under the horse's mane and down the warm side of his neck. Thane was amazed at the whiteness of the horse's coat; not one blemish or hint of color marred its perfect body. Its big gray eye looked right into Thane's.

The horse rubbed his soft nose into Thane's other hand then turned his head to nuzzle Thane's shoulder and neck as if he was trying to console him. Thane leaned his face into the horse's warm neck. The sudden sense of familiarity and affection was strange.

"You're a sweet boy aren't you?" Thane whispered to the horse as he breathed in his warm scent. He felt a tingle spread through his body as comfort settled around him like a cloak. They stood there together for a long while until, with a sigh and a final sniffle, Thane pulled away. He rubbed the horse's neck one last time then reluctantly turned and climbed up the ladder to the loft.

He grabbed his sword from under the small pile of hay and lay down. He pulled his cloak tight around his body and curled up on his side. The wooden sword was clutched in his hands for what little protection it could offer. He was asleep before his head touched his makeshift hay pillow.

Chapter Ten

Whyte Wyndmyl Inn & Tavern

It seemed like only moments later when Thane heard footsteps and voices enter the stables below him. He opened his eyes. It was almost dark and for a moment he didn't know where he was. Thoughts, images, and feelings flooded through him in a rush and the loss of Natty hit him full force in the chest again. He couldn't breathe as tears rushed to his eyes. He was a mess. Would he ever stop crying?

"Thane? Thane, are you still here?" Orphan called out into the darkening stables.

"I'm up here." Thane answered, his voice breaking with emotion.

He quickly scrubbed the tears and the sleep from his eyes with one hand and rubbed the pain in his chest with the other. He took a deep breath to steady himself before he crawled over to the edge of the loft and looked down. Orphan and Taliesin were standing in the center of the stables looking up at him.

"We're back!" Orphan stated the obvious.

"Yeah, I'll be right down," Thane replied as soon as he thought he could speak without his voice cracking.

He returned the sword to its hiding place under his bed of hay. He reached up to make sure that his hair was covering his ears and then patted his shirt to make sure the medallion was safely tucked away. He didn't want a repeat performance of the unpleasant scene with the Bard. He climbed back down the steep wooden ladder. Someone had lit the lamps on the wall while he slept. The soft amber light illuminated the two figures in front of him.

Thane was amazed. The Bard was almost unrecognizable. It was hard to believe that this was the same disheveled man who had been hunched over himself earlier. He was clean, his hair was brushed and tied back. His beard was trimmed and combed. He was wearing clean dark breeches and a white long-sleeved billowy shirt tied neatly at his wrists and throat. A long, light blue woolen cloak was draped over his shoulders and fastened together by an intricately carved silver broach. The broach had a dark green stone embedded in the midst of multiple interlocking, silver filigree circles. Circles, Thane noted, that looked similar to the designs on his own medallion.

"Please accept my apology for my earlier behavior. I was a bit...indisposed," the Bard said with an uncomfortable cough. He put his right hand across his chest and with a low bow; he cleared his throat and introduced himself. "I am Taliesin, The Bard."

"Umm, yeah, I'm Thane," Thane replied. He wasn't sure if he should bow back or just stand there. He chose to just stand there and wait.

An uncomfortable silence descended as Taliesin continued to stare at Thane, looking at him as if he was expecting him to say something else. Thane stared back at him with a puzzled expression on his face. What else was there to say?

"Yes, well enough of that," Orphan interrupted the uncomfortable silence. He walked behind the Bard, grabbed a small bundle from the bench, and tossed it to Thane as Taliesin turned and walked out.

Thane did a double take as he caught the bundle to his chest and focused on Orphan for the first time. He had freshened himself up as well. His red hair was somewhat clean now. It looked as if he had attempted to pull a comb through it but it still tumbled wildly about his shoulders to frame his small face. His clothes were well worn but they appeared to be spotless and well cared for. It was obvious to Thane that Orphan wasn't as ill treated as he had first believed. In fact, Orphan seemed to be getting along just fine here.

"You'll need to get cleaned up too. Here are some clothes and a cloth to wash with. There is a barrel of rain water outside that you can use to rinse the dirt off of yourself," he waved his hand vaguely in the direction of the back door.

"As soon as you get changed, come to the kitchen. Tilda will tell you what she needs you to do," he babbled on. "I'm going back to the tavern. Tilda is getting busy and I need to get in there and help her. I'll see you inside." With that, Orphan turned and headed in the direction of the tavern.

Thane looked down at himself and realized that his shirt and breeches were covered in mud and Natty's dried blood and he had a long tear down his left sleeve. To make matters worse, he had bits of hay stuck to the whole mess. At least there was no blood on his cloak. With a sigh, Thane went outside.

Clean rain water was in a large barrel outside the door just where Orphan had said it would be. He took his time scrubbing his face and his hands as they were filthy. When he removed as much of the blood and dirt as he could without actually climbing into the barrel, he went back inside the barn. He scooped up the clean clothes and carried them up to the loft to change.

The rough woolen breeches Orphan had given him were a bit too short and the sleeves of the shirt were a bit too long but he was grateful for them just the same. It felt good to get out of his dirty clothes. He folded them up and laid them down next to his hay bed, his cloak, and his sporran. Even though they were nasty, he couldn't afford to lose them. They were all he had now. Maybe Orphan would tell him where he could wash and repair them.

After he fastened his belt and knife around his waist, he clambered down the ladder. He rushed across the courtyard and through the back door of the kitchen. He was determined to help out where he could. Maybe if he showed them how much he could help, they would really let him stay. He found Orphan with Tilda in the kitchen. He was relieved to see that Tally was not there.

The evening went by quickly as there was a lot to do in the kitchen. The work was not hard but it was steady and Tilda was kind. He scrubbed the dirty mugs and dishes from the common room. Often he found himself elbow deep in the washing basin or standing next to Orphan or Tilda drying the dishes with a rough cloth.

Molly, a pretty young serving girl from the village, took orders from the customers. Tilda loaded the trenchers and Molly and Orphan ran them back and forth to the common room. The three of them chattered nonstop about everything and nothing. Thane just listened.

Markus came into the kitchen at one point to get a large mug of ale. He stopped abruptly when he spotted Thane. His ruddy face scrunched up and he frowned at him. He looked as if he was trying really hard to remember something and it was causing him intense pain. Eventually he gave up, grumbled to himself about flying vegetable peels and left. It looked like Orphan was right. Markus either wasn't very smart, or he had really had a lot to drink. Maybe it was a little of both.

That evening when the chores were done and most of the dishes were put away, Orphan came into the kitchen to get Thane. He grabbed the cloth out of Thane's hands, flung it on the table and pulled him out of the door to the main part of the inn.

"Come on!" Orphan said. "Tilda said we're done for the night. Let's go listen to Tally sing."

Thane had not been anywhere but the kitchen, on raids, or in the stables in the Reiver's village. He had never been inside a tavern. This was the largest room Thane had ever seen. It was full of people sitting at a dozen tables that were scattered haphazardly about the room. The Bard was sitting on a low stool in front of an immense stone fireplace playing a small lute and singing. His eyes followed the boys as they scooted along the wall until they came to a table in the far corner of the noisy room. They sat together, their backs against the wall and listened to Taliesin sing ballads. He had a soothing, expressive voice that pulled listeners into his tales as he painted pictures of great heroes and epic battles.

Thane leaned his elbows on the table, rested his chin in his cupped hands, and closed his eyes. He let Tally's voice wash over him as The Bard strummed his lute and told a tale of a great love between a handsome dark Irish Prince and a beautiful flaxen-haired Færie.

A prince was out hunting on the western edges of his land one evening when he stumbled across an enchanted waterfall deep in the woods. He had traveled all over his lands for many, many years but he had never before come across anything like this waterfall. It seemed to appear out of nowhere and shimmer in the fading light of dusk.

As he knelt at the water's edge to drink, he heard a gentle footstep, and looking up, he gazed upon the most beautiful woman he had ever seen. She had stepped through the curtain of water made by the falls.

She was tall and ethereal, her long pale hair surrounded her heart shaped face and small pointed ears and tumbled in soft waves about her shoulders and down her back.

The prince stood up and reached his hand out to help her.

Startled, she looked at him through sapphire blue eyes. Then swiftly turned to go back the way she had come.

"No wait!" he said and he reached out to take hold of her hand. "Who are you? Where did you come from?"

"Please, you must let me go," she begged him. "I will be in grave danger if I am seen." She whispered as she halfheartedly tried to pull her hand from his.

"It is too late, you have already been seen. I am alone and I will tell no one," he pleaded. "Come sit with me."

She looked back through the mist at the waterfall and hesitated. She was intrigued as she had never met a human before and this one was kind and handsome. His raven black hair was parted down the middle and fell just past his shoulders. She looked into his black eyes. She felt that she could see straight into his soul.

So, she stayed with the prince and passed the night with him by the edge of the water. They spoke of their lives and of their hopes and dreams. Finally, at daybreak she stood to go back through the waterfall with a promise to return the following evening.

For the next fortnight, Cianán, the Prince and the Færie Alyse met at the waterfall each evening at the gloaming.

Till one evening, Alyse appeared to him in tears. She had been forbidden by the Fæ Council to continue to return to him. She begged Cianán to go with her; to live with her people in the West. She promised him immortality. He could be with her forever and would stay young, healthy and handsome, just as he was, as long as he never left her lands.

Cianán was devastated. For as much as his heart wanted to, he could not leave his people. For he was not just a prince; he was the heir to the throne. He could not abandon his duty.

She told him that she would not return. She had fallen in love with the prince but it was against the laws of the Fæ for her to remain in the human realm.

Cianán swore to her that he would not give up hope. He would return to the forest every gloaming until she came back to him.

The prince was true to his word. He went back to the forest every evening before sunset for weeks, but neither the waterfall nor the beautiful Færie appeared to him.

One evening, the prince sat against a tree in despair. His forearm was draped across his bent knee and his shoulders were slumped in hopelessness. He had tried, in everyway he could, to discover the entrance to the Gateway, but to no avail. It was truly hidden. He had lost her. He closed his eyes and rested his head on his arm in defeat.

He felt a hand touch the top of his head and when he looked up, the Færie was standing before him. Tears, like twin diamonds were glistening on her cheeks. He jumped to his feet and pulled her into his arms.

"I have watched you every eve from behind the hidden waterfall. Why have you not given up?" she cried into his neck.

"I will come with you, into the West. I will do whatever I must do because I cannot live my life without you," he pledged to her.

"No! I have spoken to my father. He has agreed to let me stay with you," she said.

"That's it? It is that easy?" Cianán asked, hope in his voice.

Alyse didn't answer.

He took her face in his hands and said, "Tell me, Alyse! What did he say?"

"I cannot return to my people…ever. I will not be able to cross the gateway…and…I am to be mortal."

"No!" he cried.

She reached up to rub her thumb across his chin and said, "I have already spent endless years alone, Cianán, I will not spend the rest of eternity without you."

And so the prince married his Færie. He became King Cianán. Alyse ruled by his side as his beautiful mortal Queen.

After a couple more songs about battles and famous warriors, Tally packed up his lute and left the common room without a word to the two boys sitting quietly in the corner.

Later that night, Thane lay on his new straw bed and listened to Orphan move around behind his makeshift wall. He furtively rubbed the point of his right ear. The queen in the Bard's tale had had pointed ears like his. Did his pointed ears mean he was a Færie? It was ridiculous. There was no such thing as Færies. His ears were just misshapen.

He pulled a couple of prickly pieces of hay from under him and rolled over with his back to the wall. Questions spun around in his head. Why was Tally so scared of his medallion? Where was the Reiver's village? How did he get here? Maybe he could ask Tally or Orphan tomorrow. Exhaustion finally won out over his pondering and he fell into a fitful sleep.

Chapter Eleven

A New Life

Thane closed his eyes tighter, dragged his cloak across his face, and rolled away from the hand that was persistently shaking his shoulder. He was having an awful dream about a Hot Trod destroying the Reiver village. Maybe if he buried his head under his arms and pretended to still be asleep, Old Man Jennings would give up and he could go back to sleep and change the ending of the dream.

"Come on. You may be use to lolling about all morning where you come from, but here we have to earn our keep," an irritating voice drilled into his skull.

"Thane!" the voice persisted, even louder than before, as the hand began to shake his shoulder with more force.

Thane's eyes flew open as the events of the previous day came rushing back to him. A wave of hopelessness washed over him as he rolled over and looked into the bright green eyes of his tormentor, Orphan. It wasn't a dream.

"Finally! It's time to get up," he said as he gave Thane one last shake before turning to go down the ladder. Just before his head disappeared after his body, he told Thane that there were clean clothes next to the far wall for him.

Thane took a deep breath and sat up slowly. He groaned as every muscle in his body tightened in protest. Although he was still very tired, he forced himself to move. He rubbed the sleep and sadness out of his eyes.

He figured it was just about dawn as the stables were suffused with a soft gray light. He dressed hurriedly and wondered if everyone else was still asleep. The only sound he could hear was Orphan's voice as he crooned quietly to the horses below. When he finished dressing, he checked his hair, and stomped his feet into his boots then climbed down the rickety ladder.

Orphan was already gathering water and food for the horses. He tossed Thane a bucket.

"As soon as we feed the horses we can get something to eat from Tilda. Everyone should be up by now. Well, everyone but Tally. He is usually passed out until noon," he said in a matter of fact voice as he glanced over his shoulder at the closed door behind him.

Thane didn't have much to say as they fed and watered the horses. He found that Orphan talked enough for the both of them. He was happy to discover that he was not expected to say much of anything. Orphan was content with his occasional mumbled replies.

"Embarr," Orphan continued chattering as he pointed across the stables at the beautiful white horse "has been Tally's ever since I've known him." Thane looked over at the horse and would have sworn the horse cocked his head to the side, and looked right back at him. Intelligence shown from his bright eyes!

Before Thane could comment on the horse's unusual behavior, Orphan blathered on, "...the two brown horses belong to Marsden so they stay at the inn all year round. She is Nutmeg," he said pointing at the older brown mare behind him, "and that is Cinnamon," he indicated with a wave of his hand toward the young stallion. "We take care of them and any other animals that belong to the travelers staying at the inn."

When they finished with the horses, Orphan dragged Thane out of the stables toward the kitchen for a small meal. The scent of baking bread hit Thane's nose as soon as he walked through the door into the sunlit kitchen. The thought of eating food still made his stomach feel funny but he realized that it wouldn't do him any good to starve. He needed to force something down his throat. He had not eaten much since he had been with the Reivers the day before.

He sat down between Orphan and Marsden and, to his surprise, once he started eating he couldn't stop. The honey was sweet, the bread was warm and fresh, and the cheese had a nice sharp bite to it. He glanced up as he reached for his mug of spiced cider and found both Tilda and Orphan staring at him. He swallowed a mouthful of food; his face flushed.

"Uh, hungry are you?" Orphan asked with a snicker.

Embarrassed, he started to push the bread and honey away but Tilda put her hand on his shoulder and said, "Don't you worry, son. You eat as much as you want."

She turned to Orphan with a frown and scolded him, "…and you, you leave him be!"

Thane turned his attention back to his food and he ate until he wasn't feeling sick from fear anymore but from overindulgence! When he was finally done, he rubbed his bulging stomach and followed Orphan back to the stables.

They spent the rest of the morning shoveling out horse stalls. For the first time since leaving the Reivers, Thane felt some measure of calm. This was a job he knew well! He was able, for a little while, to forget the upheaval of the last couple days in the familiar chores and comforting earthy smells of the stable.

Marsden came for them just as they were finishing up the last stall. He told them to go outside and clean up, then head into the kitchen for the noon meal. As soon as everyone was finally gathered around the long kitchen table, Tilda and Molly brought over the food. It looked like a feast to Thane who had never seen so much food in one place.

Tilda had prepared a fragrant fish stew. She made sure everyone had a good large serving of it, especially Thane. She winked at him as she put an extra spoonful in his trencher, then she turned back to the simmering pot to make plates for the folks in the common room. Molly was constantly going out of the kitchen with full plates and coming back in with empty ones.

The boisterous meal was like nothing Thane could ever remember being a part of before. He was used to eating in the stables, in the kitchen with Natty, or on the trail with the Reivers. Here almost everyone talked at once, often interrupting each other's sentences to make sure their own opinions or stories were heard. Orphan, Tilda, and Molly chattered nonstop. Sarcastic comments were tossed in now and again by Marsden and Markus. Thane thought that must be what a big happy family would be like at meal time. He felt a bit awkward and out of place. He noticed that he and The Bard were the only silent ones at the table.

Tally finished eating first, rose quickly to his feet, and mumbled a quiet "thanks" to Tilda. Without a word to anyone else, he made his way around the table and across to the backdoor. He turned for a moment at the door, looked at Orphan and barked, "Bring the boy and meet me behind the stables." He slammed the door as he left the kitchen.

Thane wondered what was behind the stables and if he should be nervous. Did he do something wrong? Was he going to be beaten? Thane darted a quick glance at Orphan, who didn't seem concerned, so Thane shrugged his shoulders and finished eating. He was used to getting beatings with the Reivers, so how bad could the old man be?

After helping Tilda clean the dishes and tidy up the kitchen after the meal, Orphan and Thane headed out to find Tally. He was sitting on a bench next to the back door of the stables with the yellow cat curled up in his lap. His long fingers paused in mid-stroke on the cat's back. He glared up at them as they stood in front of him. His eyes lingered briefly on the small lump just visible under Thane's shirt.

"Tell me boy, can you read or write?" Tally asked Thane.

"Ah, no sir." Thane answered, shifting his weight from one foot to the other. He was beginning to feel uncomfortable under

Tally's intense scrutiny. At least it didn't look like he was going to be beaten…yet.

"What? You can't read? Or write? What about numbers? Are you telling me you can't do numbers?" Tally asked as if he was offended because Thane could not read or write. "What have you been doing for the last four years?"

Thane thought it was a really odd question. "I have been working in the sta…"

Tally cut him off before he could finish the sentence with a sharp "I don't want to hear your excuses."

"But, I…" Thane began but didn't get far before Tally interrupted him again.

"I don't want to hear your excuses," he repeated impatiently. "You are here now. You will apply yourself to your studies along with Orphan! Understand?"

Thane stood and glared back at him. He was starting to get angry. The Bard's rudeness was unfair. It wasn't as if the Reivers were going to teach him reading and numbers. He took a step backward. He wasn't sure he wanted to learn anything from this man. Orphan grabbed him by the arm and pulled him forward. He sat at the Bard's feet and Thane reluctantly allowed Orphan to yank him down to sit next to them.

"Of course he will, Tally!" Orphan answered for him as he squeezed Thane's arm tight as if to say "shut up and do what he tells you."

"Yeah. Of course I will." Thane mimicked and turned to glare angrily at Orphan as well.

Orphan was given the task of teaching Thane the alphabet and his numbers. They were both given a hornbook to practice writing and arithmetic. Tally spoke almost exclusively to Orphan. He only addressed Thane directly when he needed to correct one of his answers.

The reading, writing, and numbers lessons were actually easier than Thane expected them to be, and he found he caught on with surprising ease. He learned his letters and numbers after only one demonstration by Orphan. By the end of the first couple hours, he was actually reading short sentences in Latin and manipulating small combinations of numbers.

"You obviously already knew how to read and do your numbers," Orphan accused Thane as he slapped the manuscript shut in annoyance.

"Who taught you? Why did you lie to us?" he demanded.

"I wasn't lying when I told you I never learned how to read," Thane insisted although a part of him secretly agreed with Orphan. He felt as if the lessons were just a review. It all seemed very familiar to him but he had no recollection of his life before the Reivers and it was certainly nothing he learned while he was with them.

"Humph!" Tally snorted loudly and mumbled something just under his breath. He gathered up his books, rose and walked away without saying another word to them.

Orphan stared after his retreating back with his mouth open. "I don't understand what is going on. He is never rude to anyone." They watched until the Bard disappeared around the corner of the barn. Orphan turned to scowl at Thane as if Tally's bad manners were all his fault.

"Fine," Orphan said as he stood up too. "Don't tell us! Keep your secrets. I don't care anyway. Let's get back to the kitchen. It's time to help Tilda prepare the evening meal."

Thane watched him stomp away just as Tally had stomped away. He couldn't afford to alienate his only friend but he didn't know what else he could have said to him.

Thane and Orphan were both unusually quiet that evening as they helped Tilda serve and cleanup the evening meal; each lost in his own thoughts and each still just a bit angry with the other. Thane was sure that Orphan believed he was lying about the lessons and Thane was angry that Orphan didn't believe him. What made Thane even angrier was that he secretly agreed with Orphan. He must have been taught to read by someone but as hard as he tried, he couldn't remember where he might have had lessons like the ones Tally was giving Orphan.

The strained mood was broken later that night when Markus stumped into the inn with some of his friends. They grabbed a seat by the kitchen door while Markus raucously demanded that Thane and Orphan bring his friends a round of ale. Their mutual dislike of Markus brought them both back to common ground as their differences were rapidly put aside in favor of insulting the obnoxious group. When their chores were finished, they again found themselves at a corner table in the common room listening to Taliesin the Bard sing.

The days fell into a comfortable routine for Thane. He found that most days at the inn were much the same as his first day. He only saw the Bard during the noon meal, at their lessons and then from across the room during his evening performances. Thane had tried a number of times to get him alone. He was sure that Tally knew something about what had happened to him, but Tally always seemed to be going somewhere else. In fact, Thane was convinced the Bard was going out of his way to avoid being alone with him. So after the first few days, he just stopped trying.

Their first meeting was never mentioned. Neither was Tally's strange outburst although the incident seemed to hang between them. Sometimes, Thane would turn and catch the Bard staring at him with a worried frown across his brow when Tally thought no one was looking. It was terribly unnerving.

卌

"Thane, wake up. Thane, you're dreaming. Wake up."

Thane's eyes fluttered open to find Orphan hovering over him shaking his shoulder. Thane's first conscious thought was "It's still really dark. Why is Orphan already dressed?" Orphan dropped his hand off of Thane's shoulder and leaned back on his heels.

"Are you all right?" Orphan asked him.

Thane looked up at him and sighed. "Yeah, I'm okay." He pinched the bridge of his nose and closed his eyes tightly. He was drenched in sweat.

"That sounded like a bad one. Who is Natty?" Orphan asked as he swung his legs around to the front so he could rest his chin on his knees.

Thane rolled over onto his side to face Orphan. "Natty was the cook at the village I lived in. She was killed the day the village was attacked...the day I got here."

"I'm sorry." Orphan whispered. "Were your parents killed there too?"

Thane sat up and shrugged his shoulders. He shivered as the cold morning air hit his damp skin. He pulled his blanket up around his shoulders and scooted back to lean against the short wall behind him.

"No they weren't. I can't remember my parents. The only memories I have are of the years I spent with the Reivers. I can't remember anything from before that. There's just nothing there." Thane answered honestly.

"Thane, how did you get here? To Writtle I mean?" Orphan asked.

Thane put his head back, closed his eyes again and took a deep breath. "I have no idea, Orphan. One moment I was standing next to Natty's dead body by the village well, and the next moment there was a blinding blue light. I felt like I was being ripped apart from the inside out," he shuddered. He wasn't sure if it was from the memory or the cold air.

"The next thing I knew, I was waking up at the well just outside of town. Everyone I knew and everything familiar was gone."

"I know you probably don't believe me about this either but that's what happened. Honest!" he opened his eyes and stared through the dark at his friend.

Orphan was silent for so long that he thought Orphan probably did think he was lying and was mad at him again.

"I believe you, Thane," Orphan finally whispered.

"You have nightmares…a lot…and I hear you thrashing around at night. You also talk in your sleep. Look at you." He motioned his hand toward Thane. "You're all pale and sweaty. You can't lie about that." He paused again then whispered conspiringly, "I also think that Tally knows more than he is letting on about you."

"Yeah, well if he does, he's not going to tell me! I think he hates me," Thane complained.

"I don't think he hates you exactly. I've know him a long time and I have never seen him treat anyone the way he treats you. It is almost as if he is afraid," Orphan said. They both fell silent.

Thane looked at Orphan and turned the conversation around to ask Orphan about his life. He rattled off his own questions in rapid succession with barely a breath in between.

"Where are you from?"

"Why do they call you Orphan? I still think that is a stupid name by the way."

"Didn't you know your parents?"

"How did you wind up with The Bard?"

Orphan chuckled softly, and when Thane finally took a breath, Orphan interrupted his questioning. "Whoa, slow down." He put his hand up to stop Thane's interrogation.

"I don't remember my parents either." Orphan said. "I lived with an old couple when I was a small child, but I don't remember much about life with them. I remember her warm soft arms and his big hands."

"We lived in a simple two room cottage just outside of a small village a long way from here." His eyebrows drew down in a frown. "Alfred, the old man, died when I was about five. I guess the responsibility of caring for me and of being alone was too much for his wife, Anne. Not long after he passed, she took me into the village and gave me to Tally."

He paused for a moment as if thinking back on that day. "I remember crying for days for Anne. Tally was patient and kind, and, eventually, I guess I just stopped missing her. I have been traveling with him and Embarr since then. We've been here at the inn for a little more than a year. Anyway, we really don't have time to talk about Tally and me now."

He got up and briskly brushed the straw from his breeches. "Tilda will be taking the bread and scones out of the oven by now. Let's get some while they are still warm." He turned around, slid his feet into his boots and then hurried down the ladder.

Thane watched him disappear before he too slowly got up and dressed. He glanced over at Orphan's curtained bed. In the months that Thane had been at the inn, he and Orphan were rarely up in the loft at the same time except to sleep. In fact, Orphan was usually up and dressed before Thane and was almost always under his blankets behind the curtain before Thane came up to the loft for the night.

He thought about how strange it was that Orphan would take the time to dress before he woke Thane from what he had to have known was a really bad nightmare. In fact, now that Thane thought about it, he had never seen Orphan without clothes. Reivers changed in front of each other all the time. Maybe he was embarrassed to be seen naked. Was Orphan badly scarred or deformed?

With a shrug, he crawled to the edge of the loft, swung his legs over the edge and climbed down the ladder. He paused to rub the top of Embarr's face as he passed his stall on the way out.

"I'll be right back!" Thane reassured him.

Embarr bumped his shoulder with his nose and snorted in reply.

The kitchen was washed in soft yellow light from the small oil lamp in the middle of the kitchen table and the glow from the fireplace. Orphan was already sitting at the kitchen table with Tilda chattering on about something or other. Markus was across from him scowling into his mug. Marsden was standing next to Tilda stealing scones out of the basket in front of her.

Tilda and Marsden both looked up as Thane entered the kitchen. Marsden cleared his throat and said, "Well, I see everyone is up early this morning."

Tilda reached up, poked him in the ribs and nodded at him.

"Ah, yes, well...Tilda said..." she poked Marsden in the ribs when he paused, "I mean Tilda and I were thinking, that...well...with the cold weather approaching and with less people staying at the inn and all," Marsden shifted from one foot to the other, "that you boys should have your own rooms for the winter."

He cleared his throat, fluttered his mustache with a cough and continued, "Now don't be getting all comfortable and all. Once the weather warms up again and people start wanting rooms, you will have to go back to the loft in the stables."

"Yes, Marsden," the boys chanted together. Orphan was grinning. "Thank you, Marsden!"

"Well, what are you waiting for? Get back to the stables, both of you. Go on now! Won't have you boys slacking." Marsden growled while Tilda stood behind him smiling and nodding her head in approval.

Orphan grabbed Thane by the arm and dragged him towards the door.

"Hey, wait a minute...I didn't get anything to eat yet!" He turned back to grab a scone from Tilda's basket. He mumbled, "Thanks!" as Orphan yanked him out the door.

"Hey! What are you rushing me for?" Thane said through a mouthful of apple scone. He pulled his arm from Orphan's grip and tripped his way across the yard toward the barn. "I'm hungry and the scones are warm!" He whined as he rushed to keep up with Orphan who was almost at the stables.

"Didn't you see Markus' face? He was about to start arguing with Marsden." Orphan was rambling on, his mouth moving as fast as his feet. "He won't be happy about this. He really doesn't like that Marsden and Tilda have taken us all in. He is sure not to like us moving into the inn. Last winter I slept in the stables and, boy, was I cold...for months! I don't want to give Marsden any excuse to change his mind. So, come on. Let's clean out the stalls and feed the horses."

After the boys finished their chores that evening, they settled in to their usual table in the common room to listen to Tally. His last ballad was a sad tale of a beautiful Fæ Princess and her lost mortal love.

Niamh, of the Golden Hair,
Was a Fæ daughter of Manannán mac Lir,
She fell desperately in love,
With the mortal warrior Oisín.
Eternal happiness and youth,
She offered to him in the Land of Promise.
Together they traveled on her magical horse
To Tír inna n-Óc,
Where they lived and loved.
Of their blissful union a boy and a girl were born.
Happily together they lived
And Oisín felt not the passing of time,
Yet he began to feel homesick.
Longing filled him for his family,
And for the sight of the rich, green hills of Inis Fáil.
Niamh, sensing his sadness,
Lent to him her magical horse.
A grave warning,
She gave to him.
Do not let thy feet touch the earth,
Or you will be as you would have been.

Oisín eagerly agreed,
For his kin he did miss.
With promises to return to his love,
He traveled to Inis Fáil.
Reaching his village,
He was distressed to discover
Three hundred years had passed.
While he remained young,
His family was long since dead and his town lay in ruin.
As Oisín traveled past the town,
He came upon a family working their fields.
Oisín leaned down to help the farmer move a rock,
From the horse he tumbled.
As his body touched the earth,
The years fell upon him in an instant.
And a very,
Very old man he did become.
The horse returned to Niamh alone,
Where, in paradise, she mourns the loss of her love
For all eternity.

Tally was just strumming the last notes on the lute when Tilda walked over to the boy's table and tapped each of them on the shoulder. They were so intent on the Bard's tale that they both started.

"Go get your stuff and meet me up on the top floor. I have your rooms ready," she said over the increasing noise of the room.

THANE

Thane and Orphan wasted no time. They rushed out to the stables, gathered up their meager belongings, and were waiting in the third floor hallway before Tilda had a chance to get back up the stairs with clean sheets.

She laughed out loud when she saw them both standing there with their arms dripping clothes and weapons. Huge smiles were plastered across their faces. She opened the first door and nodded to Orphan to enter. She went a little further down the hall to the adjacent room and opened that door for Thane. She gave them each a set of clean sheets then wished them good night and left them to settle in.

Thane pulled the door shut behind him as he stepped into his new room. He breathed in the sweet smell of the lavender Molly had sprinkled on the rush mats that were strewn across the wooden floor. He tipped his armful of stuff on the bed then went to the window to admire the view through the thick glass of the window. Just below him he could see the roof of the kitchen and the small rear courtyard. The path that led to the stables was just visible.

He turned back to let his eyes wander over the room. The head of the narrow bed was pushed up against the wall he shared with Orphan's room. There was just enough room for him to walk between the dresser and the bed to get out the door. Although it was small, it seemed like a palace to Thane who had spent the last four years sleeping in his cloak on piles of smelly, old blankets in horse stables or out in the forests of the Borderlands.

Thane arranged his few belongings in the short chest. It took very little time to put the few clothes he had into it. His wooden sword, knife and leather sporran were laid carefully under his clothes.

It took him awhile to figure out how to make the bed. It looked so easy when he watched Molly do it. He would no sooner tuck one end of the sheet under the mattress then the other end would pull free. Finally, he was done. He stepped back and looked at the results. It didn't quite look like it did when Molly made it but it would do.

He took off his breeches and tunic and laid them across the three legged stool by the window. He snuffed out the candle on the small table as he climbed into the freshly made bed and snuggled himself into the clean coarse linen sheets. It was so quiet that he could hear Orphan moving around on the other side of the wall as he too settled into his new room.

He had been in these rooms many times before to help clean them but never thought there was a chance he would be allowed to sleep in one of them. He smiled and closed his eyes. For the first time in his memory, he fell asleep feeling safe and content.

He drifted in and out of wonderful dreams of a smiling woman. She had long blond hair and pointy ears just like his and bright sapphire blue eyes. She kissed him on the cheek and tucked him into a large four poster bed and covered him with fine, soft blue sheets that smelled of Lavender. The woman sang softly to him in a language that sounded familiar but he couldn't understand. He woke up the next morning feeling warm, comfortable and happy.

Chapter Twelve

The Nightmares Are Real

The winter months were long, uneventful, and often boring. The cold and occasional snow kept most travelers away and when the weather was really bad, even the local villagers stayed in their homes in the evenings. After their chores in the stables were done, they spent most of the afternoon with Tally and their studies. It wasn't long before Thane was reading almost as well as Orphan.

In the evenings, Tally continued to tell stories and sing songs by the fireplace regardless of how few people were in the common room. Orphan was learning to play the lute so he would often accompany Tally at the fireplace when there were only a few people in the room.

One night in late winter, a fierce blizzard blew in. After a simple meal was served and cleaned up, everyone gathered around the fireplace in the common room. Two travelers who had been stranded at the inn by the wild weather were settled comfortably at a corner table. Thane and Orphan were sitting in their usual place. Marsden and Tilda were at a small table to the right of the fireplace. Markus sat away from the group with his head down on his arms on a table.

Tally sat with his lute in his usual corner by the fireplace singing ancient songs. The music seemed strangely familiar to Thane and after a couple of songs, Thane began to hum along. Soon, he was softly singing verses here and there with the Bard. Tally looked up at Thane and stopped singing abruptly. Thane finished the final cadence alone. Tally stared at Thane as an uncomfortable silence fell across the common room.

The Bard sighed and mumbled to himself, "Might as well start with a history lesson."

He put his lute down next to the wall of the fireplace then turned back to the small group gathered in front of him.

Tally began his tale in a soft, soothing voice:

A long time ago, when the earth was still very young,
It was a place of darkness and flame.
Volcanoes erupted endlessly,
Liquid fire traveled for miles from
The peaks of exploding mountains.
Ash and smoke spewed into the sky
And blanketed the world in darkness,
It blocked out all light from the moon
And warmth from the sun.
Into this darkness,
A fierce wind blew the ash from the sky
And extinguished the flames.

THANE

The Earth split open,
Water welled up from deep beneath the ground.
Danu, the goddess of life,
Bubbled up from the well and flowed across the earth.
The spring became a stream,
The stream became a raging river.
The sun began to peak through the gloom,
Green grass and flowers sprang up at the river's edge.
The pure, blue waters began to wash away
The poisons from the earth,
As winds cleansed the poisons from the sky.
Life began to flourish along the banks of the river,
Plants and animals thrived.
A Sacred Tree grew out of the fertile soil,
Fed and nurtured by the waters of the Danu.
The tree was called Bíle,
The God of All Knowledge.
The Goddess Danu and the God Bíle joined together,
To create the first Færies of Danu.
The male, Dagda,
The Righteous God.
The female, Brigid,
The Goddess of Wisdom.
They were commanded to go out and populate the earth,
To build great cities to honor
The Goddess Danu and the God Bíle.

"Awe, Tally!" Markus bellowed out rudely from the back of the room. "You goin' on about those dang Færies again! 'ow about singing some of 'em tales about ogres or dragons?" he belched out.

Tally cleared his throat but didn't respond. His eyebrows drew down over his eyes as he looked over at Thane and focused intently on him for just a moment, then abruptly gathered up his belongings and left the common room.

The awkward silence was broken when one of the travelers banged his chair against the table as they got up to return to their rooms. Tilda and Marsden rose without a word and went back into the kitchen to close up for the night. Orphan and Thane headed up the stairs to their rooms. Orphan was unusually quiet.

He mumbled "Goodnight" and with a last glance at Thane, he softly closed his door.

Thane couldn't fall asleep. He tossed and turned as he went over and over the story the Bard told. It was familiar to him somehow, like a tale that had once been told at bedtime. Eventually, he fell asleep only to dream about great ships full of Færies riding on billowy clouds. The clouds became dark and stormy as the Færies got closer to land. Thunder and lightening shook the ships.

Thane jerked awake as he realized that the thunder was actually someone pounding on his bedroom door and the lightning was the sun shining brightly through the window in his room.

Orphan cracked the door open and poked his head in. "Are you still in bed? Markus is looking for you, so you better get up and get out to the stables before he finds you up here still asleep. I'll try to sneak you out some bread. So hurry!" He left quickly, shutting the door behind him.

His dreams forgotten, Thane whipped the blanket back and flew out of the warm bed. He threw on his clothes and boots and hurried down the stairs and rushed out the back door. He just managed to stop himself from falling as his feet slipped and slid on the slushy snow outside the kitchen door.

He stared around the courtyard at a silent world that was completely covered in a thick blanket of white. A few tree branches were so weighed down with snow that they were touching the ground. The sun reflecting off of the snow was so bright he had to squint just to see where he was going. He followed the path that had been made through the snow toward the stables. It looked like many feet had already made the trip back and forth.

Thane stopped to watch Markus struggle to walk back from the stables on the narrow path through the snow with his arms full of wood. His feet flew out from under him. Wood went flying up in the air. His arms swung furiously, like two windmills, as he tried to catch his balance. With a loud bellow, he toppled back and landed hard on his back. He was half buried in the snow with his legs and arms akimbo.

Thane stuffed his fist in his mouth to silence his laugher. His eyes ran with tears as he watched Markus, moaning loudly with wood scattered all around him, struggle like an upside-down turtle trying to lift himself up out of the deep snow.

Thane turned and slid back into the kitchen, through the common room and rushed out the front door of the inn. It would be worth trudging through the deep snow to circle around the side of the long building. If he could sneak unseen into the back of the stables, he could avoid being seen by Markus. Hopefully, he could manage to stay out of the reach of his fists. Markus was bound to be in a really bad mood after his fall, especially if he discovered that Thane had witnessed it.

The stables were warmer than outside but not by much. There were two other horses in the stables besides Embarr, Cinnamon, and Nutmeg and even their extra body heat was not enough to make much headway against the bitter cold outside. Thane was very grateful for the warm bedroom he just left. He rubbed his hands together, grabbed a pitch fork and got to work.

⁂

The snow melted rapidly as the weather began to warm up. All around the inn the world was coming back to life. The grass was turning green, trees were beginning to unfold tender bright green leaves, and the happy, yellow faces of daffodils were popping up everywhere. Thane and Orphan were asked to move back into the stables when the rooms started to fill up as travelers began to arrive at the inn again.

As spring progressed, Thane's nightmares got worse. More often than not, he would wake up in the middle of the night shivering violently and soaked in cold sweat. He would roll over to find Orphan's concerned green eyes peering at him from under his burlap curtain. Orphan never asked about the dreams but Thane could tell that Orphan was worried about him; Thane was worried too. He wasn't sure what bothered him more, that he could only remember bits and pieces of his dreams or that the bits and pieces he did remember terrified him.

He was usually able to fall back asleep, but tonight was different. These dreams were, if possible, even more intense. He remembered everything this time.

After he had been jolted awake for a third time, he sat up. He pulled his knees to his chest, wrapped his cloak tightly around himself and leaned back against the wall. Thane was too afraid to fall back asleep. He couldn't shake the image of a tall man with pale eyes that flashed with a burning red light. It stayed with him and was frighteningly clear.

Orphan had not awakened again after the first time and Thane hesitated to wake him even though he was desperate for the company. What would Thane say? Please wake up and sit with me because I am afraid? He huddled against the wall listening to the hushed sounds of the night and never felt so alone. As soon as the first gray light of dawn began to lighten the dark corners of the stables, he dressed silently and crept from the loft.

Thane found himself struggling to stay awake during his morning chores. Orphan was unusually quiet and kept sliding anxious glances in his direction as if he wanted to say something but didn't know how to begin. Thane was relieved when they finally headed to the kitchen for the noon meal. Maybe food would help wake him up a bit. At the least, eating in the kitchen would give Orphan someone else to stare furtively at.

Rubbing the tiredness from his eyes, and not really paying attention to where he was going, Thane stumbled through the back door to the kitchen. He bowled right into Tally who was coming out of the kitchen carrying a mug full of some unidentifiable brown liquid. Tally had no sooner righted the cup when Orphan rushed up behind Thane and barreled into his back. Thane was thrown forward into the Bard again who in turn went crashing backwards into the door frame. This time the full contents of the mug spilled down the front of Tally's shirt. The Bard looked down his nose at Thane.

Taking a deep breath in through his mouth and breathing out through his nose in an obvious effort to control his temper, Tally said, "It seems to be time to teach you a few lessons in self control young man. You need to work off some of that excess energy."

He squinted at the dark circles under Thanes eyes. "Orphan tells me that you have been having nightmares."

Thane turned and shot Orphan a glare but didn't respond.

The Bard shrugged and continued, "He also said you have a knife and a wooden sword hidden in the stables that you flail about killing imaginary monsters with when you think no one is looking. Go get them both and meet me behind the stables after your meal. You come too Orphan, inasmuch as you don't seem to have any more self control than he does."

The Bard shoved his empty cup into Thane's hands and without waiting for them to acknowledge his command; he walked away, brushing his hands down the front of his shirt to wipe away the mess. He walked around the corner of the stables still grumbling.

When he was out of sight, Thane rounded on Orphan. "Great!" he snapped. "What did you go blabbing to him for? It's none of his business! Sometimes, I swear, you are worse than a girl!" He slammed the cup down on the table that was just inside the kitchen door, then he too turned and stomped away without waiting for a reply.

Thane was so angry he was shaking. The last thing he wanted to do was to spend time with Tally. The Bard had barely spoken to him in weeks. In fact, he had even stopped giving them lessons. He would just hand them leather bound books and send them off to read. Thane had asked Orphan once where Tally had found all of the expensive manuscripts, but Orphan said he had no idea. Now he was facing having to spend hours with him again. He wanted to have sword fighting lessons but not from Tally. The Bard still made him uncomfortable.

Thane entered the stable door, climbed up to the loft, and threw himself down on his pile of straw. He became even more enraged when he realized that not only was he angry, but he was also very hungry. He reached under the nearest pile of straw and pulled out his sword, knife, and the sporran full of his treasures.

He stared down at the leather bag. He hadn't opened it since he'd come to the inn. Sitting down with his back to the wall, he laid the sword across his lap, slipped the knife into the side of his left boot and tipped out the contents of the bag. He let them fall through his fingers onto the wooden floor in front of him. Memories washed over him as he picked up each item and thought back to the years he had spent collecting each of the little pieces.

He had been frequently left to his own devices on raids with the Reivers, so he scavenged for little treasures of his own while the men were reiving. Some things he gave to Natty while others he hid in the little leather pouch she had given him. He picked through the small items and examined them one by one: a rusty key; a couple of clay marbles; and a piece of smooth, flat, green, glass. His favorite piece was a small silver horse head that had probably been either an emblem or device from some dead man's helmet. In the woods, around the Reiver village, he'd found a couple sharp animal teeth, a beautiful blue and white feather, and a long narrow stone of smooth clear crystal. Natty had given him a tiny ball of red yarn once when he was a young child because he said that he had liked the color. At last he ran his fingers along the blue ribbon he had been so eager to give to her.

He missed Natty fiercely at times. His chest still ached when he thought of her. He had been at the inn for almost a year now and was not really unhappy. In fact, he liked Tilda, Marsden, and Orphan. Even Markus wasn't too bad if you stayed out of reach of his fists. It was the Bard that puzzled him the most. There was something strangely familiar about him. Thane just couldn't shake the feeling that he was forgetting something important. As comfortable as he felt here, there were times he thought that maybe he wasn't really as safe here as he wanted to believe he was.

With a sigh, he gathered up his pile of treasures, stuffed them back in the leather sporran, and shoved the bag back under his bed of hay. Resigning himself to spending another long afternoon under the Bard's critical gaze, he got up, and grabbed his wooden sword. He headed back down the ladder and reluctantly made his way out to the rear of the stables.

Tally was seated under a tree not far from the edge of the clearing just outside the rear door of the stables. Orphan was sitting next to him whispering animatedly to Tally. When he saw Thane, he abruptly stopped talking and stared down at his hands. He didn't look up as Thane approached. Tally pushed himself to his feet, and stood watching Thane walk toward them. He held out his hand for the sword, "Let me see it."

Thane handed the sword over to Tally and stood waiting, his hands hanging at his side and his eyebrows drawn down over his eyes in a belligerent scowl. Thane refused to look over at Orphan. He was still angry with him. The rational part of him knew he was being unreasonable. He knew that Orphan was worried about him and only wanted to help, but he couldn't help feeling betrayed. He had his nightmares under control and it was nobody's business if he woke in a cold sweat, shaking in fear almost every night. He had it handled. He didn't want the Bard to think he was weak.

The Bard held the sword up, examining it. It looked like a toy in his long slender hands. The blade was flat, with a dull edge, and was carved out of some type of pale red wood. Tally traced a finger along the intertwining circular designs on the hilt. He swung the sword around and slashed it through the air.

"Where did you get this?" Tally asked as he held it up to his face and looked down the etched length of the blunt wooden blade.

"It was stolen on a raid," Thane said with some defiance.

Tally sliced it through the air a few more times. "Humph...not bad balance for a piece of wood. Who ever made this knew what he was doing," he mumbled to himself. He handed it back to Thane. "Alright, now show me what you can do."

"What? Right now?" Thane asked, glancing down at Orphan for the first time to see if he was watching. He wasn't...yet. "Here?" he squeaked. Why did his voice have to do that now, in front of Tally?

"No, tonight when we're all in bed! Of course, right now. Come on. We don't have all day!" Tally barked back, an eyebrow rose in an expression that said he was rapidly becoming annoyed.

Thane grit his teeth, bent his knees a bit, gripped the hilt firmly with his left hand and swung the sword in a diagonal from left to right and then from right to left. He lunged and thrust the sword forcefully forward toward Tally's abdomen.

"Ho!" the Bard snorted and laughed. "You really stink!" he said between chuckles. "Where did you learn to flail your arm around like that?"

Thane's eyebrows were drawn together in an angry frown. "I taught myself," he said through his teeth.

"Well, that much is painfully obvious!" Tally continued to snicker.

"You know what?" Thane protested in anger. "I don't need you! I didn't ask for your help! I DON'T WANT YOUR HELP!" He swung away to leave.

"Thane!" Orphan finally spoke. He jumped up and ran around to the front of Thane. Orphan tried to stop Thane's retreat with both hands flat against his chest. "Wait. Stop being such an idiot. He's trying to help you." Despite digging his heals in, Orphan was being pushed back by Thane's angry advance.

"Yeah, well he has a funny way of showing it," Thane snarled, trying to knock Orphan's hands off of him. "Get out of my way!"

"You just don't understand," Orphan said to him and with one last hard shove he managed to push Thane back a couple steps. Thane stopped. His whole body was tense with anger.

Orphan tentatively lowered his hands and turned back to address Tally. "It's time Tally. You have to tell him what you told me yesterday. He has to understand what is happening to him. He has nightmares almost every night now, Tally. Please, I know it is hard for you, but he has to know."

Thane paused and turned to stare from Orphan to Tally then back to settle on Orphan's anxious face. "Understand what?" Thane asked, a sick feeling beginning to sink into his empty stomach.

"What happened to you! Who you are! What you are! Thane, what we are. It was no mistake that you were sent to this village," he turned back to Tally. "Please Tally, tell him."

The Bard's shoulders slumped like the life had drained right out of him. With a sigh, he turned and walked back over to the tree he had been sitting under. He slowly lowered himself down and despite the warmth of the day, drew his cloak tight around his shoulders.

Orphan pulled cautiously at Thane's sleeve until he walked back toward the Bard and tugged on his arm until they were both sitting at the Bards' feet. Tally was staring down at his hands. He was silent for a long time. Thane felt the sick knot of fear in his stomach grow.

Whatever Tally had to tell him, it didn't look like it was going to be a happy tale.

Finally, Tally looked up at Thane, took a deep breath in through his nose and asked softly, "Do you remember your parents or anything that happened before you lived with the Reivers?"

Strange, it was the same question that Cessford had asked him the night of their last raid. Thane shrugged and said "No, not really. I've had dreams of a woman with long, blond hair and beautiful blue eyes but she's never very clear. I am not even sure she's my mother."

"That's the only thing you remember?" asked Orphan.

"Yeah," Thane said with a frown. "The first clear memories I have are of waking up in some sort of burial crypt. I was laying on the floor next to a crumbled empty tomb that had been broken down the middle. I wandered around in a forest for some time before the Reivers captured me. I was with them for four summers. One afternoon we were attacked while returning from a raid. The next thing I knew, there was this awful pain throughout my body, a flash of light, and I was waking up against the well just outside of town."

"But you remember nothing from before you were with the Reivers?" asked Tally again.

Thane was silent for a moment, shrugged his shoulders and said, "Nothing."

"What about the nightmares? Orphan told me you are having them almost every night now," Tally asked softly.

Thane glared at Orphan again before saying, "I have had the dreams Orphan is talking about for as long as I can remember," he reluctantly admitted. "They seem so real sometimes, but they are just dreams."

Orphan said, "Tell him about them, Thane. You can trust him."

Thane looked between Orphan and Tally. He had never told anyone about his dreams, not even Natty. Maybe it was time he shared them with someone. Maybe Tally knew something and could tell him what the dreams meant.

Thane took a deep breath and began, "I dream about a nobleman and an evil wizard. They're arguing..." Thane recounted the dream for them. He didn't leave out any details, "...then I have this awful pain, there's a flash of silver blue light and I wake up."

"It's just a nightmare, right?" he finished his throat dry from talking. He looked at the Bard who was now sitting with his face buried in his long slender hands and his shoulders shaking.

"Right? Tally?" Thane asked again, the sick feeling in his stomach was riding up his chest and beginning to choke him. Orphan reached over and put a hand on Tally's knee. He looked over at Thane and said, "The boy in the dream, his name was Nathaniel right?"

"Yes, how do you know that?" demanded Thane.

"Taliesin was the royal Bard to the nobleman in your dream," Orphan whispered.

Thane started to smile, "Yeah, very funny Orphan…you've been listening to my nightmares for far too long. You are making this up," he said as he looked from Tally to Orphan. "I don't think it's funny."

Tally lifted his head and looked at Thane. Thane's smile faded quickly. Tally's eyes were filled with tears, and deep lines of grief were etched on his face. "Why would I be dreaming about a nobleman I've never met?" demanded Thane.

"Martha, the head cook, spoiled that little boy rotten. He adored her and she him. She called him 'Thane.' Don't you understand me, boy? Thane was her nickname for little Nathaniel. You are not having nightmares Thane, you are reliving a nightmare," Tally insisted, his voice hoarse with emotion.

Thane jumped to his feet. His hands were clenched at his side, silver light flashed in his dark eyes, and his face was flushed with fear and anger.

"You two are crazy! I don't know what you're playing at! I'm nothing...a stable boy. DO YOU HEAR ME! I'M A STABLE BOY," he shouted. His whole body was shaking now. They were wrong. Wrong!

He turned and ran. He could hear Orphan and Tally calling out to him, the sound of their feet pounding the ground behind him, but he didn't care. He just ran faster, blindly turning to run into the woods. Branches of trees whipped at his face and bushes caught his clothes. He ran and ran until he couldn't run any longer. He stopped at a small waterfall. He dropped down on his knees next to the bubbling stream. He buried his face in his hands just as Tally had done, doubled over and cried. He cried for the beautiful woman. He cried for the nobleman. Finally, he cried for the scared little boy he had been.

The memories were coming back to him in a rush now. They were tumbling into his mind even faster than the water was tumbling over the rocks. Martha, smiling down at him, as she cuddled him in her lap laughing and wiping the fruit juices off of his chin with her apron as he ate his fill of pastries.

He remembered his mother, the beautiful woman from his dreams, tucking him into bed at night, as his father stood behind her looking over her shoulder. He recalled many, many happy days walking in the gardens below his bedroom window with his mother; the feel of the sun shining on his face and the fragrant scent of flowers in the air. He remembered his favorite white horse, Embarr, a gift to him from his Færie grandmother on his fifth birthday. He would ride Embarr for hours along side his father, Cianán. His father, a tall, handsome, smiling man with jet black hair and black eyes…black hair and black eyes just like his own.

And finally, he remembered Taliesin, the Bard. How many nights had he spent sitting at the Bard's knee, listening to the very same tales and songs that he had heard him sing all those nights in the Wyndmyl common room? He'd worshipped Taliesin; had loved the vivid pictures he painted with the soft comforting sound of his voice. How many nights had he demanded he be allowed to stay up and listen to Taliesin; only to fall asleep at the Bard's feet and need to be carried to bed by his father.

How could he have forgotten Damien, his best friend and Martha's youngest grandson? Even though Damien was almost two years older than he was, they had been inseparable, incorrigible and always in trouble. What happened to them all? Where were they? How did he get away? Did anyone else make it out of that nightmare alive?

Thane sat at the edge of the stream with his knees pressed up to his chest, his arms wrapped tightly around his legs. He cried until there were no tears left. Finally, he curled up on the ground and fell into an exhausted sleep.

Chapter Thirteen

Tally's Tale

Thane slowly became aware that his name was being called. He opened his eyes and realized he was still lying by the side of the little waterfall. It was now almost dark. He concentrated on the sound of the water rushing over the rocks and tried to ignore the persistent voices. He felt the ground shaking beneath his face as horses cantered closer to where he lay and recognized Tally's and Orphan's voices calling out to him, but he was too overwhelmed to care.

He closed his eyes again and pulled himself up into a tighter ball. Maybe they wouldn't find him, and they would just go away. Before long, he heard the rustling of nearby bushes as they stumbled through a narrow opening in the woods and heard them come to an abrupt stop behind him. Thane squeezed his eyes even tighter and wished with all his might for them to leave. They didn't.

"Looks like he fell asleep," Thane strained to hear Tally's whisper over the babble of the water.

"I'll stay here with him for a while," Tally quietly directed Orphan. "You go back to the inn. Tell them we went for a ride and that we'll be back soon. I don't want to worry Tilda and the last thing we need to do right now is attract unwanted attention to ourselves by disappearing."

"Okay," Orphan whispered back. "Are you going to be alright? You're really pale."

"I am fine." Tally sounded anything but fine to Thane. His voice was hoarse and unsteady.

"The fates of the Fæ rest on the shoulders of this heartbroken little boy, and I am just not sure I am up to the task of preparing him for what is ahead." He cleared his throat. "Go now. We have been gone a long time already," Tally ordered.

After a moment, the ground shuddered under Thane again as a horse turned and rode away. Thane sighed to himself. Tally was not going to leave him alone. He opened his eyes.

Twilight was painting the sky a deep blue gray and shadows were spreading a blanket of darkness over the forest and the stream. Thane was still curled up on his side with his arms wrapped around his body when Tally put his hand on Thane's shoulder and gently shook him.

Startled by the sudden contact, Thane pulled himself away from the hand. He rolled away from Tally and pulled himself up to sit facing the waterfall as he scrubbed the mud and the tears off of his face with the back of his hand. Tally lowered himself so he was sitting down next to Thane and placed his hand on Thane's back. This time Thane didn't pull away.

They sat together in silence watching the water cascading over the moss covered rocks. Finally, without looking at Thane, Tally began to speak. His voice was soft and soothing but still a little unsteady.

"When I first met your father, he was just a little boy. He was strong willed and arrogant, much as you would expect the son of a clan chief to be, but he was also kind, generous, compassionate and tolerant," Tally shifted a bit on the hard earth before he continued.

"As the years went by, I watched as he grew into an amazing young man. Even though he was as strong and skilled as any knight in your grandfather's garrison, I never saw him take a life if he could avoid it." Tally paused and took a deep breath. "Your father was a good man, Thane. I loved him like a son."

Tally slid a sideways glance at Thane, "He would be very proud of you."

"For what? I haven't done anything but run away and shovel out stables," Thane said with a snort and a bit of a snuffle. His soft words were barely audible over the rush of the water.

"You have survived," Tally said firmly. "Survived to grow and thrive. You have become an astonishing young man, Thane, strong, honest, and trustworthy. I know you had difficult times with the Reivers, but while you were with them, you were hidden; safe and protected. You have learned the value of hard work; a lesson not easily taught to a spoiled young prince I might add," he said with a sad sort of chuckle.

Thane shrugged but didn't respond.

Tally got to his feet and began to pace back and forth behind Thane.

"I was in the castle the day Zavior and his forces attacked," Tally said softly. "I heard the creatures you called Roki screaming and his soldiers beating down the doors. I looked out my bedroom window and saw you running around the church toward the crypt. A Roki was following not too far behind you and I was so afraid for you. I didn't think about what might be happening inside the castle, just that you were running outside alone and there was a monster following you."

"I slid quickly through the servant's entrance and followed. When I got to the small stone building, I was surprised to find Embarr at the entrance, desperately pawing at the door, and neighing in fear."

Tally stopped to look down at Thane. "To this day I don't know how he got out of the stables and past Zavior's men. It took all my strength to pull him way from the crypt and tie him to the nearest tree."

He resumed his pacing. "I headed into the entrance of the crypt and followed the sound of a roaring Roki, through the catacombs, and down to Monpier's tomb. I must have arrived just as you disappeared because I found the Roki howling like he had been denied his favorite meal and clutching what looked like a piece of your blanket. Monpier's empty tomb was broken open down the middle and dust clouded the air."

Tally paused, took a deep breath and continued. "The Roki turned as I entered the catacomb. I'll spare you the details; we fought and I killed him. I searched through the catacombs but you were gone."

"By the time I ran out of the crypt, the castle was on fire and Zavior's army and dozens of Roki were already overrunning the battlements. I am ashamed to say I mounted Embarr and we fled into the woods. That was five years ago. You were just seven." His voice shook.

Tally folded himself up again to sit next to Thane. They sat in silence for a while, each of them lost in their own memories.

"Not a day has passed since that night that I have not regretted, with every fiber of my being, that I did not go back into the castle to try to aid your parents. I have hated myself even more this past year when I realized that you didn't die, and I blamed myself for running away and not staying to look for you. I resented that you had been sent here and the responsibility for your care and training had been thrust upon me with no regards to my desires. I felt guilty for not wanting the burden of that responsibility."

"I never asked you to…" Thane began defensively.

"No you didn't," Tally interrupted, "but make no mistake about it; you were sent here to me and I will do everything in my power to protect you."

"I know now that I could have done nothing to save your parents. They were already dead and you had already left the tomb. Your tale has eased my conscience, Thane, and for that I thank you. As for being responsible for you, I will deal with my feelings about that eventually." They sat in silence for a while listening to the water tumble over the rocks. Eventually, Tally stood up.

"It is getting dark, Thane, and it is a long way home. We need to head back." He held out his hand to help Thane up.

Thane looked at Tally's hand then raised his eyes to gaze up into the face of the man he had once loved almost as much as he loved his own father. He saw the differences now. This Tally looked much older. His hair was almost all gray now. Grief and despair had etched deep lines in his face. It was his eyes that held the greatest change. Where they once sparkled with life and happiness; they were now dulled with sorrow and hopelessness.

Thane reached up and hesitantly grabbed hold of his hand. He let Tally pull him to his feet and then into the circle of the Bard's arms for a brief hug before Tally turned to get the horse.

Thane stood right where Tally left him. He was having a hard time taking it all in. This morning he was just a stable boy going about his business and trying to get through his day one chore at a time. Now he was overwhelmed by memories of another life, life as the privileged son of a clan chief and a Fæ princess.

Tally walked over to the tree Cinnamon was lashed to and untied the reigns. He climbed into the saddle and rode back to Thane. Tally held his hand down to help Thane climb up behind him. They rode slowly away from the waterfall, following Orphan's trail. Thane wrapped his arms around Tally's waist so he wouldn't fall from the horse and rested his face against Tally's boney back, head down, shoulders slumped.

He felt drained.

They rode back through the moonlit forest in silence. After quite some time, the lights of the town finally came into view. Thane was stunned at just how far he had run. As they got closer to the inn, Tally pulled Cinnamon to a halt. He turned around in the saddle and put his hand on the arm Thane had around his waist.

"It is vital that you not breathe a word of this to anyone. There are many who would wish you and Orphan harm, Thane. Zavior has spies everywhere. You must stay hidden and trust no one but myself and Orphan. You understand?"

Thane shrugged, "Yeah, I guess."

Tally turned around and they continued on in silence.

"Who would want to hurt Orphan? Why did the old lady leave him with you? You have been together a long time, right?" Thane questioned Tally.

"Yes, we are together," said Tally. "We will talk about Orphan tomorrow."

They entered the rear courtyard and rode straight into the stables. Tally slid down after Thane. As Tally secured Cinnamon in his stall, Thane headed toward the ladder to the loft. Embarr blew his lips at Thane as he passed him, but Thane didn't acknowledge him.

"Thane," Tally called after him.

Thane stopped but didn't turn around.

"Please come to the kitchen with me. You need to eat something or Tilda will be out here herself looking for you."

Thane took a deep breath, squared his shoulders and followed Tally.

In the kitchen, Tilda was cleaning pots and Orphan was drying them. They both looked up as Thane and Tally entered. Thane was grateful to see that no one else was around tonight.

Tilda looked at Thane's torn and dirty clothes and pale, tear streaked face and crooned softly. "Thane…" She made a move to rush over to them, but Tally stopped her with a shake of his head. She frowned at him but didn't comment any further. She stepped back to the pots and said quietly, "Marsden has been looking for you both."

"I went for a ride with Thane. We had some things to discuss. I'd appreciate some stew and ale, if it is not too late, Tilda. Stew for Thane as well if you don't mind," Tally said in a matter of fact voice.

Tilda nodded and turned to fill two bowls with a thick, fragrant, dark stew. She put the bowls on the small kitchen table by the wall between the fireplace and the window. As Thane and Tally sat, she added the bread. They ate in silence. Orphan was glancing anxiously at them as they ate but somehow managed to hold his tongue.

The only sounds in the room were the spoons scraping the sides of the bowls as Thane and Tally ate in silence. Thane pushed his food around the bowl for a bit before finally giving up the pretense of eating. Even though he hadn't eaten any lunch, he wasn't very hungry and wasn't sure he would get much past the tight knot in his throat.

He stood up on shaky legs and handed his almost full bowl back to Tilda. He mumbled a soft, "Thank you," to her and headed out the back door.

The stables were quiet. Embarr was still at the gate of his stall and waiting for Thane. When he walked past his stall, Embarr blew his lips at him again and shook his head. He was even more determined to get Thane's attention this time.

Thane went to him and put his arms around *his* horse's neck. He buried his face deep into the long white mane and breathed in his musky smell. "What a good boy you are," he mumbled through the long coarse hair.

He now remembered the many hours they had spent together when he was a small boy. "I guess you didn't forget me did you?" he whispered to the horse.

They stood in silence together for a bit, then, with a sigh and one last nuzzle from Embarr, Thane turned to climb up to the loft.

Thane found his sword lying across his blanket. Orphan must have brought it back with him from the clearing. Gratefully, he picked it up and shoved it back under his pile of hay. Reaching into his boot, he pulled out the knife and put that in the hay next to his sword as well. He undressed and crawled under his blanket. Thane lay on his back, with his arms behind his head and stared at the rafters that crisscrossed the roof.

It seemed like hours before he heard Orphan and Tally come into the stables below. He rolled over to face the wall. He didn't want to talk to anyone. Maybe they would think he was asleep and leave him alone. He could hear Orphan whispering but couldn't quite make out what Orphan said although Thane thought he heard his name spoken.

Tally's door shut softly, and Orphan finally climbed the ladder. To Thane's surprise, he went straight to his curtain. Thane could hear the rustle of Orphan's clothes as he undressed. He was grateful to be left alone. It was a long time before he finally fell asleep and for the first time in a very long time, he didn't dream.

Chapter Fourteen

Sword Practice

It was a somber group that gathered behind the stables the next afternoon. The sun was tucked securely behind heavy gray clouds that had been threatening rain all morning. Thane and Orphan sat at the feet of the Bard just as they had many times before, only this time, a feeling of foreboding lay upon the threesome.

The morning chores had been completed in silence as Thane had not had much to say to anyone, and for once Orphan was reticent. The noon meal was an equally quiet event. Now they sat around looking anywhere but at each other.

Tally broke the awkward silence. "Thane, I know that all of this has been a great shock to you, but there is more that I feel you aught to know."

"There's more?" Thane repeated speaking for the first time since last night.

"Thane, you asked me about Orphan. Who would want to hurt him? How we met?" He paused and looked at Orphan who nodded at him to continue.

"Well, as I told you, I left the castle that night on Embarr. We traveled together for some months through the forests and hills of Ireland."

"Ireland?" Thane interrupted him. "I'm from Ireland?"

Tally nodded, "Well, your father's from Ireland. Don't interrupt me boy!"

He adjusted the folds of his cloak tighter around his shoulders and began again, "Anyway, about six months after I left the castle with Embarr, we boarded a pirate ship and headed across the sea to the West Coast of Scotland." Tally held up his hand to silence Thane when he opened his mouth to ask another question. "We spent a few more months traveling through the Highlands before we found a pub near Inverness that would grant us room and board in return for nightly performances."

"One afternoon, an old woman followed Embarr and me through the streets to the pub. She sat huddled under an old cloak and ordered a mug of ale that she didn't drink. She sat there all night, clutching the mug tightly in her gnarled old hands; just listening to me sing. Well, I didn't think too much about it because…well…I'm very good aren't I?" Tally said in a matter of fact tone.

"When I was done, she rose and left as quietly as she had come. The next night, she returned with a small child. This time she stayed when I had finished. She waited until everyone else had left the common room then approached me. She placed the hand of the sleepy child in mine and told me a strange story." He paused, lost for a moment in memories of another time and place.

"What did the old woman say?" Thane asked eagerly.

"The small child had been left with her on a wild night three years previously. A beautiful young woman, with long flowing red hair and vivid green eyes, rode out of the ocean on a white horse near the cottage where she lived. She wore a long, brilliantly white robe belted at her slender waist with a thin gold chain tipped with brightly jeweled ends. A small child lay nestled asleep in her arms."

"She handed the child down and begged the old woman to hide her child for it was in grave danger. She told the old woman, that when the time was right, a traveling Bard would appear to her on a white horse. She was adamant that her child should be left in the Bard's care." Tally paused for a moment and Thane saw him swallow hard before he continued.

"The old woman cried as she described how the beautiful woman had climbed down off of the horse and tenderly kissed the child on the forehead. Then, before the old woman's eyes, the woman started to age. Lines upon lines appeared on her face and body. She seemed to fold up upon herself as if the weight of many, many years pressed down upon her skin. She got older and older until there was nothing left of her but dust. Then, a dark cloud passed overhead and the wind howled and swirled. The old woman spoke of how she watched in horror as the ashes and robe of the woman were blown out into the sea by the wild wind. The white horse reared up on its hind legs and bellowed an anguished cry to the sky before it turned and galloped back across a turbulent sea. The only thing that remained behind was the child wrapped in a silken blanket and the golden belt."

"I have been with Tally ever since," Orphan added quietly.

Thane looked back and forth between the two confused. "I don't understand. Who was she...the beautiful woman? Where did she come from? Why did she think Orphan was in danger?"

"She was Orphan's Mother," Tally said.

The Bard turned to Orphan and nodded in encouragement. "Go ahead. Show him." When Orphan hesitated Tally said, "As you said last night, he needs to know."

Orphan rolled up on his knees and knelt in front of Thane. He met Thane's eyes defiantly then pulled his thick red hair back away from both of his ears.

Thane jumped to his feet.

"What the hell are those?" he squeaked, staring down at Orphan's small pointy ears in shock. He reached up to the points on his own ears and covered them almost as if in self defense. "You have them too?"

Orphan snickered and said, "Obviously!"

"And you're also a Færie prince? Why didn't you tell me?"

"Don't be stupid. I'm not a prince. I guess, like you, I am half Fæ." He shrugged and pulled his red hair back down to cover his ears. "I told you I don't know much about my parents, but apparently my mother was a mortal."

"Is there anything else I need to know?" Thane demanded of them. It seemed like every time he thought he understood the people around him; they threw something else at him.

"No. What else could you possibly need to know now?" Tally said quickly. Orphan opened his mouth as if to say something else but snapped it shut when he saw the look on Tally's face.

Tally abruptly changed the subject. "Thane, you held the sword with your left hand yesterday. You never use your left hand to do anything else. Why did you do so with the sword?"

Thane looked between Tally and Orphan. Neither one of them would meet his eyes. He got the feeling that they were still not telling him everything. He wasn't sure that he could handle any more disclosures so he didn't press them for answers. He followed Tally's lead and let his questions drop for the time being.

"Because that's the way the Reivers fought I guess," Thane said a bit defensively.

"I spent many years traveling through the Boarder Lands and knew of only one clan that fought left-handed. What clan were you with?" Tally asked.

"The Kerrs," Thane answered.

"Master Asiag and his shadow young Master Avril?" Tally's lips curled up in a fond smile when Thane acknowledged his guess with a nod.

"I knew them well. A proud clan they are! How were they? Is Old Man Jennings still alive? He was older than dirt last time I was there. What about Natty? That woman made the best scones in all of Scotland," Tally rambled on happy with the change of subject.

Thane's eyebrows flew up and disappeared under a wave of his black hair. "Hey, wait a minute! You were there? You're the traveling storyteller they were always talking about; the one that sang ballads about Færies and monsters?"

Tally's usually cynical expression softened and laughter lit his eyes. For a moment, he looked like the Bard from Thane's memories.

"So you were told about a traveling bard, huh? I guess that could have been me. You were with them for four years you said?"

"Yeah." Thane retorted. He was beginning to feel a bit annoyed that Tally seemed to be so fond of the Reivers.

"Boy, are you going to make me drag answers out of you one word at a time?" Tally was beginning to loose patience again. "Tell me about them. What exciting adventures did they take you on?"

"Exciting adventures? Is that what you think life with them was like...one big exciting adventure? You want to know what it was like for me...living with them? I didn't go on exciting adventures...I went on long boring raids. When we weren't raiding, I lived on the floor in the back of the castle stables with the horses. I was even less than a servant."

Thane's sadness was rapidly turning into anger again. How could The Bard sit there and talk about the Reivers like they were happy, fun, caring people; like they had cared about him. "If it wasn't for Natty always sneaking me food, I'd probably be dead."

"I don't understand. They are good people," Tally said frowning back at Thane.

"Yeah? Well, now they're dead people!" Thane said harshly.

"Natty, Old Man Jennings, Frammel, and many more... probably the Kerr and Avril as well!" Thane continued with a bitter expression.

As much as he resented the way he was treated by some of the Reivers, he knew that there were some there that had looked out for him. Cessford and Avril never treated him badly exactly; they just never stopped anyone else from treating him badly.

"WHAT? What do you mean 'they're dead?' What happened?" Tally's face lost what little color it had left in it.

It took some time for Thane to tell them every detail of the Reiver's last raid.

"Then, we were followed back to the village by an English Hot Trod. It had been a fairly easy raid as those things went, and I guess the Reivers just got careless. The soldiers snuck up on us and brutally attacked the village as we entered. They killed everyone; as many people as they could while they set the buildings on fire," Thane recounted.

Thane continued his story. As he described the man on the black horse, who he now knew to be Zavior, Tally stood up abruptly and began to pace in front of the boys. He stopped to stare down at Thane.

"Asiag and Avril spent many long nights barraging me with questions about the Fæ. By the time I left the clan, they knew the old tales and prophesies almost as well as I did." Tally began to pace again.

After a few more minutes he said, "Answer me this: Did he ever see your ears?"

"Yeah. I guess. I didn't start to cover them until I had been there awhile. I got in a fight with the other kids in the village one afternoon after they started to make fun of me. I have been very careful ever since then to make sure they were covered." He frowned over at the hair covering Orphan's ears. Orphan fidgeted under Thane's reproachful gaze.

"There you go! I have no doubt he would have known you were Fæ the first time he saw you. It would not have taken him long to figure out precisely who you were. Your coloring would have told him much as well. He was protecting you. That is the only explanation."

Tally stopped pacing. He folded his arms across his chest, and seemed quite satisfied that he had found justification for The Kerr's ill-treatment of Thane.

"Asiag knew! I would bet my life on it. He would never have allowed anyone to be treated badly without a really good reason." Tally insisted.

Thane leapt angrily to his feet and faced Tally. "So he figured since I was a Færie he would treat me like a servant? Do you know how many times I was beaten by Frammel? How many times he tied me to the back of the stables without food? I don't understand how you can stand there and say they were protecting me." Thane raged at him. Years of swallowing his anger at the Reivers came pouring out of him.

Orphan remained on the ground between them, his head swiveling back and forth to look from one to the other.

"Don't you see?" Tally argued back, "He knew that by treating you as nothing special, you would be seen as nothing special; you would be invisible."

He shook his head and said, "Who would look for a Fæ Prince in the guise of a Reiver stable boy?"

Thane opened his mouth to respond when Orphan jumped up and stood between them. He frowned at both of them before interrupting them by saying, "Would you let it go for now Thane? Tally? I thought we were going to learn to fight?"

Tally and Thane glared at each other over Orphan's head for a moment longer. Tally shrugged and sank back down onto his stool. Orphan plopped down on the hard ground next to the Bard and pulled Thane down beside him.

Thane propped his elbow on his bent knee and stared down at the dirt. He was trying hard to control his anger but his brain was bursting with unanswered questions. Was Tally right? Cessford had told him on that last raid that he might know where he was from. Then, during the battle, he had mouthed the word "run" to Thane. Did that mean he really was protecting him? Had The Kerr really known all along who and what Thane was? Did that mean Natty knew as well? Why had she never told him? Why would they keep something like that secret?

Lost in his own thoughts, he was startled when both Orphan and Tally stood up abruptly and started to head back toward the kitchen. Thane scrambled to his feet and ran to catch up to them. He heard Tally tell Orphan to meet him tomorrow afternoon in their usual place behind the stables. They would begin sword fighting lessons in earnest. The only thing Tally said to Thane was, "Bring your sword."

††††

They met in their usual spot behind the stables the next day to begin their training. Thane was surprised to see Marsden amble up and stand right behind them. Both he and Tally had long swords in scabbards strapped to thick leather belts at their waists. Thane was stunned when he got his first good look at Tally's sword. It had a large green stone embedded in the pommel and was encased in an ornately carved scabbard. Where did the Bard get something so valuable? Marsden's sword, in comparison, was plain, unadorned steel with a cruciform hilt and a simple steel scabbard. The blade of Marsden's sword must have been almost four feet long.

In his hands, Tally held a plain wooden practice sword similar in size to the one that Thane was carrying. He was painstakingly wrapping strips of thick wool around the blunt blade. When he finished, he handed it to Orphan then held out his hand for Thane's sword and proceeded to wrap it with wool as well.

"We will pad them for the next couple days to reduce your injuries. It won't do any good to have you hurt and unable to complete your chores," he mumbled as he handed the now padded sword back to Thane.

"I won't pretend to be an expert," Tally began, "but I can hold my own in a fight. I have asked Marsden to lend us a hand as he is quite proficient with a blade and we could use another skilled swordsman for demonstration purposes." He nodded at the big man standing silently behind them. The boys turned around to look at him but Marsden just lifted an eyebrow and stared back at them. Since when was Marsden 'proficient with a blade'?

The blade of the Bard's sword slid from its scabbard with a hiss as he pulled it out and held it in front of him with the tip pointing skyward. "I am sure you both believe you know all there is to know about swords, but we will be going over some basics anyway."

He turned the sword so that the reflection of the sun shot bolts of light from its mirrored surface. "The blade is made of finely tempered steel. The blood grove…"

Orphan interrupted him, "I know what that is! That's the channel down the middle of the blade that lets blood drip out from the dead body?"

Marsden slapped his hand on his thigh and roared with laughter. "What fool told you that?"

"It adds strength to the blade you idiot!" Tally snapped at him. "If you will not take this seriously Orphan, I will send you inside to shovel out the stables. Now pay attention," he reprimanded.

Orphan grinned back at him; not at all cowed by Tally's sharp scolding. Tally scowled in his direction as he held up his sword and began again. He flipped the sword around with a couple quick twists of his wrist so that the point was facing down and began to identify the parts of the hilt: "pommel, grip, and guard." With another flick of his wrist, he turned the sword up and ran his finger across the blade on the sides nearest the guard.

"The blade is actually quite dull right here next to the hilt and can be held for better control when manipulating the sword or blocking with the sword." His hand was cupped lightly around the blade nearest the hilt as he demonstrated how to hold the blade without slicing open a hand.

"What you really need right now is to learn to protect and defend yourselves long enough for aid to arrive or for you to escape danger. We will begin with correcting your abysmal posture and form."

Tally and Marsden faced each other, feet apart and pointed slightly outward. Their knees were bent and their bodies were crouched in a squat. "You want to present as small a target to the enemy as you can, and give yourself as much maneuverability as possible. By standing like this you can easily shift your weight from one leg to another and have the means of turning quickly with very little effort." Tally demonstrated by moving his body in a side to side rocking motion.

Thane and Orphan practiced standing with their feet spread apart, squatting down and flexing their knees to keep loose and balanced. Marsden moved between the two and corrected their positions; adjusting a leg here and moving an arm there. When he was satisfied with their stances he stepped back.

"The most important thing to remember is that you are not fighting sword to sword. You are fighting man to man. You're goal is to wound or kill your enemy before he wounds or kills you. Therefore, you are aiming for their bodies not their swords." Marsden instructed.

"Now, observe," Tally commanded.

He nodded at Marsden who pulled his sword from its scabbard and attacked. Tally grabbed the lower blade of his sword with his left hand and held the sword horizontally across the front of his face to block Marsden's strike. With a quick flick of his wrist, he twisted his sword down and around the hilt of Marsden's blade to bind it so it couldn't move. He looped a foot around the back of Marsden's knee and took him down to the ground. Turning his wrist, Tally disentangled his hilt from Marsden's and in an instant, he swung the sword around and pointed the tip at Marsden's neck. "Use any means possible to disarm your opponent."

He looked up to make sure the boys were paying proper attention then continued, "Always aim for the vulnerable parts of the body: under the arms, neck, groin, back of the knees and ankles." Tally demonstrated by slowly swinging his sword to point toward those area's on Marsden's body. "No matter what type of armor or protective clothing they are using, they must have joints for mobility and those joints will be vulnerable." He helped Marsden to his feet and said, "Now, you two practice."

Initially, Thane and Orphan just danced hesitantly around each other, too tense and afraid to get near each other's blade to land a strike. It took a little coaching from Marsden and a lot of threats from Tally to get the boys to move closer to each other.

Finally, Thane attacked Orphan. He swung his sword from upper left to lower right and was met with an underhanded block from Orphan. He swung his arm back around and came at him again. Then they switched roles and Orphan attacked. Marsden and Tally again moved between the two and corrected their stances and swings.

Their moves were a bit awkward at first. They knocked each other on the knuckles numerous times before the afternoon was done. Even with the padding on the swords, by the end of the day, both were covered in bruises and were thoroughly exhausted. Every muscle in their bodies ached but they were smiling, sweaty, and excited. Although the practice session had been difficult, Thane thoroughly enjoyed it. It was much more fun to fight a moving target than it was to fight a stationary tree.

After their chores were done in the afternoons, they practiced guards and strikes with their swords. Tally removed the padding on the practice swords after the first week. Now, they would be able to get a better feel for how one sword slipped and slid along the other. They spent many hours with their arms in the air, wooden blade against wooden blade. They learned to sense how the pressure on the blade changed and how a subtle shift in the angle of the blade could signal the intent of the wielder. Thane found that he was often able to anticipate which move Orphan would be using by slight differences in the direction or the location of pressure he felt through his blade from Orphan's sword.

After the first couple weeks, Marsden only joined them behind the stables occasionally. Those days were challenging as his fighting style was very different from Tally's. Thane would pair with Tally and Marsden would pair with Orphan. After a bit, they would switch partners and begin again. Sometimes Marsden would just lean against the back door and silently watch them spar. Other times he would regale them with tales of his adventures as a part of King Henry VIII's troops in Ireland. It became quickly apparent from the banter between Marsden and Tally that it was not happenstance that had brought Tally and Orphan to The Whyte Wyndmyl Inn. Tally and Marsden had a long history behind them, most of which Thane was sure, they had not shared with the boys.

Thane took to the sparring drills quickly. He was actually quite good. He picked up the moves easily and was usually able to avoid

Orphan's thrusts and lunges without much difficulty. His longer arms were an advantage as he could often out reach Orphan and strike him on the head.

Orphan, on the other hand, didn't seem to enjoy the practice session as much as Thane did. Orphan was fierce and agile but not as strong as Thane. He relied heavily on his nimbleness to get under Thane's guard, because Thane held the advantage with his larger size and brute strength. Thane was sure that the difference in their size and abilities was due to the difference in their ages, although he couldn't remember ever being as scrawny as Orphan was. He eyed Orphan's thin arms and narrow shoulders and hoped he would catch up soon.

Chapter Fifteen

Nock, Mark, Draw, Loose

Tally's disposition changed drastically over the summer months. The weight of the world appeared to be lifted from his shoulders. He seemed to be more content and easy going and had stopped drinking altogether. More importantly, he no longer brooded and stared at Thane. He focused all his energy on teaching Thane and Orphan to protect themselves. He was a hard task master and knew more than he had initially led them to believe about the art of sword fighting. More often than not, Thane and Orphan found themselves falling into bed in the evenings exhausted. Thane longed for the comfort of the soft bed he had enjoyed during the winter months.

The green leaves on the trees surrounding the inn began to turn red, gold, and orange as the air cooled with the arrival of autumn. Tally and the boys once again moved into their small rooms in the inn as the weather began to worsen. Marsden also purchased Thane two new pairs of breeches as he had grown taller over the summer.

"You can't spend the winter months with your knees hanging out of the bottom of your breeches," Marsden growled at him when Thane protested at the expense. "How much work will we get out of you when you're sick?"

"Just say, 'Thank you' boy!" Tally had yelled across the stables.

Thane's voice had begun to change as well. He found he frequently croaked and squeaked in the middle of sentences. It was a bit embarrassing, so he found himself saying even less than usual.

Tally told him his birthday was November 11th and that he would soon be turning thirteen. Orphan on the other hand, had just turned twelve in the spring. He wasn't growing as fast as Thane and his voice was still as high as ever. Thane had begun to tease him about it but only when no one else was around to hear his own voice crack.

The Bard had decided that it was time for them to add archery to their afternoon tutoring and sword training. They were both approaching the age that the law required they be proficient in archery, and neither of them had ever held a bow. Tally bought two yew bows and a number of beech wood arrows from an armory in town. The boys each were given a tab, a glove that covered half of the hand they would use to pull the linen bowstring, and a brace to protect their bow hand from the whip of the string. The brace looked much like a fingerless gauntlet. Thane noticed that his bow was quite a bit longer and sturdier than Orphan's.

"Why is my bow so much bigger than Orphan's?" Thane asked.

"Because it is what the man gave me that is why. Stop complaining. How many times do I have to tell you to just say thank you," Tally blustered. "Young kids these days…no gratitude." Thane slid a sideways glance at Orphan who just shrugged his shoulders.

They made a target out of a large stack of hay and covered it with an old cloth Tilda gave them. They painted three concentric circles on it with blueberry juice. The first thing Tally demonstrated was how to handle the bows and arrows without taking out someone's eye. They were shown how to hold the leather wrapped grips of the bows in their left hand with their arm extended straight out from their bodies. The index and middle finger of their right hand would be used to hold the string and pull it back.

The first thing Thane did when Tally wasn't looking was to pull the bowstring back taut then let it go. He had not bothered to put the brace on his left hand first so when the bowstring whipped back it slapped him smartly across the fleshy part of his thumb. He dropped the bow and hopped around waving his hand and howling at the top of his lungs. An angry red welt rose across the outside of his thumb.

Orphan rolled around on the ground and laughed at him while Tally frowned at the pair of them. It was a painful lesson but neither he nor Orphan used the bows again without first putting on their braces. By the end of their first lesson, their arms were so sore from pulling the tight bowstrings back, they could barely lift them without groaning out loud.

After a week's practice behind the stables, Tally decided they were ready to use real targets. He took them to the large butts on the outskirts of town where a wide open field was set up for townsmen to practice archery. A dozen mounds of sod covered earth were lined up across the opposite end of the flat field at distances that varied between 200 to 400 yards from the archers. Each mound was relatively flat on top and held a target with a center of yellow and concentric circles of red, blue, white, and black.

Cries of nock, mark, draw, and loose, were heard up and down the line. The archers varied in age from the youngest at eight years of age to the oldest…well…Thane couldn't even guess how old he was. The old man's bow shook so badly in his hand that Thane wondered if he would be able to hit the side of a building let alone the target. Fascinated, he watched as the old man took a steadying breath and shot the arrow right into the center of his target. As soon as the arrow released, he went right back to rattling his bones in his skin.

The butts were always busy as English law required all men between the ages of fourteen and sixty to own a bow and be proficient in its use. They were expected to accurately hit a target the size of a man at 220 yards at a speed of twelve to fifteen arrows per minute. Thane didn't see how he was going to meet that qualification since it took him almost a minute just to notch the arrow and site the target properly. What would they do? Arrest him? Did they have a special jail for those who couldn't notch a bow?

Orphan, as it turned out, was exceptionally good at archery. He almost always hit the target, and at least half the time, he hit the yellow center. Thane teased him often that it was only because his bow was so much smaller and easier to handle. In reality, Thane knew it had nothing to do with the size of their bows. Thane just didn't seem to have the patience to be still and focus on his target. His arrows tended to land in the dirt in front of the mound, shoot wildly to the side or careen over the top. Thane was so bad he even hit the target next to his once.

"Are you aiming at the worms, Thane? Slow down and concentrate!" Tally yelled at him during their third week of practice at the butts.

Orphan, on the other hand, could become so still that it didn't seem as if he was even breathing. He never once missed the target. Within another month, Orphan could not only hit the target, he hit it within the yellow and the red circles of the target every time. He took great joy in ribbing Thane whenever his arrow missed its mark.

||||

Tally came into the stables early on the morning of Thane's thirteenth birthday. He sat on a stool, leaned his head back against the wall, folded his hands neatly in his lap and watched as Thane painstakingly ran the brush over Embarr's white flanks. He was silent for so long that Thane almost forgot he was there until he spoke.

"You and that horse were inseparable you know," Tally reminisced. "You would sit for hours upon him with not one bit of fear and ride into the fields like you were going to conquer the world," Tally smiled sadly. "On one hand, your mother was afraid you were going to get lost or hurt and was determined to keep you safe and close to home. Your father, on the other hand, was equally determined to make you a confident and skilled horseman."

He lifted his sad brown eyes to look right into Thane's dark ones. "You are so much like your father," he said as he ran his eyes up and down Thane's tall, lanky body. "You look like him. You walk like him. Do you know that you even tilt your head to the side in the same manner as he did when you are puzzling over something?" He sighed.

"I miss them both, every day. I think to myself that if I miss them this much, how much more their child must miss them."

Thane's hand stilled mid-stroke on Embarr's side. He swallowed the lump that had formed in his throat and turned away from Tally to put the brush and the rest of his tools away. After a few minutes, he quietly shut the gate to Embarr's stall and walked over to sit on the floor next to Tally. He leaned back and rested his head against the wall with his legs stretched out in front of him.

"I didn't really remember them until…well…until recently, but I do miss them," Thane whispered.

"Embarr was a gift to you from your mother's mother, your Færie grandmother. Did you remember that?" When Thane nodded he continued, "He is unique Thane. He is powerful and he is magical. He knew who you were the moment you first walked through those doors," he waved his hand in the direction of the stable door.

"Embarr rightly belongs to you. The time has come for you to learn each other's ways again, Thane. To do that you must take full responsibility for him. Caring for his needs is not enough, you must take him out and ride him." Tally got up and put a hand on Thane's shoulder for a moment. "Love him well," he said as he walked out of the stables.

Thane sat where Tally left him for a long time mulling over the past and wondering about the future. He looked up to find Embarr looking back at him. What was he going to do with a magical horse?

THANE

Thane did as Tally advised and took Embarr out for long rides after his chores and weapons practice were done. It was clear that although Thane had forgotten Embarr, Embarr had not forgotten Thane. The horse responded to his every move as if he were an extension of Thane's body.

Orphan was given permission to ride Nutmeg, Marsden's brown mare, so that he could accompany Thane and Embarr. The mare was not fast but she was steady and eager to please. The four of them spent many happy hours exploring the countryside together.

††††

"Orphan. What do you really know about Færies?" Thane blurted out one cold winter morning when they were walking together into town. They were on their way to the blacksmith to pick up a new iron hook for Tilda's kettle in the kitchen.

"What do you mean?" Orphan stopped and glanced around to make sure no one was listening. After he was sure they were alone, he leaned into Thane and whispered. "I know they have pointy ears," he chuckled at his own joke and started to walk again.

"Don't be stupid! I mean, what do you know about what they can do? The Fæ are supposed to be powerful, right...like Lír and his wife? So, if we are supposed to be Færies, does that mean we have powers too? Do you know how their powers work?" Thane was bursting with questions.

The previous night, Tally had sung a ballad about the Children of Lír. Lír was the God of the Sea whose second wife cursed her step children to live as swans for 900 years. Thane lay awake for hours thinking about the Færies and their powers. If he and Orphan were truly Fæ, did that mean they could do something like that? If he had powers, why had he spent so many years being beaten by Frammel?

"Do you think we could turn someone into a swan like Lír's second wife did to his kids?" Thane asked.

Orphan snickered, "I don't know. Why? Who do you want to turn into a swan? Wait!" he said. He turned to move in front of Thane and skip backwards, facing Thane. "Maybe we could try it out on Markus!"

"I'm serious," Thane said frowning at Orphan's silliness.

"Hey, me too!" Orphan said laughing out loud. "Although, now that I think about it, he'd make a much better boar!" Orphan laughed uproariously at his own joke. Once he finally settled down enough to walk calmly beside Thane again he said, "I've never done magic. Have you?"

"I don't know. Maybe," Thane replied.

"Maybe, what?" Orphan said. "Tell me!"

"Something strange happened once. The boys in the Reiver village were beating me up. They were all piled on top of me, punching me. Then all of a sudden, there was this bright blue light. The next thing I knew; they were all flying off of me. They were thrown twenty feet away from me and landed on the ground crying in pain. I was left untouched by the light, lying right where I was, all alone. It was like a huge wind lifted them off of me and threw them across the dirt. Do you think that was magic?"

"What were you doing just before the light?" Orphan asked.

"Getting the snot beat out of me. I told you!" Thane stopped and stared at Orphan.

He thought back to how he had felt. "As I was under the pile of boys on the ground, I remember feeling really angry that they were calling me names, and I was really scared because they were hurting me. I wished someone would come along and just get them away from me. The next thing I knew, they were gone."

Orphan was frowning at him, serious now. "That sounds like magic to me," he said with just a little bit of awe in his voice.

"We need to see what Tally knows. Maybe he can tell us something," Orphan suggested. He turned on his heel and headed into the warmth of the blacksmiths shop without another word.

††††

The following day, after sword practice, Thane and Orphan were sitting against the back wall of the stables for a quick rest before they walked to the butts for archery practice. Even though it was cold, the sun was warm and the stables blocked most of the chilly wind. They were quite comfortable. Tally was sitting on his stool leaning back against the wall with the large orange cat in his lap. His eyes were closed and his hands were folded neatly across the top of the sleeping cat. It almost looked like he was sleeping too.

"Tally, what do you know about Fæ powers?" Orphan blurted out.

Tally cracked an eye open and looked at him curiously. "What do you want to know?"

"Can all Færies do magic? Do all of them have powers like Zavior, the man from Thane's dream and the Færies in the old stories?" Orphan asked.

"As far as I know every Færie has a basic power they draw from within themselves. In addition to that basic power, many have a special gift as well," Tally began. "The…"

"Did my mother have a special gift?" Thane interrupted.

"She had the ability to manipulate water. Your mother's father was Manannán mac Lir, the son of the Sea God Lir," Tally explained as he turned to look at Thane. "It may be a talent that is passed on to you. You will have to wait and see. But as I was saying before you interrupted me, the Fæ have an inherent energy that allows them to manipulate objects in the world around them."

"Can you teach us to use powers like real Færies?" Orphan asked innocently.

"No! I don't think that is a good idea," he said firmly. "Do you see any pointy ears on me? I know very little about Fæ powers and even less about how they are used."

"But Tally, you said we needed to learn to protect ourselves. How can we do that if we can't fight the evil Fæ?" Orphan argued back.

Tally stared at Orphan for a moment with his mouth slightly open. It looked like Tally had not given much thought to it before. The thought of fighting a Færie wasn't a pleasant one.

"I'll consider it, but I'm not sure I would know where to begin," he stood up abruptly. The cat meowed in protest as he fell unceremoniously from his lap and darted into the warmth of the stables to find another place to nap.

"Come. Let us move on to the butts before it is too dark to see."

Orphan winked at Thane behind Tally's back and grinned. "He didn't say, 'No,'" he whispered to Thane.

Chapter Sixteen

Fæ Powers

It stormed for a solid week that spring. The sun was tucked securely behind a gray and black patchwork of angry, dense clouds. They had not been to the butts for the past few days as the rain made the bows slippery and difficult to grip, and it was too windy to practice with any hope for accuracy. Thane was grateful for the break from archery. He was lousy on a good day and was looking forward to having another afternoon free from Orphan's constant teasing and 'helpful advice.' He swore each of his arrows had little brains of their own sitting smartly between the goose feather fletchings. Whenever he began to gain a bit of confidence, the little brain would say, "Let's go this way instead." and would promptly fly away in a direction of its own choosing. He was frustrated with his lack of progress. The only way he would ever be able to defend himself with an arrow would be if his attacker charged at him and impaled himself on it.

Since sword practice had been cancelled the last few days, Thane and Orphan assumed it would also be cancelled today. They planned on spending the afternoon in the warm dry kitchen with Tilda and Molly. They were sitting at the kitchen table laughing at a story Molly was telling when Tally walked in.

"Then lil' Benny emptied 'is belly of stew all over me Da's lap!" Molly was laughing so hard, tears were running down her face. "And me Da, not being 'imself a man with a strong belly mind you, he took one look at Benny and 'e threw up 'is stew too!"

Tally crossed his arms over his chest and stared at the lot of them.

"The dogs, leapt in and started fighting at they feet to lick up the mess. I had to shoo the dogs off of the two of 'em with a broom! By the time I'd got the beasts outside, Da and Benny was licked clean and sound sleep in front of the fire." She finished her tale with her hands on her hips and a huge smile plastered across her face.

Tally scowled at them. "What are you two doing sitting in here? I've been standing outside waiting for you to begin sparring drills and here you sit laughing and joking as if you have no other responsibilities," Tally barked at them. Molly quickly grabbed a tray of food off of the table and slid quietly out the door.

He gave them both a gentle cuff on the back of the head and barked, "Get your swords and go out back. There is a break in the rain. We are going to spar for as long as we can before the skies open up again."

Orphan and Thane didn't wait to be told again. They ran out of the kitchen and up to their rooms. They were still sleeping in the inn as Tilda and Mardsen had not asked them to move back to the stables at the end of winter. The boys were told they would be allowed to stay in their rooms on the top floor of the inn indefinitely. Although Tilda said it was so they could keep a better eye on the boys and keep them out of trouble, Thane had felt there was more to it than she said. He wasn't about to question his good fortune. He liked his soft bed.

They grabbed their practice swords, stomped their way back down the stairs to the kitchen, out the door, and headed to the back of the stables. They found Tally leaning against the wall. He was staring up at the darkening sky with his eyebrows drawn down in a frown when they burst around the corner.

"What took you so long?" he asked. "Let us begin."

The rain had made tiny crooked rivers and ponds in their practice field. Thane and Orphan were finding it almost impossible to get their footing in the soggy mud to lunge or block. At one point, Thane's boot got stuck in the mud, he couldn't retreat fast enough, and Orphan slapped him hard on the side of the head with the flat of his blade. Thane's foot pulled out of his boot as he fell backward and landed hard in a puddle. Even with his head throbbing, he laughed at the sight of the empty boot standing up, perfectly straight, in front of Orphan.

After half hour, they had both fallen down so many times that they were covered in mud from top to bottom and were thoroughly enjoying themselves. Soon, it began to drizzle and before long the rain was again falling in sheets. Finally, Tally threw his hands in the air and gave up.

"Go get cleaned up and put your weapons away. Meet me inside the stables," he ordered them. "Make it quick!"

They ran up to their rooms, washed off what little mud the rain hadn't already rinsed from them. They changed clothes and were back in the stables within a half-hour. They were a bit apprehensive about what Tally might have planned for them.

Tally was standing next to Embarr's stall in the dim light of the stables. He was moving his hand down the horse's neck in long deliberate strokes. He turned slowly around as they entered and stared intently in their direction for so long that Thane and Orphan began to fidget uncomfortably.

"What's wrong?" Orphan asked him.

Tally ignored him and spoke instead to the horse, "Well, Embarr. Shall we see what they can do?" Embarr blew a breath out of his lips and nodded his head.

Orphan and Thane glanced questioningly at each other as Tally settled himself on the bench in front of Embarr's stall.

"Sit," the Bard said as he waved his hand toward the floor in front of him. Embarr stood behind him peering over Tally's shoulder, looking like his self-appointed advisor.

"I think I have a basic understanding of how Fæ power works," Tally began, "as I have spent some time with Færies. Thane, your mother and I had many conversations about Fæ powers...powers of glamour, telepathy, levitation, manipulation of the elements...you get the idea."

"She told me her powers were an innate ability to manipulate the world around her; an ability that was as much a part of her as her ability to walk or talk. It is my understanding that usually these powers don't begin to develop fully until the Færie reaches young adulthood, but can emerge in times of great stress at a much younger age. I suspect that you have both experienced some type of magic before now. Am I correct?"

Orphan shrugged his shoulders and Thane nodded hesitantly.

Tally pulled two very damp leaves from the pocket of his robe and placed a leaf on the floor in front of each of the boys.

"So, I imagine that all you need to do is focus on what you want to happen, and it will happen." Tally glanced over his shoulder at Embarr who had been listening to the Bard's instructions with interest. He turned back to the boys.

"We'll see what we can accomplish. Maybe we can find a more suitable teacher in the future," he grumbled.

He pointed a hand at the leaves lying on the ground in front of them and said, "I want you to focus all your attention on a leaf. Feel the weight of it in your mind. Imagine lifting it. See it floating in front of you. Begin," he commanded, then sat back and watched.

Thane and Orphan both leaned closer to their leaves and stared intently at them. They were both frowning in concentration. The only sound heard in the stables was the rain as it began to batter the roof above them.

The minutes stretched on...nothing happened.

"Maybe we need to know the magic word for lifting?" Orphan looked up at Tally for more directions.

"Magic word? Don't be ridiculous! There is no magic word. Were you not paying attention Orphan? It is power that comes from *within* you. You are not pulling it out of the air with a stick like some common wizard! Now, be quiet and let me think!" he berated him.

"Humph" Tally finally said after a few more moments of them all frowning and staring down at the very still leaves. Two pairs of eager eyes darted up to his expectantly. Embarr leaned over the door of the stall, shook his head and snickered. Tally cleared his throat and said, "Okay, well, maybe we need to take a step back. Pick up the leaf with your left hand."

They reached out together and each lifted a leaf between their fingers.

"You see!" he cried out.

Thane and Orphan jumped, startled at the loud exclamation from Tally.

"You didn't have to think: 'left hand, reach out, grab the stem, pinch stem between thumb and finger, and pick up the leaf.' You just did it. This skill is no different from walking, archery or sword fighting," Tally explained again.

Embarr nodded his white head up and down behind Tally's back and whinnied.

"Lay them back down in front of you and try it again," Tally said.

Brows furrowed in concentration, both boys leaned forward with their elbows propped on their knees and frowned down at the leaves again. Minutes passed in silence and once more, nothing happened.

Tally scratched his beard in contemplation and mumbled, "Hmm...maybe we are missing something."

He got to his feet and paced in front of Embarr's stall. Three pairs of eyes watched him walk back and forth; tugging at his beard as if he could pull the answer out of it. His cape billowed out around him, stirring the leaves in his wake.

He stopped abruptly in front of the boys.

"I think we are trying too hard. This should be natural for you." Embarr whinnied in approval again.

"Focus. You can see the leaf on the floor. Now reach out with your mind, as you did with your hand, and gently lift it."

Thane gasped as his leaf wiggled. Embarr nodded and stomped his feet excitedly as Tally stood over them grinning. "That may have been just a bit of breeze but we will take it as a simple success! Settle down. Settle down. We'll try it again."

They worked at it until Thane and Orphan could both make their leaves wiggle. Thane caught on more quickly than Orphan did. By the end of the hour, he was able to nudge the leaf at least a little bit with each try, and once even managed to lift it off the ground.

They went back to their chores feeling both elated and deflated. They were excited to have been able to move their leaves at all; at the same time, they were disappointed that they had only moved them a little bit. Tally promised to give them more time to practice another day.

Chapter Seventeen

Playing With Fire

Thane and Tilda were washing up the pots in the kitchen the next evening, when Orphan came storming in from the common room. He was covered in onions and bits of fish and gravy. He slammed the tray of dirty dishes down on the table, ripped the cloth from around his waist and tossed it on top of the tray and huffed. Tilda and Thane both turned to look at him in surprise.

"I want to hit that man!" Orphan snarled. "Jared is a fool! He just barreled past me on his way out the door and knocked the tray full of food onto me..." he fumed, pacing back and forth in front of the table, "...without even an 'excuse me!' He makes me so mad!" he seethed as he stomped his foot in anger.

Thane and Tilda glanced at each other trying not to laugh. Unfortunately, Orphan caught the look they shared and got even angrier.

"What are you laughing at? It's not funny!" He turned and stormed out the back door vowing, "...to get even with Jared someday."

Well, someday arrived sooner than any of them expected. The following week Orphan and Thane were in the back corner of the common room clearing tables of dirty dishes when Jared stumbled in. His eyes were bloodshot. He had obviously already been drinking. He weaved his way over to a table full of his noisy friends. He walked up behind the shortest man at the table and with a smack of his hand, shoved him off his chair, on to the floor. The small man landed hard on his rear-end with a solid flump.

He opened his mouth and started yelling, "HEY! WHAT THE HE..." When he looked up and saw that it was Jared who had dumped him on the floor, he quickly changed his tune. "...EY! Jared! How nice of you to join us..." he sniveled.

The other men at the table burst out in rowdy guffaws. Markus came stumping out of the kitchen, caught sight of his friends and headed over to join them. He walked up behind Don, the small man who was still sitting on the floor, and slapped him on the back of the head. Markus pulled a chair away from another table and sat down next to Jared.

Jared looked down at the man on the floor and bellowed, "DON! Go get us some food and ale from the kitchen!"

Don scrambled to his feet and ran toward the back room to find Tilda.

"The great big bully! I wish somebody would put him in his place!" Orphan said looking up from wiping the table and scowled in the direction of Jared's group.

Don reappeared with a tray laden with trenchers of fish stew and tankards of ale. He was a bit unsteady on his feet from drinking all afternoon and the ungainly and heavy tray was making it even more difficult for him to maneuver through the crowded room to the table.

Orphan glared at him and said, "He should dump it right on top of Jared's head!"

As Don turned to place the tray on the table between Markus and Jared, Markus stood up. Markus caught the edge of the tray with the point of his shoulder. It was as if time slowed down and every sound was magnified tenfold.

The tray tilted.

"Noooo..." Don cried as he struggled to balance the tray but two of the trenchers slid forward and bumped into the jugs. The jugs tipped off of the tray spraying their contents across Jared's face and chest in a giant wave of ale.

Don frantically tried to regain some control of the wildly swaying tray but it was useless. The trenchers, full of fish and onion stew, followed the jugs off of the tray. They hovered over Jared's head for a fraction of a second, flipped over in the air, and dropped their gooey contents right top of him. The whole room was staring at them in silence.

Jared sat there stunned. A bread trencher sat upon his head like a cap. Fish and goo dripped from his eyebrows, ran down his cheeks and dribbled onto his chest.

There was a collective gasp from the watching crowd. Someone snickered. Soon the whole room was full of laughter and jeers. Jared stood up and pushed Don violently out of the way. He pulled the bread off of his head and threw it to the floor in a fit of rage. He turned and stormed angrily out of the room leaving a trail of fish stew and ale in his wake.

Thane looked at Orphan with his mouth hanging open. Orphan looked back at Thane equally stunned and just a bit pale.

"Nah. You couldn't possibly have done that!" Thane finally said. "Could you?"

They turned to look at The Bard. He was sitting on his stool by the fireplace frowning intently at both of them.

Thane grabbed Orphan by the shirt sleeve and pulled him out of Tally's sight into the kitchen. "I think we better wash dishes for a bit!" Thane said.

✝✝✝✝✝

Before long, spring's blanket of bright colors had transformed into the equally vivid colors of summer. For Thane and Orphan, the days passed in a blur of chores and training. When they weren't helping out at the inn, they were either out riding horses, training at the butts, sparring with their swords or being tutored by the Bard. Thane continued to excel at sword fighting while Orphan perfected his skills at archery.

They were not able to practice using their powers as often as they would have liked. With the warmer weather, the inn was very busy. They had to be careful that they would not be observed or disturbed.

Although they were equally matched in their Fæ powers, Thane found he could easily lift heavier objects than the much smaller Orphan could. Did the difference in their abilities reflect their physical selves somehow?

Tally encouraged Thane and Orphan to take advantage of the extra daylight hours of summer to ride Embarr and Nutmeg further out into the fields and woods surrounding the village. The boys were more than happy to follow his advice.

They were exploring the fields south of town one afternoon when Orphan began to complain about how little time they had been given to practice their powers. Tally had been angry with them since the incident with Jared and the trenchers.

"Do you think Tally will ever let us do anything besides lift and move rocks and buckets of water?" Orphan complained loudly over the heads of the two galloping horses.

"Eventually, I guess," Thane replied with a shrug. He wasn't sure he wanted to learn anymore about his Fæ powers. If he was totally honest with himself, he would have admitted his abilities actually frightened him. He was perfectly content to concentrate on sword fighting. He was good at it and there was no mystery to it. Hit the other person before they could hit you. He found his powers perplexing and often hard to control.

Embarr and Nutmeg carried them across field after field until they came upon a stream that cut through an open meadow about an hour outside of town. The horses stopped and eagerly drank from the cool water.

Hoping to distract Orphan's thoughts from their Fæ powers he said, "Hey, this looks like a good place to stop. Why don't we rest here for a while?"

The boys hopped off of the horses and left them loose to nibble on the long grass and dandelions and drink from the stream at their leisure. Thane and Orphan kneeled at the edge of the same stream. They cupped their hands and drank their fill of the cold water as well. Their thirst quenched, they lay back on the grass to stare up at the fluffy white clouds drifting across the sky.

Thane watched as a small white pig climbed up a mountain and morphed into an eagle. It looked as though an invisible hand was pulling silken strands from one white lump and gently sculpted them on to another white lump. He marveled at the sky as his eagle turned smoothly into a dog.

"I think we have lifting down pretty well, don't you?" Orphan said to the sky.

It took a moment for Thane to realize that Orphan was not going to let their earlier conversation go. With a sigh of resignation, Thane rolled onto his side in the grass to face Orphan. He propped his head on his hand and answered hesitantly, "Yeah, I guess."

"I asked Tally about learning to make fire yesterday…asked him if he could teach us to do it. He got mad and yelled at me, 'Why do you need to learn to make fire?'" Orphan mimicked. "Then he stormed away before I could say another word."

"You're surprised he yelled at you?" Thane asked puzzled. "He always yells at us."

"Not like this he doesn't. He got a bit pale and very angry. Maybe he is afraid of fire. You think he had been burned or something?" Orphan asked. They lay there in silence for some time. Thane plucked at the grass between them waiting to see where the conversation was going.

"I feel it Thane," Orphan whispered urgently, his green eyes boring into Thane's dark ones. "The fire, I mean. I stare into the fireplace at night and sometimes I swear I can feel it tingling on the tips of my fingers. I think we can do it on our own. All we need is somewhere to practice. Somewhere we won't be seen."

He sat up abruptly, looked around and grinned excitedly. "Like right here! We can practice right here. There is no one around for miles so we won't be seen or interrupted."

Thane sat up warily and looked around at the small stream and the open field. Orphan was right. This place was perfect. Still, he hesitated. He wasn't sure why he hesitated, but Tally must have a good reason for not wanting to teach them to make fire. Thane didn't think it was because Tally had been burned.

Orphan was not going to be swayed. He was determined to try to make a fire. Thane acquiesced. He could see that for whatever reason, Orphan was going to do it; with or without his approval. He was afraid that if he didn't help him; Orphan would try it on his own when Thane wasn't around and get hurt.

Thane suggested they each make a stone circle to contain the flames so that they wouldn't set the field on fire. They filled the small circles with sticks, dried grass and leaves. When they were done, they each knelt in front of a circle and stared hesitantly at each other.

"I don't think this is a good idea. Suppose it works?" Thane tried one last time to change Orphan's mind.

"Stop being such a baby! I know we can do this, Thane. I can feel it." Orphan said with confidence.

Thane sighed and asked, "So, what do you think we have to do?"

"I don't know. I guess we just imagine it there…don't you think? It can't be any harder than lifting, can it?" Orphan leaned forward. He stared into the circle of stones. "I'm going to try." He reached his right hand out as if caressing the air above the little pile of dried debris.

Thane was stunned when the dry grasses began to smoke. Within seconds, flames were licking at the leaves. Thane jumped to his feet in shock as undulating tongues of orange and yellow multiplied, rapidly filling the circle with flame.

Thane panicked and quickly kicked dirt into the stone circle and stomped on it until all the flames were extinguished. Orphan had not only created a flame on his first try, he had created an inferno. Thane was glad they hadn't tried that behind the stables. He tore his eyes away from the ashes and stared at Orphan's flushed face.

"I never expected it to work!" Orphan exclaimed excitedly. "I mean I did, but I didn't. You know!" He turned to look up at Thane, his eyes shining with excitement and said, "Stop being such a coward and sit back down. You try!"

Thane sat back down hesitantly. He stared intently at the dried debris in his circle of stone. The sound of the horses whinnying nervously behind them were distracting him.

Nothing happened.

"Concentrate Thane. Feel the heat," Orphan whispered.

They sat in silence for a while, both staring fixedly at the small circle in front of Thane. Slowly, a thin thread of smoke rose from under the small pile of leaves.

As soon as Thane looked up at Orphan, the flame fizzled and died.

He tried again.

Another thread of smoke slithered through the air only to dissipate rapidly in front of them. Thane shrugged his shoulders and gave up.

"It's getting late. We need to go," Thane said as he hopped to his feet and kicked dirt into the piles of stones then kicked the stone circles apart. He mounted Embarr and turned to watch Orphan as he climbed happily up on Nutmeg. They turned together and headed back towards town at a canter.

"Thane, do you suppose it is harder for you to make fire because your mother was the daughter of a sea god. Do you think it is so easy for me to make fire because I am related to some sort of fire Færie or fire God? You need to try to make water do something next time...like make it rain or control the stream." Orphan babbled all the way back to the inn. He was too excited and self involved to notice how quiet Thane had become.

Thane was frightened by how easy it had been for Orphan to make fire and how quickly and aggressively the fire had grown. He wondered just what Tally was really afraid of?

̶|̶|̶|̶|̶|

By late summer, Thane and Orphan were becoming more daring in the use of their powers. They had begun to practice them surreptitiously when doing their chores and were careful that no one, especially Tally, was looking. They were sure he wouldn't approve.

One afternoon, as it was beginning to get dark, Markus trudged around the corner of the inn leading a horse and small carriage towards the stables. He had just passed in front of the door to the kitchen when it eased slowly open. Half a loaf of bread and a hunk of cheese sailed through the opening. The meal crossed in front of him and floated along until it disappeared around the far corner of the stable.

Markus dropped the reins and ran back the way he had come.

"Ghosts!" He yelled at the top of his lungs as he disappeared around the corner of the inn.

Two heads poked out from around the side of the stables. Huge grins were plastered across their faces and their cheeks were stuffed full of bread and cheese. Chewing as quickly as they could, they swallowed their stolen snack, and they ran to catch the spooked horse before he disappeared with the carriage.

They paid dearly for the prank that night. It didn't take the Bard long to ascertain that it was Thane and Orphan who had made the food float across the yard, and that it was not the work of a mysterious spectral being. He was furious with the pair of them. He lectured them for what seemed like an eternity on stealing, on using their powers for ill gotten gains, and on being morally responsible for their actions. On and on and on he went until their ears were ringing.

"You have the power of the gods," he railed at them. "That power comes with great responsibility and great temptation! It is never, ever to be used for personal gain or to torment another being!"

Thane didn't think he had ever seen Tally so upset. They were sent to bed without their evening meal and he refused to hold any of their lessons for the next two weeks.

For weeks following the incident, Markus would creep across the courtyard and the door to the kitchen with his head and shoulders hunched and his eyes nervously darting all around looking for flying food. Although he never found out exactly what happened that day, he must have figured out that the boys were somehow responsible for the mischief. He took great pains to avoid being anywhere near Thane and Orphan. In fact, he rarely ate meals in the kitchen anymore.

Although Thane understood all the reasons Tally was angry with them, he was secretly enjoying Markus' uneasiness. He thought that it had been worth all the trouble they had gotten into with the Bard.

Chapter Eighteen

Betrayed

After the incident with the bread and cheese, it was weeks before Tally relented and let them use their powers. Although Orphan was frustrated with their lack of practice, he was as hesitant as Thane was to try anything behind Tally's back. Neither one of them wanted to disappoint the Bard again.

The days had begun to get shorter and cooler as the summer drew to a close. Tally didn't want them riding alone after dark. They found themselves staying much closer to the town than they had during the summer so they could be sure to be back at the inn well before nightfall.

Late one afternoon, as they were returning to the inn along the west side of town, they spotted a column of red smoke. It was coming from the forest just on the other side of the field that they were riding through. Laughing and joking with each other they decided they had just enough time to sneak over and spy on whoever was making the smoke.

They leisurely picked their way through the forest and headed in the direction of the oddly colored smoke. Before long they realized that the deeper they traveled into the forest, the heavier the air felt and the quieter the birds became. The trees were still thick with leaves so the forest was very dark; shafts of eerie orange and yellow light filtered through the canopy.

Thane noticed that the closer they came to the source of the smoke, the more nervous Embarr became. It was getting difficult to control him. Embarr began tugging against his lead, pulling his head to the side, trying to turn back. Thane could feel Embarr's fear and his reluctance to go any deeper into the now silent woods. Thane was puzzled. Embarr had never acted like that before, but Thane was too curious to leave without getting a look at the fire.

"What's the matter with Embarr?" Orphan asked frowning at them.

Thane was struggling to go forward while Embarr was sidling backward. Embarr had never refused to obey Thane before and it was beginning to make Thane uneasy.

"I don't know what is wrong with him!" He confessed in frustration. "He keeps pulling back and fighting me...like he doesn't want to go any farther. Maybe he is just getting tired."

Finally, Embarr came to a complete stop and refused to move forward. Thane jumped off of his back in a huff and stared at him. "What's wrong with you! Come on!" He pleaded as he tugged on the reins. Embarr shook his head and held his ground. Thane gave up.

"Fine! You stay here." He ordered and tied his reins to a tree.

He turned to face Orphan who was just jumping down off of Nutmeg.

"I'm going to see who's out there. Are you coming?" Thane asked him more aggressively than he intended.

"I don't like this," Orphan whispered.

"What? Are you scared?" Thane taunted.

"Something's wrong. I think we should go back and tell Tally." Orphan argued, with his brows furrowed. Nutmeg began to get skittish and was dancing about next to Embarr and pulling on her reins.

"It would take too long and we are already here. Wait with the horses then if you're too scared! I'll be right back." He turned and headed in the direction of the smoke.

Slowly and quietly he crept forward making sure to stay hidden behind trees and bushes. He nearly cried out loud when a hand grasped his shoulder. For a brief moment he imagined that a giant, with a face much like Frammel, had caught him. He expected to be hauled in the air by the scruff of his neck. Instead, he looked back to find Orphan standing right behind him his eyes wide with fear. He looked past him to see that he had tied Nutmeg to the tree next to Embarr. Both horses were pulling on their reins, struggling to free themselves.

"What are you doing? You scared the skin off of me. Are you trying to get us caught?" Thane hissed at him as his heart slid back down into his chest where it belonged. He was grateful he hadn't wet himself!

"Sorry!" Orphan growled a whisper back at him. "I can't let you go alone, and you are too stubborn to go back for help."

"We're not babies! Why would we need help? We're just going to look. Now, be quiet and follow me," Thane said as he turned toward the smoke.

They continued to sneak through the underbrush until they began to hear voices at the edge of a small clearing. Two men were standing by a large red and orange fire that was spitting and sizzling, belching columns of red and orange smoke into the air. A black horse and a brown horse were tethered to a tree on the opposite side of the clearing. Thane immediately recognized the brown horse as Cinnamon, the young stallion from the inn. He was tugging on his reigns and pawing nervously at the ground. He wasn't any happier about being here than Embarr and Nutmeg were.

"Let's see if we can get closer so we can hear what they are saying," Thane whispered.

They edged their way slowly around the clearing. As they got closer to the two men they realized that one of them was Markus. His face was flushed red and shining with sweat. He removed his hat and began twisting it between his beefy hands.

The other man had his back to them. He was tall and thin. His long blond hair fell across his shoulders and splayed across his long black cape.

Markus looked like he would rather be anywhere but at this clearing. "What is he doing here?" Thane whispered motioning to Markus.

"Shhh...listen!" Orphan said. His fingers were digging into Thane's arm.

"There is something unnatural about the boy. I am sure he is the one you seek," Markus babbled, nervously shifting his weight from one foot to the other. "He has black hair and unnatural black eyes. He showed up here about the time you said you lost him."

"Tell me where he is you fool and stop sniveling!" The robed man rudely interrupted Markus' nervous chatter.

"He is working for my pathetic brother at the Whyte Wyndmyl Inn in town. If you will just give my bag o' silver I will take you right…"

Markus gasped as the man lifted his right hand. Markus' thick hands flew up to clutch his throat as he struggled to breathe. His face began to turn bright red, then a sick shade of purple. He looked up pleadingly at the robed man as he fell to his knees in front of him. Horrible gagging and coughing sounds were coming from his open mouth. Then finally, silence. He fell forward on his face, his arms tucked awkwardly under his body, his hands still clutched tightly around his neck.

"Greedy fool!" The man in the black cloak sneered. "You have no need of silver now."

The man in the black cape lifted his head and swung around, his black cape billowed out around his legs. He looked directly at the copse of bushes where Thane and Orphan were hiding as if he could see right through the leaves. His eyes were glowing red.

Thane gasped as he saw him clearly for the first time. It was Zavior, the man from the Reiver's village…with the braided beard…the man from his nightmares…that killed his mother and father. The sneer on his face turned into a satisfied smile as he turned back to look down at Markus's still form. He gave the body a firm kick with the toe of his boot then turned away and stood in front of the fire.

"It's him!" Thane stumbled back into Orphan, knocking him over and landing on top of him in a tangle of arms and legs. The bush they were hiding behind shook wildly. Dirt and dust exploded around them forcing them to cover their faces with their hands till they could breathe without sneezing.

"That's the man from the village who led the soldiers to the Reivers. It's the man who killed my parents," he whispered frantically into Orphan's ear.

"The Færie from your dreams?" Orphan whispered back, his eyes, still tearing from the dust, were now growing wide with fear. "Are you sure?"

"Yes, I'm sure!" Thane's blood ran cold and he sat immobile. Unable to move, his gaze locked on the tall man and Markus' unmoving body.

"We need to get back…Now! We must warn Tally." Orphan pulled Thane back to his knees.

They glanced back at the clearing and saw that the darkly cloaked man had walked back to the fire. His arms were outstretched and raised high above his head. He lowered his right hand to point at the flames then raised it rapidly in the air in front of him.

An explosion of fire and blinding red light lit the clearing. A monstrous creature, Thane recognized as Zavior's Roki, parted the flames as if it were stepping out from behind a bright red curtain. It stepped out of the fire and paced menacingly behind the tall cloaked figure. It was soon followed by another and another…

Thane was staring at the fire transfixed. Images of another time and another fire seemed to overlap this one; the memory momentarily blinded him. Orphan frantically tugged at Thane but he couldn't budge him. Thane wasn't able pull his eyes away from the scene unfolding in front of him. It was happening all over again and he felt as scared and helpless as he did that night so long ago.

Orphan put both hands on either side of Thane's face and turned his head away from the fire to face him, forcing Thane to look him in the eyes. It took a minute for Orphan's scared pale face to register with Thane.

"We need to get out of here. We need Tally. Now, Thane! Come on, please move!" Orphan begged as he squeezed Thane's cheeks between his shaking hands. He was finally able to break through Thane's shock and fear to get him moving. Thane shook his head trying to clear it. He let Orphan lead him back the way they came.

They threw themselves on the horses and turned to ride in the direction of the village. Embarr, frantic to get away needed no extra encouragement. Thane berated himself as he realized he should have paid more attention to Embarr's unease. He had obviously felt the presence of danger.

They galloped through the now dark forest, across the wide field and down through the middle of town, scattering townsfolk before them as they went. They bolted into the courtyard behind the inn and almost ran over Marsden in their haste.

"Slow down you two!" Marsden yelled. "You want to hurt someone! I'll forbid you to ride those horses if you can't be more responsible."

"Where's Tally?" Orphan shouted, ignoring Marsden's reprimand.

Marsden raised his eyebrow at Orphan's rudeness but answered, "In the kitchen with Tilda. What's wrong Orphan?" He grabbed Nutmeg's reins and rubbed a calming hand down the horse's neck.

"What is all the commotion about out here?" Tally burst out of the kitchen door with Tilda on his heels, her apron flapping about her.

"Didn't I tell you two I wanted you back before dark!" His eyes swept over the horses. They were panting and foaming at the mouth. "Orphan! Thane! You know better than to ride those horses so hard!" he scolded them as he rushed forward to stand next to Marsden.

"Tally!...in the woods with Markus! He killed him. Markus told him where we are Tally! He's dead! We watched him kill him. There was a fire and monsters. Tally we must leave. He knows we are here." Orphan was so frantic, that the words were tumbling out of his mouth too fast. Each sentence was making even less sense than the sentence before.

"Whoa, slow down. Who is here? Who killed who? What does Markus have to do with this?" Marsden asked as Tilda came up next to him and looped her arm through his.

Thane took a deep breath and explained. "We were riding in the field west of the town when we saw a strange red smoke coming from the trees in the forest on the other side of the valley."

"Thane wanted to see who was camped out there and find out what they were burning," Orphan broke in. "I told him we should have stayed away from there!"

With a glare at Orphan, Thane continued. "Yes, and then we wouldn't have found out what Markus was up to, right?" Thane argued back.

"Well, I..." Orphan started to yell back, leaning forward on the horse.

"Boys!" Tally interrupted with a shout. "What did you find? Who was it?"

Orphan dismounted quickly.

Thane nudged Embarr closer to Tally and continued with his explanation. "We found Markus talking to a tall man in a long black cloak. It was Zavior!" He described what happened in the clearing then finished by saying, "Markus told him where I am. He told him exactly where to find me," Thane said.

"Then Zavior killed Markus; choked the life right out of him without laying a finger on him. He turned to look right at where we were hiding, like he knew we were watching. I don't know why he didn't attack us then. He just turned back to the fire and made these huge horrible monsters come out of it." Orphan finished. "We left and rode straight back here...as fast as we could."

Thane got off of Embarr. "I don't understand. What is going on? Why is he here?" "Why would he kill Markus?" Thane asked. "What does he want with me?"

Tally put his hand on his shoulder. Thane wasn't sure if Tally was trying to comfort him or trying to steady himself.

"Thane, our time here is done. We have been found. I thought we would have more time but it is not meant to be. We must leave. Now! Zavior wants YOU and the medallion. He will stop at nothing till he gets both. Go pack up what you need from your room."

When the boys both stood there staring at him, he repeated in a firmer voice, "Go get your things, both of you. We leave immediately."

"No, I don't want to run away again. We can fight! I know how to fight now!" Thane argued fiercely. He pulled his shoulder away from Tally's grasp and glared at him.

"You are not strong enough to face him yet. Think, Thane!" Tally insisted. "He killed your father, a powerful knight, with ease! Your parents fought him and died so that you could escape. Do not, in your arrogance, waste their sacrifice. You cannot defeat him yet, you still have too much to learn."

Tally stared into Thanes eyes. "Not yet, Thane," Tally added softly. "Now go get your things. You too, Orphan. Quickly! We leave immediately."

Thane reluctantly turned and stormed into the inn, with Orphan right behind him. They paused at the doors to their rooms and looked at each other. Thane's hands were fisted at his side and his jaw was clenched. Slivers of silver light flickered in his eyes.

"Thane, you have to trust Tally. He knows what's best. We can't fight him," Orphan said. "So stop being so difficult and get your stuff. Hurry!"

Thane didn't reply. He turned, threw open the door to his room and stormed inside. He was quick as he didn't have a lot to gather. He wrapped his extra clothes in a shirt and tied the pile together with the sleeves, shoved his knife into the side of his boot, and lopped his dark woolen cloak over one arm. He grabbed the little sporran of treasures and wooden sword in the other hand.

He went out in the hall to wait for Orphan. Orphan rushed out of his room with a small sack slung over his shoulders, his wooden sword and a green traveling cloak draped over his arm. Their eyes met for a moment before they turned and hurried down the stairs without speaking.

Thane stopped at the bottom landing to take one last look around the common room. The tables were wiped clean and the chairs were pushed in close. The fireplace was cold and dark. They had spent so many peaceful nights here. He wondered if he would ever see it again. With a sigh, he walked back through the kitchen and followed Orphan quietly out the door.

The adults were still gathered in the courtyard. They had their heads together, whispering and gesturing with their hands. Tally stood with a small leather bag at his feet, his cape over his arm and his sword hanging from his waist. He was holding the reins of both Nutmeg and Embarr. Embarr had the bows and arrows strapped to the back of his saddle. They looked up as one when the boys came out and immediately stopped talking.

Tally cleared his throat. "Marsden has given the mare to us. We can send her back when we are safe. She will carry Orphan and me. You will ride Embarr with the extra weapons and baggage." Tally said. He took his bag, Thane's bundled shirt and Orphan's sack and stuffed them into the large leather bags hanging over Embarr's flanks. Molly rushed out of the kitchen and handed Tally some smaller bags that Thane assumed held food. Those too were stuffed into Embarr's saddlebags. She gave them each a quick hug goodbye and went back into the kitchen.

Thane looked back at Marsden and Tilda. Marsden had his arms around her shoulders, and she was leaning her thin body into his. She was holding the corner of her smock to her face. Thane could see tears in her eyes. Marsden looked furious.

"I am sorrier than you will ever know that it was one of us who betrayed you. Markus has not only betrayed you, he has betrayed his family and our honor. He has paid the price for his stupidity." Marsden held out his hand for Thane to shake it. "Take care of yourself. It has been an honor to know you. Don't forget us."

"Thanks," Thane said. Puzzled by Marsden's speech, he glanced over at Tally with a frown.

"He has known who you are for a while now Thane," Tally said reading the question in his eyes. "He has done much to protect your identity."

Tilda tore herself from Marsden's side and walked over to Orphan. She enfolded him in her arms and whispered something in his ear. Orphan's eyes grew wide and Thane was surprised to see them fill with tears. Tilda pulled away and kissed him on the head.

She turned to Thane and took his face in her hands. "You will be missed Thane," she sniffed. "Know that you will always have a home here. Take care of yourself. Take care of Orphan too! He is not as tough as he wants everyone to believe!" She hugged him tightly, pulled his head down, and kissed him on the forehead. Giant tears spilled out of her soft brown eyes, trailed down her cheek, and dripped off of her chin as she turned back to fold herself into Marsden's arms.

Thane made sure their bows and arrows were strapped securely to Embarr's side then climbed up onto the saddle. Marsden helped Orphan up behind Tally and with a last wave they galloped out of the yard and into the alley next to the inn. Tally led them through the dark and deserted streets and out of town as quickly as he could.

They made as much noise as they could to draw attention to their departure in the hope that it would keep Zavior and his monsters away from the inn. They left town on the same road that Thane had taken to the inn on his first day there. As they rode past the well where Thane first appeared, he stopped and looked around. It was so long ago.

Once they cleared the outskirts of town, they kicked the horses into a run and rode as hard as they dared in the dark. They followed the road north for some distance. Orphan rode quietly behind Tally with his face hidden in Tally's shirt. It was clear that Tally knew where he was going so Thane just followed along behind him. Eventually, they slowed to enter a path that led into the forest due east of town. They trudged through the trees until they came to a wide shallow river.

"We will make our way toward Maldon then head northeast towards Ipswich. This will be one of the most dangerous parts of our journey; the land is flat and there are not many places to hide. We are going to ride through water for a while to cover our scent and hide our tracks as much as possible. Thane, I would like Embarr to lead. He will be able to find safe passage through the water in the dark." Tally said quietly as he pulled Nutmeg to the side to give Thane room to maneuver around them. "Take it slow. It will do us no good to get injured."

They rode painstakingly up the middle of the river and followed it east for an hour. Finally, Tally called out to Thane to exit the river at the next opening. Tally said they had ridden far enough to disguise their scent and the water was getting too deep to ride safely through. The sky was just beginning to lighten the tops of the trees when they climbed up a short rocky slope to a small section of grass. They stopped close to the river so the horses could drink, eat and rest.

Molly had packed some food for them but, on such short notice, it was simple and there was not much of it. They would have to ration it if they were going to hide in the woods for any length of time. Tally wouldn't light a fire for fear of it being seen.

"Where are we going?" Thane finally asked Tally.

"We will rest here for a couple of hours then continue northeast. Before we reach Ipswich, we will head northwest toward Cambridge then turn to the north. I know of a Fæ gateway in the Highlands of Scotland. If we are lucky, we will find a way to contact your mother's people there. They are the only ones who can protect you both now," Tally said as he put the remaining food back in Embarr's saddlebag. "Get some rest. We have far to travel and you will need your strength." An uneasy silence settled on the small group.

Thane leaned back against a large log and closed his eyes. He eventually dozed. It seemed like just a few minutes had passed before Tally was shaking his shoulder and urging him to his feet.

All he said was, "Time to leave."

They stopped twice during the day to care for the horses. Tally was concerned about Nutmeg. She was not a young horse anymore and she was beginning to show signs of fatigue.

They stopped at twilight. Thane wished they could light a fire. Even though it was just the beginning of autumn, the air was very cold. They wrapped their cloaks around themselves for warmth and they laid down under the stars in silence. Thane could clearly see the outline of Tally and Orphan as they lay tucked beneath their cloaks next to him and was grateful for their presence.

It was impossible for Thane to fall asleep this time. The fear of Roki stumbling upon them in the dark had him straining his ears for the slightest change in the sounds of the forest. Thane's hatred of Zavior burned in his heart.

He turned onto his back on the hard ground and watched the full moon slowly travel across the sky, sliding in and out of billowy bright clouds, until finally, hours later, it disappeared behind the line of trees. The sun took its turn as it began to tint the sky misty blue and the birds began to sing.

Tally rose quietly and began to prepare breakfast in the gray early morning light. He nodded at Thane when he realized he was awake, and then bent over to shake Orphan awake with a hand on his shoulder. Orphan rubbed his eyes as he got up and stumbled into the privacy of the trees. When he returned, they shared another small meal of bread and cheese. No one spoke as they packed up their meager belongings and got back on the horses.

They passed the outskirts of Cambridge sometime in the late morning. The sun was directly overhead when they stopped to eat and rest the horses at a pool of water near the base of a small cliff.

Before they had a chance to dismount the horses, they heard it. Loud thrashing and growling sounds were coming from just behind the trees on the other side of the clearing. Tally and Thane pulled the horses close together and turned to face the alarming noises.

Thane pulled out his wooden sword feeling rather unprepared to face what was coming their way. Out of the corner of his eye, he saw Tally unsheathe his sword and Orphan reached for the bow and arrows he had strapped to his back earlier in the day.

A moment later, a half dozen of Zavior's Roki burst through the trees, cornering the mounted riders between the cliff and the water. The Roki stopped and waited; teeth bared and growling as Zavior, astride his massive black horse, approached slowly from behind the beasts.

Tally, Thane, and Orphan were trapped. With the pool of water to their side, the cliff to their back, and the Roki facing them, they had no way to escape. Thane couldn't take his eyes off of Zavior. This was the man from his nightmares, the man from the Reiver village. Thane was petrified with fear.

Thane heard a splash behind him but didn't turn to investigate.

"You thought to run from me and follow Taliesin?" Zavior sneered as he advanced on them. "Did you believe that old man could possibly hide you from me?"

The Roki parted to let him through. Snarling ferociously, they closed ranks behind him. Zavior continued to taunt them. "You should know by now that you cannot hide from me. There will always be someone willing to betray you. How do you think I found you in that Reiver hole you were hiding in? Your Cessford knew who you were from the moment he set eyes on you. So he hid you amongst his rabble."

Tally shot a glance at Thane. Thane knew exactly what the Bard was thinking. Tally had been right about Asiag. He had known who Thane really was.

"However, not all Reivers felt loyalty to the Fæ. Frammel couldn't stand the sight of you and whined about you to anyone who would listen. I have wondered, what is it about you that makes some want to protect you and others so eager to betray you," he said almost to himself then waved his hand in front of his face as if to brush away the thought.

"Markus was just as much of a fool as Frammel. He was jealous of your precious Bard's relationship with his dear brother and resented the attention he and his wife lavished on two stray boys. It was even easier for my spies to get word to me your whereabouts this time for he was even more vocal in his dislike for you than Frammel had been." Zavior paced on his horse in the open space in front of his Roki.

Thane felt a surge of anger supplant his fear. "We saw what you did to Markus," Thane shouted. "Why did you have to kill him? He told you what you wanted to know."

Zavior smiled coldly. "So, it was you making all the noise in the bushes yesterday! I thought I felt a presence…" he shrugged. "He was no use to me anymore."

"And what use am I to you?" Thane demanded. "Why go through all this trouble to get to me?"

"Don't you know? Has he not told you anything?" Zavior stopped his pacing to look between Thane and Tally.

"I want you to join me. Leave this fool. He is just a Bard…a coward. I know you have the medallion, Nathaniel." Zavior slowly advanced on Thane. "Together we can open the Gateway, gather the sacred gifts and take control of the West. We can return Inis Fáil to the Fæ."

"Come with me and I will let your friends go," he promised as he coaxed Thane forward with an outstretched hand.

Thane glanced sideways at Tally. He was still on his horse; his sword in one hand and a short knife in the other. Orphan was just visible behind Nutmeg to Tally's right. He was ankle deep in the water at the edge of the pool, an arrow notched in his bow, his knees bent and his face pale. He must have jumped from the horse when Zavior strode into the clearing. Despite the overwhelming odds, they were ready to fight.

Thane looked back at Zavior and the line of Roki behind him and realized that Tally was right. There was no way the three of them were going to win in a battle against Zavior. A wave of hopelessness washed over him as he realized that they were probably not going to make it out of this alive. Images of the people he had loved who had died to save him from Zavior flashed through his mind. Fury pushed the hopelessness away. He too would die before he would join Zavior.

"Never!" Thane shouted as he lifted his open hand and struggled to throw a ball of flame at Zavior. It was not much more than a spark and was easily brushed aside by a wave of Zavior's hand.

He heard a snort of annoyance from somewhere behind him and knew exactly what Orphan was thinking…that was a stupid move. He couldn't make a decent flame on a good day. An arrow went sailing past his head toward Zavior only to be brushed aside as easily as Thane's flame had been.

"No, Thane…Orphan…don't fight him…you must go. You can do nothing here. Run!" Tally yelled as he charged forward, his sword raised in the air.

"Fool! You cannot protect him. Bring me the dark haired boy and find the medallion!" Zavior ordered his minions as he stepped his horse back and let the Roki push past him.

"Kill the others," he laughed out loud, the two braids in his beard undulating. The beasts surged forward in a wall of claws, jaws, growls, and snarls.

Two Roki pressed forward to attack Tally as he sat atop Nutmeg. Fighting desperately, Tally swung his sword and managed to stab one in the neck as it was about to pull him off of the horse. The creature let go of Tally's arm abruptly then exploded into dust. Tally shook his head to gather his wits together before turning to engage the other one.

A couple of the beasts charged at Thane. Embarr reared up to kick one as Thane swung around to stab the other in the eye with his wooden sword. Thane heard Orphan cry out and turned Embarr towards the pool. Orphan was now thigh deep in the water desperately trying to fight off a Roki with a short blade. Thane watched in horror as the Roki raised his paw and slashed Orphan viciously across his side. The boy fell to his knees in the water as the Roki raised its arm for another blow.

"Orphan!" Thane yelled and charged through the water toward Orphan. He could hear another Roki crash into the water behind him.

Embarr splashed through the water and reared up again to kick the Roki away from Orphan just as Thane began to feel his insides burn.

"NO!" Thane cried "NOT NOW!"

Thane grasped Embarr's mane with the same hand that gripped his sword. He reached down with the other and grabbed Orphan by the arm. The leaves, dirt, and water began to swirl around them and through the gold and red debris he caught a glimpse of Tally being pulled from his horse and of the fury on Zavior's face as he realized what was about to happen.

Thane's vision blurred. He held on to Embarr and Orphan with all his strength as a blinding white and blue light exploded up and outwards from the water. He threw back his head and screamed as the pain in his body reached a fevered pitch and everything went black.

Chapter Nineteen

Orphan's Secret

Thane awoke with a start. He was laying on a riverbank, half in and half out of the shallow water. Cold water was rushing over his partially submerged legs. He rolled onto his back and couldn't stop himself from crying out as a stabbing pain tore through his shoulder. He wasn't able to move his left arm. He realized he must have dislocated it when he tried to pull Orphan up onto Embarr during the fight.

THE FIGHT! He sat up quickly to look around for the Roki, Zavior, or any signs of the struggle. Lights burst in front of his eyes, and he almost passed out as another wave of pain and dizziness washed over him. Squeezing his eyes shut, he let himself fall back down on the cold grass. Cradling his arm against his body, he took several deep breaths.

When the pain subsided a bit, he opened his eyes and looked around. Just feet from where he lay, Orphan was curled up on his side.

His eyes were closed and he wasn't moving. Thane could see where his shirt was torn at his waist and his side was soaked in blood. Embarr was nudging at Orphan's shoulder with his nose as if he was trying to wake him.

"ORPHAN!" He cried out as panic seized him. He pulled his legs out of the water and crawled across the ground toward Orphan; careful to cradle his arm against his body to keep his shoulder still. He stopped twice to catch his breath. He wasn't sure he was going to be able to make it across the short distance that separated them. The pain was so intense it radiated from his shoulder down through his whole body, and he was sweating from the pain and the effort of dragging himself toward Orphan and Embarr.

"Orphan!" Thane called out as he reached him. It took him a full minute to roll Orphan onto his back.

"Wake up!" Thane grabbed Orphan by the shoulder and shook him frantically with his good arm.

"Please Orphan...please...please don't be dead!" He pleaded as Embarr rubbed his nose down Thane's back encouragingly.

Orphan moaned softly and blinked. His green eyes opened and he looked anxiously up at Thane. "What happened?" Where are we?" he mumbled before closing his eyes again. "Where's Tally?"

"I don't know. I think we left the clearing though," Thane stated the obvious as he sat back on his heels. Relief flooded through him. Orphan was alive. "I don't know where Tally is. I don't even know where *we* are!"

Thane's heart stopped as he noticed the dark red blood dripping from Orphan's clothing onto the ground. The Roki must have slashed him across the stomach with its claws before they escaped the clearing.

"You're bleeding Orphan! Take your shirt off and let me see how bad it is. Maybe I can bandage it until we find help." When Thane reached for the bottom of Orphan's shirt to lift it up, Orphan slapped his hand away. He wrapped his arm around his side and rolled slowly around to turn his back to Thane.

"No. I'm okay," Orphan mumbled.

"You're hurt! Let me see," Thane argued. "You have nothing to be embarrassed about. I don't care if you have some stupid scars or whatever it is you are always trying to hide!"

"I said, 'No,' Thane! Just leave me alone."

Orphan struggled to sit up. He wrapped both arms around his side and doubled over in pain. "I'll be fine!" he growled through clenched teeth.

"Don't be stupid. You're shirt is soaked in blood and you can barely move. Why are you being so thickheaded?" Thane stubbornly argued back.

"I said I'm fine," he gasped. His breathing was rapid and shallow and his face was deathly pale. "We need to figure out where we are and what happened to Tally. That's more important than a little scratch. Really, Thane, I told you I can take care of myself," he insisted.

Thane drew back a bit with his right hand raised up in front of him in surrender. He looked away from Orphan in frustration. He studied their surroundings. They were in a small opening next to a shallow stream in a very old forest. The ground was covered in small rocks, decayed leaves, and broken branches. Thick fuzzy green moss blanketed the roots at the base of the ancient trees and covered the rocks and forest floor around them.

The trunks of the trees were so wide that Thane thought he, Embarr, and Orphan could hide behind one. A thick canopy of yellow, orange, and red leaves blocked out most of the sky and light from the sun. It made it difficult to figure out the time of day or how long they had been unconscious.

Thane looked at Orphan again. He was obviously in a great deal of pain. "Do you think you can stand?"

"I don't know but promise me...promise me you'll leave the scratch alone, Thane, please," Orphan begged as he closed his eyes again.

"You call that a scratch?" Thane started to argue again but at Orphan's irritated grunt he relented and said, "Fine! You're being really stupid you know that?"

"I need my bag," Orphan gasped out as he continued to press his arm to his wounded side.

Thane reached up and grabbed one of Embarr's stirrups and pulled himself to his feet. He had to wait for his head to stop spinning before he could untie Orphan's bag from the saddle. He dropped it next to Orphan then eased himself back down beside him. Thane leaned forward to help him untie the bag. Orphan reached inside and pulled out a clean shirt and stockings. He bunched up the shirt and pressed it to the wound under his tunic. Tossing the stockings to Thane he asked breathlessly, "Can you help me tie this around my waist to hold the shirt in place?"

When Thane finished helping him tie the two legs of the stockings together, Orphan eased himself back down and closed his eyes.

"I don't think that's going to work for very long." Thane whispered helplessly. "You're bleeding all over the place."

"Orphan?" Thane put his hand on Orphan's shoulder and shook it gently. He could tell he was still breathing but he was now unconscious. He needed to find someone to help Orphan but he couldn't leave him here alone. He was going to have to find a way to take him with him.

Thane looked around the forest in a panic. He had no idea where they were. Embarr was standing behind them with his eyes closed, his head up, and his nose sniffing the air.

"Embarr, come! Help me!" Thane yelled. "I need you to kneel down so I can get Orphan up on your back," he ordered the horse.

Embarr trotted over, bent his front legs and nudged Thane on the shoulder. Thane maneuvered himself around until he was able to slide his one good arm around the uninjured side of Orphan's body. He half rolled, half dragged him across Embarr's back until the front half of Orphan was draped awkwardly over Embarr's white neck. Thane stopped and took a few deep breaths before he hoisted Orphan's right leg up and over Embarr's back. It took several tries before it worked and with one last desperate shove on his backside, he had Orphan straddling the horse.

Embarr waited patiently on his knees for Thane to catch his breath and muster the strength to throw a trembling leg across the saddle. He finally dragged himself up and sat unsteadily behind Orphan.

Embarr got slowly to his feet and without waiting for direction from Thane, he sniffed the air again then carefully made his way through a thick stand of trees. He followed a small path that led them away from the water.

Orphan was slumped forward over Embarr's neck with his arms dangling down on either side. Thane held on tightly to the back of Orphan's shirt with his good arm. He wasn't sure how much longer he was going to be able to stay conscious himself. He was dizzy, and sick with pain and worry.

The three of them were moving slowly along a path that was beginning to slope steeply uphill. The land rose sharply up on both sides of the path. They were making their way through a pass between two enormous mountains. Thane had no idea where they were or where they should go so he let Embarr take the lead and carry them in whatever direction he desired. Thane had the impression that the horse knew exactly where he was going. They were moving along at a steady pace despite the fact that Embarr was struggling keep the injured boys balanced on his back.

Blood was beginning to soak through Orphan's makeshift shirt bandage and was dripping steadily down his leg. Long streaks of red now covered Embarr's white shoulders. Thane began to panic. He knew that if he didn't find help for Orphan soon, Orphan would likely die. He had seen enough wounds when he was with the Reivers to know that this much blood leaking from an injury could be fatal. He would respect Orphan's wishes and not look at his wound; not because he made him promise but because Thane had no idea what he could have done to help anyway.

They crested the summit of the pass. Thane pulled Embarr to a halt as they reached a small plateau. He could see for miles. He looked below them to where the land met the sea and the sea met the horizon.

On his left, a small waterfall was surging down the mountain in a ribbon of white foam. Thane's eyes followed the water from where it tumbled over the waterfall into the pool at its base. He could see where the river wove its way through the land and emptied into the sea.

He knew that Writtle was relatively close to the sea but had never seen it himself. Was that where they were? He swiftly ruled it out as he didn't see a town between him and the water. Embarr started forward on the small path that led steadily downhill in the direction of the sea.

It wasn't long before Thane began to drift in and out of consciousness. The forest was passing by him in a blur of pain colored by evergreens and the sound of rushing water. Every time his weight shifted as if he was going to slide off of the horse, Embarr would bray loudly, jerking him awake. Orphan never moved.

Finally, the pine trees thinned and bright light began to filter through the sparse branches above them. The loud roar of the sea broke through the stillness of the forest. A strange sharp odor made Thane lift his head. What was that smell? He wrinkled his nose and frowned. It was like fish and salt and wet all combined. It stank! They broke through the trees to an astonishing sight.

A thin strip of sandy white beach lay unfurled like a crescent moon before a sea of crystal clear blue water. The tumbling, crashing waves stretched as far as his eyes could see. The sound of the water was almost deafening after the quiet of the forest. He squinted through the glare of the sun. He could see a small white stone house tucked into the trees down at the far end of the beach to his right. Immense rocks were scattered around the sand just outside the cottage. Maybe they could find help there. Embarr appeared to have the same idea because he headed straight toward the house.

As they approached, the door of the house swung open. A small old woman emerged from the dark doorway. A bright red woolen shawl hung over her shoulders and tangled in the folds of her dark brown dress. She shuffled out to meet them. Thane slid off of Embarr's back. She reached him just as his legs buckled under him. She attempted to catch him but wasn't strong enough to hold him. He slid through her arms and landed in a heap on the ground at her feet. Orphan was still draped unconscious over Embarr's neck.

"Here, boy. To you, what have you let happened?" she admonished him.

"My friend's hurt and bleeding. Can you help us?" Thane mumbled as he struggled to pull himself back up. Using the stirrup hanging above his head, he held his helpless arm close to his body and managed to get his feet under him. He leaned unsteadily against Embarr as the stranger blurred in and out of focus.

Thane watched uneasily as she pulled the hair back from Orphan's face and stroked her wrinkled hand across his forehead and down around his neck. Thane swayed as relief flooded through him.

Finally, they had found help. Thane slumped heavily against Embarr and closed his eyes for a moment. He was not sure how much longer he was going to be able to remain standing.

"Inside your friend must be brought. Your help I be needing boy. To lose control now, it is not the time. To that side you must hold and to the other I will." Thane reached up with his good arm to help the old lady ease Orphan from Embarr's back. He stumbled and almost collapsed again as the weight of Orphan's limp body slid down off of the horse. With Orphan sandwiched between them, they managed to slowly half-drag, half-carry him inside the little house. They laid him clumsily on a small bed that was almost hidden from view in a tiny curtained alcove.

Thane looked down at the tiny old woman as she fussed over Orphan. The top of her head came to just under his chin. She had so many wrinkles that Thane was sure there wasn't one spot on her that wasn't covered in some type of line. She looked like she had been a full sized human at one point in her life, then someone had come along and scrunched her up into their idea of what an old woman should look like, only they didn't know when to stop. Her eyes were a crystal clear blue, so light that they were almost white, with a thin dark blue ring around each iris.

As he looked down at her, she seemed to move away from him down a long dark tunnel. She was moving farther and farther away. The tunnel was getting darker and darker. He closed his eyes and sank into the darkness.

††††

Strange noises gradually began to penetrate Thane's consciousness. He became aware that his body ached all over. The events of the last day played swiftly across his mind. He was afraid to open his eyes hoping that maybe it had all been a dream and he would wake safe and warm in the stables at the inn. Holding his breath, he peaked out from under his lashes to locate the source of the noise.

He was definitely not at the inn and the old lady was real. She had her back toward him and was tending to a large black kettle hanging from an iron hook in the fireplace. She had removed her red shawl and had her sleeves rolled up past her thin wrinkly elbows. Steam was rising in opaque swirls from the blackened iron pot. It smelled just like Tilda's fish stew. He hadn't realized how hungry he was until he felt his stomach rumble. How long had it been since they had last eaten?

"Good, now you wake. For two days have you slept."

Thane started as the woman answered his unspoken question without turning around. She added something chunky and green to the pot and stirred some more. "Ready to have a meal are you?" she cackled. "Your belly is telling me you are."

"Where am I? Where is Orphan?" Thane said as he struggled to a sitting position. He didn't feel like he was going to pass out but the effort to sit was causing him some distress. He moved his shoulder slowly around. It was stiff and still very painful but it felt like everything was back where it belonged. Could the old lady have fixed his arm while he was unconscious?

He glanced around the little cottage. There was a small window above his head. Dark curtains were pulled shut so he couldn't tell if it was day or night. The only light in the room was the soft orange glow from the fire where the old woman was still calmly stirring her pot. He found he was lying on a soft woolen mat next to the fireplace that nearly filled the back wall of the small dimly lit room. A tiny loom was set up on the other side of the fireplace. Thane saw a small square table in the middle of the room. A chair was angled away from it as if its former occupant had stood up abruptly and left. A cup sat on the table. He could see a door across the room from where he lay and assumed it led to the outside.

"Ill your friend is still, with fever. I had a hope that today she would awake but it is not to be. Much blood she lost and set with an evil poison the wound is."

"She who?" Thane asked raising his eyebrow in confusion. "Who are you talking about?"

The old woman turned to look at him with her head tilted to the side. "Two days ago, a wounded girl you brought with you. Behind the curtain she lays in a fever."

"I didn't come here with a girl! He isn't a girl! What have you done with Orphan?" Thane cried in alarm as he struggled to stand up. A wave of nausea and dizziness washed over him as the blood rushed from his head. He had just lost Tally, he couldn't bear to lose Orphan as well.

"Where is HE!" Thane demanded again. He turned and dug his fingers into the rough stone wall behind him to pull himself up; his arms and legs trembled with the exertion.

"Calm you must be now. Come, here I will show you; then eat and rest you must." She soothed.

She grabbed hold of his elbow and led him slowly across the little room to the small alcove carved into the side wall. The old woman reached up and pulled a corner of the curtain back with a gnarled hand.

Orphan lay unconscious on the small bed. Thane vaguely recalled helping the old woman lay him down on this bed just before everything went black. Orphan's eyes were closed, his face flushed and his hair was slicked back from his face with sweat. Thane could see small pointed ears peaking out from under Orphan's flat wet hair. He was wearing a thin sleeveless night shift. Thane looked from Orphan to the old lady and back to Orphan again with a frown. A knot was beginning to form in his stomach. Was this old woman trying to tell him that Orphan was a girl?

Images flashed rapidly through his mind. He recalled how Orphan never dressed in the same room with him and how Orphan always refused to swim with him in the river during the summer. If Orphan was truly a girl, that would explain why his voice did not change and why he was still so scrawny. He stared at the ears that were so similar to his and felt anger flare up inside. Why? Why the deception? How could they have lied to him for all those years?

Thane backed away from the bed Orphan lay upon, his eyes riveted on the still figure in front of him. His throat ached with anger and the pain of betrayal. That's why he...no she...had not wanted him to look at the wound. How could he have been stupid enough to have been fooled for so long? He turned away abruptly and smashed his toe against the leg of the table behind him. With a vicious curse, he limped angrily out of the cottage and down the sandy beach.

He didn't get far before pain and fatigue forced him to stop. He lowered himself slowly down onto one of the large stones that were scattered along the small strip of sand just outside the cottage. The waves were battering the small beach with a ferociousness that matched the hurt and anger building inside Thane. Why did they lie to him? Tally and Orphan knew all there was to know about his life. Now it seemed that everything he thought he knew concerning them was a lie. What other lies had they told him?

Thane sat on the rock for a while, watching the waves as they tumbled and rushed in toward him, then just as quickly, were sucked back into the churning body of water. Heavy, dark clouds hung over the tiny strip of beach threatening rain. Should he leave Orphan and just go? But where would he go? How could he ever trust anyone again?

He looked back at the cottage and wondered where Embarr was. He didn't know if he would have enough strength to get up from the rock let alone leave. He tucked his helpless arm against his stomach and bent over to rest the elbow of his good arm on his knee. Thane covered his face with his hand as he felt tears of anger and hurt begin to leak from his eyes. His world was tearing apart at the seams and he had no control over how far it was going to tear or what he was going to do with all the pieces.

The door behind him opened and closed. Thane hastily wiped his eyes and looked back to see the old woman shuffling toward him with a small bowl clutched precariously between her gnarled old hands.

She came to a stop next to him and stood in silence for a moment gazing intently at the churning waves. Thick gray clouds were crowding the sky; shoving against each other, pressing down and merging with the dark water. In the distance, it was impossible to say where the water ended and the sky began.

"All things are not as they seem my young man. Though she has deceived you, you cannot abandon her here," she said softly.

"More you will know if she awakens but warn you I must, through the night she might not survive. Eat! Strength you will need for what is ahead."

Leaning over, she placed the warm bowl gently in Thane's hands. He looked up into her face as he took hold of the bowl. He was stunned to see that her eyes were a different color today. He was sure that they had been light blue that first day they arrived. Today, they were as dark as the turbulent water. She placed a small weathered hand gently on the top of Thane's head for a moment then turned and shuffled back into the cottage.

By the time Thane managed to force a spoonful of stew past the lump in his throat, it was cold; tasty, but cold. Hunger won out over betrayal and before long he had finished every last drop in the bowl.

Fat drops of rain began to fall. Thane gathered his strength to stand. His body felt stiff and sore as he forced himself to walk back to the shelter of the cottage. The fire was blazing bright and warm, still the only light in the small room. He slid a glance over to the alcove and saw that the curtain was now held back with a piece of green wool. Orphan lay immobile and quiet. Thane was sick to his stomach with fear that she would die and at the same time so angry that she had deceived him. He thought he never wanted to talk to her again. The cold stew was now sitting like a rock in his stomach and his whole body ached.

He eased himself back down on the mat and lay on his side to stare morosely into the fire. The last hour had sapped what little energy he had and before long he fell into a fitful sleep. He dreamt of girls with strangely colored eyes swimming in the water next to the cottage. They were calling out to him…laughing at him…taunting him. Their features were swiftly changing from girl to boy and back to girl again.

Chapter Twenty

On the Beach with Embarr

The sun was shining through the open window of the cottage when Thane awoke next. It was very quiet in the small room. The old woman was gone. He sat up slowly on his mat and turned to lean his back against the wall next to the fireplace. The pain in his shoulder was now no more then a dull throb.

He stared across the room at Orphan. He…no…she was still lying on the bed in the alcove, curled up in a ball on her unhurt side and facing him. Her face was still flushed but not the burning red it had been the last time he saw her. Her breathing seemed a little bit less labored. His chest tightened again as he thought about how Tally and Orphan had lied to him. He looked away from her.

Thane got to his feet. After rolling his shoulder around slowly to test it, he made his way outside. Fat, fluffy, bright white clouds were scattered across the sky and the water was the deep blue color of sapphires. He walked slowly over to his rock and sat gingerly down onto the sand in front of it. The sun-warmed surface felt wonderful against his back. Inhaling the salty smell of the water, he closed his eyes and tilted his head back to let the sun warm his face.

He must have slept because the next thing he knew, something was rubbing the top of his head and licking at his hair. Startled, he opened his eyes and stared right up into a horse's pink nose. The little hairs around the horse's nostrils were blowing in and out with every breath it took. The horse whinnied and blew little bits of spit at him.

"Hey boy," Thane whispered affectionately to Embarr with a smile.

Embarr continued to nuzzle and nibble Thane's hair with his lips.

"Whoa! Embarr! Okay! Okay! I'm fine! I missed you too. Where have you been hiding out?" Thane laughed out loud for the first time in days. He reached up with his good arm to rub his palm over Embarr's nose and soft cheek.

"Roaming about the mountain he's been," a beautiful singsong voice called out.

Thane turned in the direction of the voice. A tall, willowy woman was emerging from the waves in front of him. Her long, pale blond hair tumbled down past her shoulders, trailed down her back and floated in the waves behind her. Her sleeveless dress appeared to be made of millions of tiny blue and green jewels overlapping each other like scales on a fish. Every part of her body above the water was dry. Her eyes mirrored the sapphire blue of the water behind her and her skin glowed with a blue-green light.

"Who are you?" Thane asked as he jumped to his feet to stand in front of Embarr. He flung his good arm out as if to protect the horse.

"I am Muirghein, Færie Goddess of the Waters," she said with a smile. "For aid, to me you were sent." She continued to walk out of the waves toward him.

"You, young Nathaniel, last hope of the Færies for peace you are. To that end, my help I will give to you."

"How do you know who I am? To the end of what?" Thane asked as he backed away from her advance, until he was pressed firmly back against Embarr who stubbornly stood his ground, unwilling to retreat. "How can you help me?"

She continued to walk toward him until she had stepped completely out of the retreating waves. As soon as her small, narrow feet touched the dry sand, she began to fold up upon herself as if she were a piece of parchment being crinkled up by a giant invisible hand. Before his eyes she transformed into the old woman from the cottage. Only her eyes remained the same sapphire blue as the water.

"Afraid you should not be," the old woman said in her usual raspy voice as she continued to shuffle towards him. "No harm will I do to you."

Thane stared at her with his mouth hanging open. How did she do that? He looked quickly back at Embarr, who stared serenely back at Thane; relaxed and unconcerned. Surely, if this old woman was going to harm him, Embarr would be struggling to get away or at the very least, showing some fear of her. He wasn't. He was just gazing at her like this was just an everyday common occurrence for him.

Thane turned back to see that the old woman was almost upon him now. He was uncertain about what he should do, so he just stood there and watched her as she toddled up to him…then toddled right on past him toward the cottage. It wasn't until she reached the front door that she turned back. He was still standing right where she had left him with his mouth hanging open.

"Standing there for what reason are you?" she queried with a lift of her gray brow.

"Uh…" he mumbled as he didn't have an answer for her. She sounded just like Orphan had on the first day they met. It was that more than anything else that finally convinced him that he could trust her.

"With me you need to come for food I will give you. Awake your friend may yet be." She shuffled into the cottage without a backward glance to see if he was indeed following or if he had taken his horse and made a run for the hills.

He shrugged and looked at Embarr. The horse calmly blinked back at him before he too turned away from Thane and ran down the beach and disappeared around a bend in the sheer cliff wall. Thane slowly followed the old woman back into the cottage. She was bent over at the fireplace fussing with the black pot, her stooped old body outlined in the light from the flames.

Thane stumbled across the room and flopped down on his mat next to the fire. He stretched one leg out in front of him and kept the other bent up next to his body. He draped his good arm across his knee and rested his forehead down on it. Nightmares had been plaguing his dreams so he was not eager to fall asleep any sooner than he needed to. Thane heard Orphan stir restlessly on the small bed across the room. He lifted his head just enough to see his...that is... her eyelashes flutter open. Her eyes were still glassy with fever.

The old woman bustled over to her and blocked most of Orphan's face from his view. Thane could just see her wrinkled hand as she stroked it across Orphan's hot brow, and he listened with half an ear as she soothed her in a reassuring voice. Strange, he couldn't make out exactly what she was crooning to Orphan, but he was pretty sure that it was not any language he had ever heard before. Before long she turned back to her pot and Thane could see that Orphan was asleep again.

He closed his eyes as relief flooded through him. It looked like Orphan was getting stronger. The old woman didn't seem to be worried, so maybe Orphan was going to be alright. He sat there staring at Orphan's flushed face. He was still trying to come to terms with not only her betrayal but the fact that his best friend was now and always had been...a girl.

†††††

Thane spent most of the next morning with Embarr. It felt good to be up and moving around, albeit slowly and carefully as his shoulder was still very tender. Even though he didn't leave sight of the cottage, it was good to be outside and out from under the watchful gaze of the old woman.

When Thane was tired, he headed back across the beach and into the small cottage. He stopped short just inside the door when he realized Orphan was awake and sitting up in the little bed. A pillow was propped behind her back and she was eating something brown from the spoon the old woman was holding to her mouth. They both looked up at Thane who was standing in the doorway with his mouth open. Orphan dropped her eyes immediately but the old woman held his gaze and seemed to admonish him with her eyes.

"Eat two more bites you will. Then, alone I will leave you to talk," she said as she turned back to shovel a couple more spoonfuls efficiently into Orphan's mouth. She patted Orphan's face with a small cloth; then stood to wash out the little bowl and spoon.

Thane made his way to the small table and sat down with his back to Orphan. The old woman paused next to him on her way out. She placed a gentle hand on Thane's shoulder and offered a last bit of advice.

"Hear her out you should before a judgment you make. Heavy with anger your heart is, but in your head anger must not rule. To make all whole, faith in her you must have." With a last glance at Orphan, she shuffled to the door and left them alone.

The silence in the small cottage was deafening. Thane looked down at the worn table and traced some of the scratches on it with the pad of his finger. He didn't know what to say or where to begin. Minutes passed painfully by; neither one eager to be the first to talk.

"Why?" Thane finally broke the silence without looking around.

No answer.

"Why did you both lie to me?" he repeated hurt and anger raw in his voice. He swung around in the chair to glare at Orphan. She was lying down again; tears were sliding silently down her pale cheeks.

He turned away again then jumped to his feet to pace before the fire.

"We couldn't tell anyone," she finally whispered; her voice still very weak. "Tally was so afraid that we would be found out. Thane, we had been on the run and hiding for so long that he was afraid to trust anyone. Then, you came along, and well, we wanted to tell you…"

"So why didn't you. Especially after that night Tally told me who I was. Why didn't you trust me then?" Thane demanded. He stopped pacing and rested his good arm on the mantle above the fireplace and gazed down at the orange and blue flames. He was still so angry. "You knew everything about me!"

"Tally was afraid that you would treat me differently if you knew and that someone would figure it out," she sighed. "Don't you understand Thane? You would have treated me differently if you had known."

He grunted a denial.

"You would have and you know it!" she insisted.

"I know you're a Færie. Weren't you afraid I would give that away?" Thane snapped back.

"Look, Thane," she was starting to get angry. He could hear it in her voice.

"I'm sorry we…" she said as she started to get up but gasped in pain. She put a hand to her side and fell back down on the bed.

Thane spun around to look at her. He could see how stark white her face was as she carefully settled back down against the pillow, pulled her blanket up, and closed her eyes.

"We were just trying to stay safe…" she mumbled, "…not only us…you…you as well…he said we must keep you safe…" Her voice was now so soft he had to strain to make out the words. "…must protect…"

"Look…you better rest. We'll talk later," he said with a sigh.

She fell quiet. He watched the slow rise and fall of the blanket covering her and felt some of his anger drain out of him leaving him feeling oddly deflated and very tired. Part of him acknowledged that he would never be able to look at her the same or treat her the same way he had when he thought she was a boy. He couldn't see how they would ever be able to go back to the easy camaraderie they had shared. He mourned the loss of his best friend. This changed everything.

He crossed the small room and stepped over to the bed to lift the blanket and gently tuck it back under her chin. He stared down at her. Her lashes, spiked with fresh tears, lay vivid against her pale cheek. She'd fallen back to sleep.

卌

The following day, Thane went outside to sit on his rock and stare thoughtfully at the water. He was beginning to love the sharp tangy smell of the sea. The motion of the waves soothed him and he found himself dozing in the weak sunshine. After a while, Embarr came galloping up the small beach, his hoofs splashing through the water, his tail trailing behind him as he danced in and out of the waves. He came to a stop in front of Thane, whinnied at him then waited with his head tilted.

Thane rolled his shoulder around testing it. He hadn't ridden Embarr since the day they'd arrived at the cottage. He was eager to get back on him and it seemed that Embarr felt the same way. Embarr knelt down, one knee in the sand and looked pointedly at Thane again.

Thane took a quick look back toward the cottage to see if anyone was watching, then, with a grin, he leapt off of the rock. With one hand wrapped in Embarr's mane, he swung his leg up and over the horse's bare back. Embarr stood, shook his head in delight and raced down the beach.

Thane felt the wind brush its aggressive fingers through his hair pulling the black strands back away from his face. Waves splashed cold against his legs until his breeches were dripping with the salty sea water. He felt Embarr's warm muscles contracting against his legs as he held on tightly; his fingers threaded through Embarr's thick white mane. All his troubles fell away from him; replaced by the thrill of speed and his love for this horse.

The morning and the afternoon flew by as they followed a narrow trail that led up through the mountain above the beach. It felt good to get away from the tense atmosphere at the cottage and the even tenser turn of events of the last few days.

They rode though trees, past many brooks and burns. He watched as small animals scurried out of his way and just enjoyed the feeling of being alive. The smell of the pines and the sounds of the forest seeped into his senses soothing him. It was strange to think that this old forest would go on, just as it always had, untouched and unconcerned with the turmoil in Thane's life.

Thane's stomach insisted, with an outrageously loud growl that reverberated clear to his backbone, that it was time to return to the cottage. He had only eaten a small piece of bread that morning and had missed the noon meal. Thane let Embarr take them back along the trails toward the cottage at a slow walk. They had gone further than he realized. It was beginning to get dark by the time they hit the beach and started across the surf. The sun hung low in the sky straining to touch its reflection on the sea.

He glanced down in the fading light and realized that they were not running through the sand at the edge of the water but actually running across the top of the waves. He screamed and let go of Embarr's mane. He went flying backwards through the air and landed with a great splash on his rear end in the waves; sputtering and swallowing mouthfuls of salty water.

Embarr slowed and turned around smartly on top of a wave. He came trotting back to Thane who sat waist deep in the water as waves crashed over him. He looked up at his huge white horse and could have sworn Embarr was laughing at him.

"I didn't know you could do that!" Thane shouted above the roiling waves, slapping his hands in the water in his excitement.

"Woo hoo!" he cried as he tried to get to his feet and was knocked down by another wave. Laughing and sputtering, he sent a spray of water toward Embarr with his cupped hand.

Embarr snickered again and trotted closer to Thane. He bumped Thane's chest with his head then leaned down for him to climb up on his back. As soon as Thane was settled on him again, they headed down the beach toward the cottage. His heart felt lighter than it had in days.

When they returned to the cottage, he jumped off the horse and burst through the door eager to tell someone about Embarr. The first thing he saw was the old woman sitting at her loom. She looked up and smiled at him. Her eyes traveled up and down Thane as he stood in the middle of the little room dripping wet and grinning.

"A good day you had?" she asked.

"You won't believe what Embarr..." he glanced over in Orphan's direction and stopped abruptly, his smile sliding from his face.

She was awake and dressed...in a dress! Her hair, clean and brushed, was scattered loosely around her still very pale face. She was wearing a light green woolen dress and was sitting on the edge of the bed with her small bare feet dangling over the side.

She glared back at him and said defiantly, "What's your problem?"

"You're wearing a dress!" he croaked back at her, stunned for the second time in as many hours.

"Yeah! So what! I am a girl!" she said irritation back in her voice. "Or had you forgotten already."

"I thought that it was supposed to be such a big secret!" he said as he shoved his hands down into the wet waist of his breeches and hunched his shoulders. He couldn't stop the bitter note from creeping into his voice.

"A boy and a girl they will not be looking for. Now two boys, is the hunt for. Quite safe she will be." The old woman prattled on, not taking her eyes from the motion of the shuttle shooting dark green wool back and forth between her hands.

"Wonderful," Thane mumbled as he sloshed over to his makeshift bed and grabbed dry clothes from the little pile of their belongings. Without another word to either of them, he turned and squelched his way back outside to dry off and change behind the cottage.

When he was finished, he stormed back inside, slamming the door behind him. Without a word to either of them, he flung himself down on his mat and turned his back on them both. The hungry feeling in his stomach was replaced by a knot of anger and just a little bit of fear as the reality of his situation slammed into him full force. He was stuck in a strange place, with a strange old woman…Færie person, and a strange girl.

"Oh…you are such an insufferable brat, Thane!" Orphan cried at his back in frustration. He could hear her moving around on the bed and the curtain being wrenched closed. Thane could hear her mumbling to herself.

"Tonight to pout I will give you. At dawn your choice you must make," Thane heard the old woman announce to the room.

He watched the reflection of the firelight flicker and dance on the stone wall in front of him. All thoughts of Embarr and his strange abilities had vanished from his mind, replaced by the image of Orphan wearing a dress. The worst part of it all was…she looked really pretty.

THANE

||||

Just before dawn the next morning, Thane woke to find the old woman leaning over him shaking him with a hand on his shoulder. He had to blink up at her a few times before her face came into focus. This close, in the light of the fire, he could see the deep lines in her face and intersecting those lines were even more tiny little lines. How old must she be to have that many lines on her face? How much living must she have done in all those years? How much knowledge did each one of those wrinkles stand for? He could see that, this morning, her eyes were light blue with little flecks of green in them. Thane now knew that the sea outside the cottage door would be calm and today the sun would be bright.

"Up you must get. Leave today we will if you so choose," she said in her odd way of speaking.

He looked past her shoulder to see Orphan up and walking tentatively toward the little table. She was wearing a brown dress and a pair of soft brown leather boots. Her hair was tied back away from her face with a dark green ribbon; her pointy ears peaked out from under her hair. Thane felt a little stab of hurt in his chest as he looked at her. He wondered how he could ever have thought she was a boy. What kind of an imbecile was he?

Breakfast was a quiet affair. Neither Thane nor Orphan had much to say to each other and the old woman was unusually quiet. They cleaned up, put the dishes away, and the old woman led them outside.

Thane hid a grin behind his hand as he watched Orphan struggle with the skirt of her brown dress. She was getting her legs all tangled up in the fabric as she walked. He felt a perverse sort of pleasure watching her trip her way across the sand. Served her right... didn't it, he thought with a snigger.

The old woman led them over to Thane's rock and motioned for them to sit. She continued on into the tumbling waves. As soon as her feet touched the water, she began to change. Her body radiated with a strange blue-green glow as she began to stretch and elongate until she was the tall willowy woman he had seen coming out of the water before. Her hair lengthened and brightened until it was glowing with a golden light. It tumbled about her shoulders and down her back. Even though Thane had seen her become the Old Woman once, he was still slightly taken aback at how quickly and dramatically her appearance changed.

He slid a glance sideways to see how Orphan was taking the transformation. Her mouth was hanging open and her eyes were wide with shocked surprise. Thane smirked, secretly pleased to know that he finally knew something she didn't.

Muirghein raised her slender arms to the sea and chanted in an ancient language in her beautiful sing-song voice. It took a moment for Thane to realize that it was the same language that she whispered over Orphan when she was sick.

The water stirred and began to bubble. It began to build upon itself until it rose straight up in the air in a wave that was twice as tall as Muirghein. It seemed to hover, suspended in front of her like an enormous blue-green wall. With another motion of her hands, she parted the wall of water and stepped up to it.

"Come. Danger Embarr would not lead you to." She said as she turned to look behind her at the two stunned youths. "Decide Nathaniel." She beckoned them forward with a wave of her hand then disappeared into the gap in the water.

Thane felt a nudge at his back and realized that Embarr had come up behind them. He craned his head around to look up into the horse's soft gray eyes. Embarr's gaze was steady and calm. Thane took that as a clear sign that it was safe to follow Muirghein. Thane jumped up, stood on the rock, and in one smooth motion, he swung his leg over and climbed on Embarr's back.

"Come on Orphan!" Thane beckoned with a wave of his hand. He was eager to see what was on the other side of the sea wall.

She turned to look up at him and hesitated. He held out his hand for her to join him. No matter what had happened between them; they were in this together. Embarr bowed low in front of her. Thane raised his eyebrows and wiggled his fingers at her again. She glanced back at the towering wave where Muirghein had disappeared, then back up at Thane. She took a deep breath, wrapped one arm around the wound at her waist and put her other hand in his. He pulled her up behind him.

She huffed and grunted as she struggled to get settled behind him while still fighting with the skirts that were now all jumbled about her legs. Thane waited impatiently while doing his best to ignore her labored breathing and awkward wiggling behind him.

Finally, with one last huff, she was firmly ensconced behind him with her hands twisted tightly in his shirt low on his back. Embarr needed no encouragement to walk swiftly across the top of the waves toward the wall of water. Orphan let out a high pitched squeal of surprise when she realized that they were walking on top of the waves not through them. Her arms slid around Thane's waist and she buried her face in his back. Thane laughed out loud when her nose poked him sharply in the back.

Inside his shirt, he felt the medallion heat up against his skin as the waves in front of them parted of their own accord. Embarr trotted happily through the blue-green wall carrying them along with him. They emerged through an immense waterfall on the other side. All three of them were dry as a bone. A flat stone threshold was at the base of the waterfall and projected slightly over an oval pool of clear blue water. The pool was surrounded by enormous ancient twisted trees whose gnarly branches were dripping with tiny pale pink flowers that hung like a canopy over a carpet of green grass.

"Welcome to *Tír inna n-Óc*." said Muirghein. "Welcome home."

Chapter Twenty-One

Tír inna n-Oc

Muirghein was standing next to two Færies who were tall and slender with light hair and eyes. Their skin seemed to glow with an ethereal white light. The woman was dressed in a long flowing robe made of a silky material that was, at once no color and all colors. A thick silver belt cinched the loose fabric tightly to her small waist. The man wore simple breeches and a tunic made of velvet in the same strange color and trimmed in silver.

"We are of the Council of Elders, the oldest of the Tuatha de Danann," the woman in the silken dress said.

Thane was taken aback by her statement. The oldest? If these people were considered the elders, then what were the young people like?

"We have waited many years for you Nathaniel," the man nodded then added, "Ceara, we welcome you here as our guest. Please, follow us. We will escort you all to the palace. There will your questions be answered."

Thane felt Orphan stiffen behind him. Who was Ceara? Were they talking about her? He turned around and frowned at her. "Another secret?" he hissed, his anger resurfacing in an instant.

"Come," interrupted Muirghein before Orphan could reply. "For questions and doubts now is not the time."

The Færies turned without another word, left the clearing and disappeared through the trees. Embarr took it upon himself to follow them and happily trotted across the still surface of the lake to follow a path through the stand of old trees. Thane and Orphan raised their hands to brush the sweet smelling flowers out of their faces. They looked up to see sunlight filtering through the canopy of flowers lighting each dangling blossom. It was like they were passing under a ceiling of millions of tiny pink lanterns.

They caught up to the Færies and continued to follow them on Embarr as he picked his way delicately through the ancient flowering trees. They crossed a small shallow stream into a dense forest of thick fragrant pine trees before, finally, they emerged from the thick knot of trees.

A magnificent stone bridge reached across a ribbon of blue water toward a blindingly white castle. The bridge's massive arching stone piers rose from the river supporting two soaring towers topped with silver spires. Swirling ornate silverwork decorated a balustrade that ran the length of the bridge connecting one end to the other. It looked just wide enough for a horse and carriage.

Thane had to tip his head all the way back to see the top of the immense castle beyond the glittering spires on the other side of the bridge. It was clinging precariously atop an enormous rock in the middle of a vast river. The castle's many circular turrets were attached to its angular sides in a somewhat haphazard manner. Each turret was topped with a pennant of blue and silver that fluttered gently in the light breeze. An oval courtyard, slightly larger than the width of the bridge was carved out of the cliff between the entrance of the castle and the end of the bridge.

Orphan let out her breath in a sigh behind him, "Oh my…"

Thane pulled Embarr to an abrupt halt at the foot of the bridge. He was scared. He knew that once he crossed that bridge, his life would never be the same again and he was not sure he was ready to face what…or who…was waiting for him on the other side.

"Wait! Where are we? Who are you really?" Thane demanded of the two self proclaimed members of the Council of Elders. "What could you possibly want from us?"

The Færies didn't acknowledge his questions; they just continued to make their way across the bridge as if he hadn't spoken. Muirghein turned to face him.

"Why have you brought us here?" he demanded of her.

"Do not fear, all will be explained in time," was all she said before she too turned and followed the others across the bridge.

Frustrated, Thane twisted around to look at Orphan. "What do you think? Do you know anything about this…Ceara?" he couldn't help the note of accusation that crept into his voice.

"Thane, I honestly don't know a whole lot more about this than what Tally sang about in his tales at the inn," she replied rather stiffly. Thane could feel her fingers clenching the back of his tunic as she leaned around him to look up at the castle again.

"Obviously this is *Tír inna n-Óc*...you know...the *Land of Eternal Youth*...Didn't you ever listen to Tally?" Orphan berated him.

Of course he had listened to the Bard but he wasn't going to give her the satisfaction of having to defend himself to her. With a shrug of annoyance, Thane kicked Embarr into a trot and they started reluctantly across the bridge. He looked down into the blue water. It was as clear as the water had been in the pool by the waterfall. He could see right through to the stones rolling around in the current at the bottom of the river. Embarr's hoofs clomped noisily across the white cobbled stones of the bridge, ringing loudly in the wake of the silent footsteps of the Elders they followed.

When they got to the other side of the bridge, they crossed the courtyard. Embarr stopped at the foot of the marble staircase that led up to two huge silver doors. A pair of armed Fæ sentries was standing at attention at either side of the doorway holding matching standards of blue, emblazoned with a silver sword. Thane stared up at the castle. It was even more imposing from this side of the bridge.

Thane hopped off of Embarr then turned and lifted his arms up to help Orphan dismount. She frowned down at his hands then slapped them away. She gathered her skirts together in one hand to hold them out of her way as she swung her leg around and slid awkwardly down on her own. Thane noticed she was gripping the edge of the saddle so hard her knuckles were white. She leaned against Embarr for a moment to steady herself.

"So, you wouldn't have treated me any differently if you had known I was a girl, huh?" Orphan sneered at him as she lowered her hands to her hips and swung around to face him.

"I don't remember you ever helping me off of a horse when you thought I was a boy!" She turned up her nose at him, smoothed out the wrinkles in her skirt with the flat of her hand and walked stiffly away from him. She made her way slowly toward the marble staircase with her head held high.

Thane frowned as he watched her. He thought he was helping her down because she was not completely healed and obviously still weak. Was she right? Was he treating her differently because she was a girl? Would he have held his arms up to help the 'boy' Orphan? Deep inside, he had to admit he might not have.

He turned back to Embarr just in time to see the tail of his horse swishing back and forth as he disappeared happily around the left corner of the outer wall of the castle. Obviously, Embarr had been here before and was eager to be somewhere particular. With a sigh, Thane turned back to face the castle entrance and realized that everyone had already gone inside.

Feeling a bit abandoned, he trudged up the stairs alone. As he made his way past the door guards, they tipped their standards forward and bowed their heads in salute. Thane acknowledged them with an uncomfortable, "Uh...hello..." and hurried in through the open doors.

The semicircular entrance hall was brightly lit by a series of silver candelabras mounted to the pale stone walls. Each one glowed with a strange brilliant white light; very different from the dim yellow glow of the flame lit lamps he was used to. He could see that the rest of the group had already reached the end of the hallway to his left and were disappearing through a set of tall silver double doors. The room was being guarded by another pair of sentries. Thane's boots echoed loudly across the white marble floors as he rushed to catch up to everyone else. The sentries held the door open for him with a bow and he entered just a few steps behind Orphan and the rest of the Færies.

Thane crossed the threshold and stepped hesitantly into the large receiving room and looked around in awe. Two matching high backed ornate silver thrones sat at the far end of the room on a raised marble dais. Plush blue velvet cushions padded the seats, backs, and arms of the chairs. A canopy of dark blue curtains hung high over the stone dais. The platform was flanked by two flaming silver torches. Intricately carved wooden chairs lined the right side of the long room on a shorter, similarly curtained platform. The walls were hung with long tapestries depicting tall beautiful people in idyllic nature scenes. To the left, dozens of long windows were sending shafts of light ricocheting off of crystal chandeliers hanging from the high vaulted ceiling. Even his vague memories of his father's castle could not compare to the grandeur and wealth displayed here.

The Færie couple from the waterfall and Muirghein stood silently in front of the center dais until a door behind it opened. The King and Queen entered the room. They were even more elaborately dressed than the council members. Each wore a long shimmering cloak over their gowns. Thin silver circlets had been woven through their golden hair. The royal pair stepped in front of the silver chairs and turned to greet the visitors.

"At your request, they have been brought," Muirghein announced with a bow.

"Thank you Muirghein. You have done well," said the Fæ King. Muirghein bowed again, quietly turned, and left the room.

"Nathaniel, come forward please," the King commanded with a wave of his hand.

Everyone turned to look back at Thane who was still standing next to the door. He slowly walked forward. The small group gathered in front of the crowned couple parted to let him through. He felt their eyes on him as he drew closer to the foot of the dais.

He looked up and with a jolt, realized the woman looked just like his mother. At least, she looked remarkably like the woman from his dreams. It took him a moment before he recognized both of them. They were his mother's parents, his grandfather Manannán mac Lir and his grandmother, Fand. She was the woman who had given Embarr to him when he was a small child.

She stepped down from the dais and enfolded Thane in her arms. She smelled of flowers and rain, and for the first time in many, many days, he felt safe and calm. He stood in her embrace until she pulled away from him slightly and looked down into his eyes.

"We have been searching for you for many years Nathaniel. Your mother hid you well." With another quick hug, she released him. She turned to look at her husband as he spoke, "You are welcome here Nathaniel. All that we have is at your disposal and available for your use. Feel free to treat this castle as your home." He reached out a hand and pulled Thane into a quick embrace as well.

"Ceara, you must also come to look on this as your home," Fand said with a soft smile in Orphan's direction, "…as once your mother did."

Manannán mac Lir interrupted his wife, "We understand from Muirghein that you both have many questions, but they must wait. We will do our best to answer them in the next few days but not tonight. Tonight we will get to know one another once again, and you will be presented to members of the Fæ Council, as well as to visiting royal deities from other realms of the Tuatha de Danann."

His grandfather turned and addressed another Færie who had come up to stand behind his throne. "Sorcha, show them to their rooms so they may rest. Have a tray of food brought up to them, and find them some decent clothes. Send for Dian Cécht. Muirghein believes Ceara's wound is poisoned and in need of the healer's attention. We will gather at twilight for the evening meal..." he turned back to Thane and Orphan and said, "...so I suggest you rest."

He held his hand out to his wife. "Fand, come let us prepare for our guests." With one last look at Thane and Orphan, she placed her hand in his and he escorted her from the room.

Thane turned to glance back at Orphan. She was pale and looked tired. Her shoulders were hunched and she was holding an arm tight to her side. She looked up and caught Thane watching her. Frowning at him, she stiffened her back. He knew pride would prevent her from asking for help even though Thane could see that she was ready to collapse from pain and exhaustion.

Sorcha approached Orphan and, without asking for permission, put an arm around her shoulder to turn her toward the door. With a nod to Thane to indicate that he should follow them, she led them both out of the room. They headed back out the way they had come, crossed the entrance hall, and turned down a long hallway that led to the opposite side of the castle.

At the second spiral staircase, Sorcha took hold of Orphan's arm. Thane was beginning to worry about Orphan. She didn't protest Sorcha's help, and it seemed to be taking a lot of effort for Orphan to ascend the stone steps. They climbed the staircase to the top level and headed down a hallway that curved to the left. Sorcha opened the third door they came to and indicated to Thane that he should wait outside.

She led Orphan into the white and gold room. Thane watched as they made their way slowly across a thick white rug to an enormous bed. Curious, he stepped inside the room for a better look despite Sorcha's directions. He needed to assure himself that Orphan was not going to be in any danger.

Sorcha pulled back the thick white covers on the bed, removed Orphan's cape and helped her to lie down. Thane was startled to see how much blood had seeped through her dress. The Færie reached down and loosened Orphan's boots and removed them from her feet before tucking the fluffy covers around her.

Orphan looked over the Færie's shoulder at Thane. He stiffened, prepared to be on the receiving end of a biting comment from her, but she just nodded at him and closed her eyes with a sigh. He frowned. She must be feeling pretty awful if she didn't even have the energy to snarl at him.

He backed quietly out of the room and waited for Sorcha to finish fussing. To distract himself from what was going on in Orphan's room, he looked around the hall. The walls curved away from him along both sides of the hall. He could see more doors leading away from either side of the room he was standing in front of. A thick green rug covered the stone floor. The intricate circular designs on the rug reminded Thane of the silver broach Tally had always worn on his blue cloak. There were no windows in the hall. The only light came from the silver torches mounted on the walls between each set of doors.

Sorcha pulled Orphan's door quietly behind her as she joined him in the hallway. Without a word, she led Thane to the door to the left of Orphan's. This room was decorated in dark blues and silver. The ornate wooden bed was carved with images of dragons and mountains as was the large fireplace against the left side of the room. Dark blue velvet curtains matched the bed covers. The rug had the same interwoven designs that he had seen in the hallway. Windows lined the curved outer wall opposite the door, just as they had in Orphan's white room.

"I will return for you later this evening. A meal will be brought up for you. I suggest you eat and rest as the evening will be a long one." She tipped her head in a bow and left softly closing the door behind her.

Thane paced in front of the windows. He was too restless to sleep. He heard voices pass in the hallway outside his door and guessed that the healer was going into the room next door to help Orphan. Why was her wound still bleeding? Shouldn't it have been close to being healed by now? What if they couldn't help her? He stopped in front of one of the windows and leaned his hands on either side of the frame and looked out.

The window was made of exceptionally clear glass. It was so thin that it didn't look like there was anything between him and the world outside. He ran a fingertip across the glass. It was smooth and cool to the touch.

Looking through the glass, he saw that they were on the back side of the castle. The river flowed past the massive cliffs far below his window. On the opposite bank, the trees and bushes seemed to rise right from the water making a solid wall of green. The sky above the trees was the most incredible shade of blue with small fluffy white clouds scattered about it.

He stared out the window lost in thought. He sifted through every corner of his memory and although he could remember his grandparents, he couldn't recall ever being in this castle. The whole 'prince' thing was making him really uncomfortable. That wasn't who he was…no matter what they said. Why did he get the feeling the Færies were hiding something from them? How did they know Orphan's mother?

A soft knock broke him out of his reverie. He crossed the room and opened the door. Sorcha was standing in the hall with a tray laden full of food and drink.

"Come in," Thane stepped back and swung the door wide to let her in.

She placed the silver tray on a small table between the windows and pulled off the cloth that was covering it. The tray was full of pastries, meat pies, and fruit. She reached for a round glass jug and poured out a light amber liquid into a tall, silver and glass tankard then turned to him with a smile.

"Eat. You will feel better. If you would like to change after you rest, there is a wash basin in the corner and some cloths to dry yourself. I will bring you some clean clothes when I return. Shall you require anything further, pull the cord next to the door, and someone will come to assist you. Sleep well Prince Nathaniel." She bowed respectfully as she passed him to leave.

He nodded awkwardly, uncomfortable with all the deference.

Thane closed the door softly behind her and resumed his restless pacing. More bored than hungry, Thane decided to sit at the small table and pick at the food. His stomach started to grumble as the mixed sweet and spicy smells hit his nose. The meat pies were fresh and warm. The pastries were covered in honey and the fruit was so juicy it dribbled down his chin. The drink was some kind of thick sweet nectar. Before he knew it, he had eaten more than half of the large meal. Sorcha was right. He did feel better.

He toed off his boots and laid down sideways across the bed on top of the covers. He folded his hands behind his head and stared up at the designs on the ceiling. Silver dragons were twined around a dark blue ribbon that wove around the outer edges of the ceiling. His eyes traced the blue line around the room as it wove in and out of itself with no apparent beginning or end.

He was still restless but was not feeling as anxious as he had felt earlier. Just as he started to dose, he heard voices coming from the hall outside his door. He got up and slowly eased the door open a crack to listen.

"She has been infected by the poison of an evil Fæ beast. The wound will not heal on its own. I will make a poultice of herbs and an antidote made with the liver of a sheep and coal to draw out the poison. I cannot guarantee it will work as she is not yet reached immortality and she is, after all, half human. I will do what I can," a man's voice explained.

"Dian Cécht, did you see the mark on her thumb?" a woman's voice queried.

"Ugh! Yes. Didn't you know?" the man answered with a question of his own.

"No, and I don't think Zavior knows either, he believes her to be dead. We have a powerful weapon. We must..." the voices trailed further down the hall until Thane could no longer hear them.

What was all that about? What weapon? He wondered.

He cracked open the door and looked out into the hall. Once he was confident the Fairies were gone and the hallway was empty, he slipped out of his room. He trailed his fingers along the smooth stone wall as he tiptoed down the hall to Orphan's room. He put his ear to her door. There was only silence.

He knocked softly. When no one answered, he turned the doorknob and eased her door open just wide enough to poke his head in. Orphan was lying on her side in the bed. Her eyes were open and she was staring right at him peeking into her room.

"What are you doing, Thane?" she asked tiredly.

He slipped his body through the door and shut it quietly behind him. He stood with his back pressed hard against the wood of the door. His hands gripped the knob as if for moral support and he stared at the floor.

"I heard the healer leave," he shuffled his feet and said, "I just wanted to make sure you were okay." He looked up at her and added, "I'll leave if you like."

She was silent for so long that he turned to go. "No, don't go. It was kind of you to check on me." She shifted a bit into a more comfortable position and continued to talk. Thane turned back to look at her, one hand still anchored to the doorknob in case he needed to make a quick getaway.

"What do you think is going on? Did that woman who brought us up here tell you anything? The healer poked around my scratch a bit and grunted a lot, then left without saying a word to me," she rambled on sounding a bit annoyed.

Thane walked slowly toward the bed. "I heard them leave. The man…whom I'm guessing was the healer?" he paused and waited for her affirmation. She nodded and he continued, "…said that you had been poisoned by an 'evil fæ beast'. Do you think that means they don't know what Zavior's Roki are?"

She lifted her shoulder in a little shrug. Feeling more secure in his welcome, he edged closer to the bed until he was close enough to wrap his arm around the tall bed post and lean one knee up on the bed.

He looked down at her and said, "Anyway, he was going to try to fix up some kind of poultice or something."

She looked even worse than she had when they first brought her to her room. Her skin was so pale it was transparent and her eyes had dark circles under them.

"You look pretty awful!" he blurted out before he could think twice about the wisdom of voicing his opinion.

She frowned up at him, "Well…thanks! I feel better now."

Thane's eyes widened in dismay for a moment then he started to smirk, "You wouldn't have minded looking awful when you were a boy."

Orphan narrowed her eyes to glare at him and started to say, "You are an idiot…you're…you're…" she paused then began to laugh.

"You know what? You're right!" She giggled then gasped, holding on to her side and smiled up at him. "I would've thought it was great."

Thane sank down on the corner of the bed and grinned back at her.

"Is there anything you need; anything I can do?" He looked around her room and spotted a tray similar to the one that was brought into his room earlier. It looked like it hadn't been touched.

"Have you tried the food they brought in?" Thane asked as he hopped off of the bed and walked over to the tray.

"It's really good!" He said as he lifted the cloth from across the tray and described some of the food to her.

"Tell me what you want and I will bring some of it over for you," he said as he picked up a honey covered pastry and bit into it.

"Bring a little of everything," she said as she scooted herself toward the headboard of the bed until she was sitting with her back up against the white pillows, her legs gathered up underneath her, and one arm wrapped around her waist.

Thane folded some pastries and fruit into the cloth that had covered it, laid it on the bed next to her, then went back to fill a glass with the same golden brown nectar he had had earlier in his room. He handed her the glass. Careful not to jostle her, he climbed up on the bed and sat in the middle of it facing her with the food between them.

Thane picked at a meat pie and watched as she took small bites of a pastry and sipped some of the juice from the glass. He was surprised to see that some of the color was coming back into her face. She wasn't as pale as she had been when he first walked in.

He glanced at the glass she had in her hand. He remembered how much calmer he had felt after he drank the juice in his room and wondered what it was made from. His eyes fell on the hand she was holding the glass to her mouth with. He could see the small scar etched across the back of her thumb. He had noticed it before but had never thought much about it. It was just a scar. What had the healer found so interesting about it?

"You know that crescent shaped scar you have on your thumb?" Thane asked motioning to her left hand with his pastry.

She glanced down at it, tipping the glass to get a better look at it and sending the contents sloshing about wildly, almost spilling the sweet liquid onto her lap. "Yeah, what about it?" she said through lips sticky with honey as she quickly righted the glass in her hand.

Thane leaned forward and lowered his voice to whisper, "The two Færies who left here were talking about it…your little scar. They said Zavior thought you were dead? How did you get it anyway? And why would Zavior care that you have a scar or know if you were dead or not?"

She looked puzzled. "I don't know. I've had the scar for as long as I can remember. I asked Tally once if he knew how I got it.

He got annoyed and asked me why I cared. He never really answered my question."

"What did they mean 'Zavior doesn't know'?" Orphan asked. "That's strange. He doesn't know me. I never saw him before that day he killed Markus in the woods."

Thane stopped chewing and frowned. "Did you know your mother stayed here?"

He swallowed abruptly as another thought dawned on him. "Is there something else you need to tell me 'Ceara'?" he asked, anger edging his voice again.

"No," she replied hastily. "I honestly think you know everything now. At least, you know as much as I do. I don't know much about where I was before I was given to Anne and Alfred. I told you I don't remember my parents," she shrugged and looked right into his eyes "and I never heard the name Ceara before today."

They both fell quiet as they chewed; each lost in their own thoughts.

Orphan looked up unexpectedly and said in a rush, "Thane, I am really sorry. We never meant to hurt you. We were only doing what we had always done; what we thought was best at the time."

Thane slowly lifted his eyes to hers. He stared at her and realized that she was still the same person. She had the same wild red hair, the same emerald green eyes, and the same infuriating smile. He felt the tear in his heart heal just a little as he finally began to forgive her.

"I know Orphan. I guess a part of me understands." The corner of his lip lifted in a little smile. "I might have agreed with you if you had been keeping the secret from someone other than me."

"Just promise me you'll never lie to me again," Thane said in a rush.

"I won't. I swear!"

He was shocked when she impulsively leaned forward and threw her arms tightly around his neck. Thane fidgeted uncomfortably under her fierce hug. She groaned as her movements pulled at the wound in her side and released him just as suddenly as she'd grabbed him. The cloth full of food toppled off of the bed and scattered its contents across the floor. She held her breath as she sank awkwardly back into the pillows and closed her eyes.

With a short nod of acceptance, Thane shoved himself off of the bed. Tossing the cloth and the bits of food back on the tray, he took the cloth and tried to rub some of the honey out of the rug. He finally gave up when all he managed to do was spread the mess around and rub it even more deeply into the fine white threads. He clumsily straightened the covers back over her bed and walked toward the door.

"I'd better go back. Get some rest Orphan. I'm sure I'll see you later."

He slid a last glance at Orphan as he put his ear to the door to listen for any noise from the other side. After a moment, he slowly cracked open the door and stuck his head out to make sure there was no one out there. Confident the hall was empty; he slipped out and returned to his own room.

Once he was back securely in his room, he laid down across the bed. He was so tired he didn't even bother to get under the covers. His brain barely had time to register how soft the velvet felt under him before his eyes fluttered closed and he fell into a deep dreamless sleep.

Chapter Twenty-Two

A Royal Feast

He awoke hours later to the sounds of Sorcha moving quietly about his dimly lit room. At some point while he was asleep, someone must have pulled the heavy blue drapes shut because the only light in the room was the soft yellow glow from the fireplace.

She was setting out a small basin of water and folded linens on top of the dresser on the other side of the room. On the chair next to the small table, she had draped clean clothes. Black leather boots were propped against the leg of the chair. His sporran, bow, arrows, wooden sword, and Tally's bag were propped up by the fireplace next to a three legged stool that had his extra pair of breeches and a tunic folded on top of it. Someone must have gone back for them. How strange. Did that mean he would not be returning to the cottage? He would miss the small beach retreat. He had found some peace in watching the movement and listening to the sounds of the waves.

Sorcha had gathered up the remains of the meal. What little food he had left on the tray had been covered with the white cloth. He wished she would just leave the rest of the food there but was too unsure of himself to ask her for it. He was hungry again. She glanced in his direction as he sat up in bed. With a sweeping wave of her hand she lit the candles on the small candelabra across the room from the bed. Soft amber light flickered in the room casting shadows against the walls. She laughed at his raised eyebrows and open mouth.

"You have been asleep for hours. It is time to get up." She said. "Water and linens have been provided for you to wash with." When he didn't reply she continued, "Fresh clothing is laid out next to the table. The guests will be gathering in the Throne room for a short reception before the evening meal. I will return for you within the half hour to escort you down." She picked up the tray of left over food and started to leave. Thane called out to her just as she reached the door.

"How is Orphan…uhh…Ceara?" he asked.

She paused long enough to reply, "She is still very weak but insists she is well enough to join you for supper." That said, she turned and left.

Thane sat on the bed for a moment longer then threw his legs over the side and stood up. He reached his arms up above his head and stretched. He felt great. It was the strongest he'd felt since the fight with Zavior. In fact, his body felt completely healed. His shoulder wasn't stiff and he could swing it in a full circle without any hesitation or pain. After his talk with Orphan, the heavy weight of hurt and anger was lifted from his chest as well.

He made his way over to the dresser and looked at himself in the mirror. His black hair was standing on end and he had a long crease down the left side of his cheek from the pillow. His clothes were a wrinkled mess. With a quick glance at the door, he shed his clothes and let them fall in a messy pool on the floor at his feet. He did his best to wash up with the smallest cloth. He used it to briskly rub his face, desperately trying to scrub the wrinkle from his cheek. He washed the sleep from his eyes and rubbed the cloth over his hair and the rest of his body. Once he was dry, he turned to pick up the clothes from the chair.

The breeches were made of dark blue velvet. They hung loosely around his hips so he tied them up with a thin length of pliable black leather he found in the pile. His tunic was made of the softest material he had ever felt. It was the same blue color as the breeches but was made from a tightly woven material and fit snuggly across his chest then flared slightly as it fell from his waist to his hips. Silver piping and embroidery were stitched along the hem and collar, in the now familiar circles. The boots were fashioned out of supple black leather that matched his belt and fit him perfectly.

Walking back to the mirror, he reached up and combed his fingers through his damp hair in an attempt to tidy it. Stepping back, he looked himself over from head to toe. Not bad he thought. He felt a little ridiculous in the fancy clothes but at least he no longer looked like a stable boy.

There was a quick knock on his door. He took one last look in the mirror, shrugged his shoulders and walked out to meet Sorcha in the hallway. She acknowledged him with a nod and silently led him towards the stairs. He glanced at Orphan's door as they passed. There was no noise coming from inside her room. Hopefully, she was up and getting dressed because he was sure he didn't want to face this dinner alone.

Sorcha left him at the entrance to the receiving room. One of the Fæ sentries held open the door and bowed him through it. He slid quietly in to the room and stood next to the door as it gently closed behind him.

Through the tall windows, he could see that the sky was now washed in pinks, purples and deep blues. Chandeliers illuminated the inside of the room with their strange white glow. There were perhaps two dozen Færies gathered in groups of threes and fours around the room. He was struck again by the incredible youth and beauty of the Fæ. Every one of them stopped talking and turned to stare at him.

Thane backed up a couple steps toward the door not quite sure this was really where he wanted to be. He didn't fit in with all these beautiful beings. He had just put his hand behind him to reach for the door to leave when he saw his grandmother. She caught his eye from across the room and beckoned for him to come toward her. She broke away from the small group she was with and met him halfway.

"Where do you think you are sneaking away to?" She smiled at him as she looped her hand under his arm and maneuvered him to the front of the room. "You can explore to your hearts delight later, but first we need to get this over with," she whispered conspiringly.

His grandfather joined them as they stepped up on the dais and turned in front of the ornate chairs. With Thane positioned between them, she placed her arm comfortingly around his shoulders.

Before they could begin, the doors opened again. Thane looked up over the heads of the Fæ, interested to see who else would be joining them. It was Orphan. Thane couldn't take his eyes off of her as she was led to the front of the room. A deep green velvet empire waist gown flowed around her as she walked. Gold embroidered trim lined the sleeves and hem. Her red hair had been swept up into a loose knot at the nape of her neck with gold ribbons and was shining in the Fæ light. She looked nothing like the boy that had been his best friend…until she looked up at him and stuck her tongue out at him.

Sorcha brought her to stand next to his grandfather on the other side of the dais.

Manannán mac Lir held his hand up for attention and everyone stopped talking to gather around the front of the dais.

"Welcome my friends." There was a smattering of applause. Most of the Færies just stared at Thane and Orphan with open curiosity.

"Tonight we honor the return of my grandson Nathaniel and Lúgh's granddaughter Ceara."

There was an immediate buzz of conversation from the assembly. His Grandfather raised his hand again for silence.

"There will be time enough to address the issues that their return presents in the coming days. Please, let us put speculation aside for tonight and be glad of their homecoming." Even though it sounded like a request, Thane had the distinct impression that it was understood by all to be an order.

Thane stood awkwardly next to his grandparents with his hands hanging at his side wishing desperately that he was someplace else. After years of trying to blend into the background, he was finding it difficult to stand still in front of all those people and be the center of attention. He could hear bits and pieces of the murmured conversations of the small crowd surrounding the dais.

"Uncanny!" whispered one Færie.

"Has his father's black looks about him," muttered another.

"…her standing there as if she…" said another.

"Look at his eyes," gasped one woman. "Unnatural…"

"Come!" Manannán mac Lir interrupted the Fæ's uneasy chatter. "Let us celebrate." Thane's Grandfather took hold of Orphan's elbow, his Grandmother took hold of his and they guided them out through a side door.

They entered a large circular room that formed the base of one of the large turrets they had seen from the outside. An enormous round table dominated the center of the room. It was laden with bowls and dishes that were overflowing with many different types of food and drink. The room was surrounded by long windows curtained in long dark blue velvet drapes similar to those in the receiving room. The walls and the floor were startlingly white.

The Færies headed to the table and took their places in front of chairs as if they had assigned seating. Thane's grandmother pulled him forward and led him to an empty seat at the table next to a pair of large ornate chairs that were obviously the King's and Queen's. She sat on the tall chair that was being held out for her by a simply dressed Færie as her husband settled into the chair next to hers.

Once his grandparents were seated, the other Færies followed suit. Thane awkwardly skirted around his chair and sat down. He was feeling out of place and unsure of himself. Orphan eased herself down on the seat next to Thane's with a quiet sigh. She looked as uncomfortable as he did.

Meals at the inn looked like beggar's fare compared to what was laid out in front of them. Dish after dish was brought to the table and no sooner was one plate emptied, than another was slid into its place. He remembered how shocked he had been at how much food Tilda had made the first time he had eaten in the kitchen at the inn but that was nothing compared to this. He couldn't identify most of what was being served and was afraid to eat anything he couldn't put a name to. The last thing he wanted to do was to spit something he didn't like out in front of all these perfect people. He desperately wished that Tally was here to guide him through this meal.

Thane kept his head down and ate in silence. The bread was soft and warm. He couldn't get enough of the baked fish he thought was salmon because it was crusty on the outside and pink and flakey on the inside. He nibbled out of the bowls of berries, roasted nuts, and sticky cubes of confection that tasted like roses. His glass was kept full of the sweet juice he'd had in his room.

The meal passed in a blur of sounds, smells and tastes. He looked around at the other guests at the table. He recognized a few of their names from the ballads Tally had told at the inn but most of them were totally unfamiliar. They were all beginning to blend together in his mind with their tall lithe bodies and beautiful faces.

He listened to their conversations with half an ear as the Council began to discuss plans for training Thane and 'Ceara'. The Fæ Council spoke about them as if they were not sitting right at the table with them. He didn't want to look like a fool so he was happy to let the conversation continue to move around him. He could feel the stares of his dinner companions. His cheeks began to burn in embarrassment.

By the time dessert was brought, he was so tense he thought he was going to explode. He caught Orphan sneaking something small and red from her mouth and sliding it back on her plate when she didn't think anyone was looking. He unclenched his hands on his knee and tried to relax.

His grandfather waved his hand to indicate that his plate be removed. A server quickly whisked his plate away as he folded his hands together on the table in front of him. Brilliant blues eyes turned to Thane and Orphan.

"You are not the first children born of Fæ and mortal," the king began as the rest of the Fæ guests settled in to listen. "More often than not, those children are born human…" his Grandfather began.

He told them of another of the Tuatha de Danann, Titania, who fell in love with the Chief of the Mac Leòid Clan in Scotland. She was granted permission to marry her love and against all odds, she became pregnant shortly after their marriage. She gave birth to a baby boy. As the Gods would have it, he was born mortal. The Council demanded her return to the land of the Tuatha de Danann for it would have been torturous for her to watch as the child aged and died and she remained young. She left him a silken blanket which she imbued with the power of her protection. The mortals call it the Færie Flag of Dunvegan Castle. It is carried by their clan into battle as a good luck talisman to this day.

As the story was coming to an end, a tall man with a hooked nose entered the dining room. It was obvious to Thane that this man was not one of the Fæ. He looked familiar but Thane couldn't remember where he had seen him before. Maybe he had been a visitor at the Reiver village or the inn. Who was he and what was he doing here? Instead of taking a seat amongst the Færies, he stayed near the doors. He stood with his arms crossed over his chest, his feet braced shoulder width apart, and leaned back against the wall.

"...I tell you this story because I want you both to know how unique you are," his grandfather finished his tale. "Children of mixed marriages who are born mortal should be left with mortals. You both were born Fæ and not meant to live in their world anymore than they are meant to live in ours." He paused and looked up at the stranger leaning against the wall and his brows drew down in a frown. "You are here now and that is all that matters."

"Nathaniel, tell us how you came to be at Muirghein's cottage," his grandmother asked. "How did Ceara receive such a nasty wound?"

Thane's stomach dropped at being asked to address the table. This was not a conversation he wanted to have in front of all these strangers. He certainly didn't want to have to describe his failure in the fight against Zavior in front of all them.

He cleared his throat and began.

"Well, we were heading north to a Færie gate in Scotland with Tally...um...our friend, Taliesin the Bard, when we were attacked by a Fæ named Zavior and the creatures he has created that he calls his Roki." He looked briefly at Orphan before continuing, "We tried to fight them off. Tally yelled at us to run then charged Zavior himself.

Next thing we knew we were somewhere else and Zavior, Tally, and the Roki were gone." Thane stopped to swallow the lump in his throat. "Embarr brought us to the cottage. We don't know what happened to Tally. We think he was killed by Zavior."

The silence around the table was deafening. He looked up to see all eyes on him except Orphan's. She was staring down at her hands.

"We have had grave reports from the other side concerning Zavior," Manannán mac Lir's voice broke the silence. "Taliesin the Bard is not dead; he has been taken captive by the Formoire."

"The Formoire?" Thane questioned. "Isn't Zavior Fæ?"

"Zavior has aligned himself with the forces of the Formoire" a Fæ sitting across from Orphan answered with a hard edge to his voice. "Fæ or not does not matter now. He is out of our control."

Thane sat stunned. He was both thrilled that Tally was alive and terrified at the thought of him in the hands of Zavior. He had been so sure that Tally had been killed. How had he survived so many Roki? Where would Zavior have taken him? He looked around the table at the beautiful Fæ and wondered how they could sit there and be so calm and indifferent. He scanned the room looking for someone willing to help Tally. He caught the eye of the man in the back of the room.

"You'll rescue him, right?" Orphan asked the King impatiently.

Thane's eyes swung back to his grandfather. "You must have a way to get to him…to get him out!" he said.

"Calm down, children," Manannán shook his head sadly. "We can do nothing to help him now. We cannot openly interfere in the interactions between the Formoire and the humans. It would mean war between our peoples," his Grandfather said firmly.

"What do you mean you can't interfere? Of course you can interfere. Zavior's one of you isn't he. You have to help Tally!" Orphan shouted. She was on her feet seemingly unaware that she was now shouting at a King. "It was not his fault. He was protecting us."

"The last time we gave aid to a human, it proved to be a mistake," he replied as his focus shifted briefly to the back of the room. Thane followed his eyes to the man standing by the door. Was he the human his grandfather was referring to?

"So you plan on leaving him in the hands of Zavior. Don't you understand? He will torture him or kill him," Thane argued.

"Nathaniel! That is enough!" his Grandfather's booming voice interrupted him in a tone that said Thane had gone too far. "I will hear no more about it and that is final. We are here to celebrate your return not to plan a rescue mission for a mere mortal. Now, sit down Ceara!" he commanded.

She looked down at Thane. He nodded shortly. She reluctantly sank back into her seat. There seemed to be nothing left to say.

Thane could feel the anger and worry radiating from Orphan in waves. Her knee jostled his as it bounced up and down under the table in agitation. Thane wasn't surprised to hear Orphan ask to be excused a short time later but was startled when she kicked him in the shin. It took all his will power to not cry out. He looked at her out of the corner of his eye and quickly realized that the wide-eyed look she was giving him meant she wanted him to leave as well.

Thane immediately turned to his grandfather and said, "Ah… Sir, may I be excused too. It has been a long day and I'm pretty tired."

"By all means," Manannán mac Lir granted permission to them both then stood up to address the table. "I would like to thank you for sharing our joy in finally finding our grandson Nathaniel and in welcoming both he and Ceara back." Thane scrambled hastily to his feet as the Fæ around him began to stand.

Sorcha appeared at their side to escort them back up to their rooms. As they walked out the door, Thane paused when he noticed that the strange man was gone. He shrugged and followed Orphan and Sorcha as they made their way in silence through the hallways and up the winding stairs. They made no comment as Sorcha bid them goodnight. "All will look better in the morning." She said as she shut the door behind first Orphan and then Thane.

Chapter Twenty-Three

A Stranger's Aid

Once alone, Thane paced restlessly around the room. He couldn't understand how his grandfather could leave an innocent man captive. Did he lack compassion? Well, Thane couldn't sleep curled up nice and comfortable in a warm soft bed knowing that Tally was out there possibly being tortured or about to be killed. He had to do something.

He cracked open his door and peaked outside. The hallway was deserted. He slipped out of his room and crept to Orphan's door. He knocked softly inwardly cursing the fact that she was now a girl and he couldn't just barge in. He could hear noises coming from inside the room.

"Orphan. It's me! Let me in!" he whispered through the door while looking over his shoulder to make sure no one was watching.

The door opened and a small pale hand reached through the crack and pulled him swiftly inside. He stood in the middle of the floor with his mouth open. Orphan had already changed into her old breeches and tunic in the short time that she had been back in her room. She looked like a he again. His best friend was back…sort of…

"Can you believe them?" she ranted as she turned her back on him and stalked toward the dresser. Her small bag was open and she had begun to pack.

"Well, I'm not crawling into bed and going to sleep like a good little child! I'm leaving. I'll find a way to free him myself."

He let out the breath he hadn't realized he'd been holding and said, "I feel the same way! Wait for me. I'm coming with you."

He eased back out of the room, snuck down the hall, and into his own. He quickly changed into his old clothes just as Orphan had done. He folded his new clothes and put them back on the chair next to the table. He hesitated when he picked up the new boots. They were sturdy and comfortable and his old ones were beginning to pinch his toes. He put the new boots back on his feet with a twinge of guilt. It wasn't like he was stealing, they had been given to him.

He laid the wooden practice sword across the pillows on the bed. It would be of no use to him where they were headed. After wrapping his extra clothes and sporran up in his spare shirt, he grabbed his cape, Tally's bag, his bow and arrows, and his dagger then slipped quietly from the room.

Once back in Orphan's room, he joined her on the end of the bed. "Do you have a plan?" he asked softly.

"No," she said miserably. The fight seemed to have drained out of her in the short time he had been gone. "I can't figure out how we are going to get out of this Færie land let alone find Tally.

They sat in silence. Each lost in their own doubts. Not only did they have to get out of the castle but they had to find a way to leave Tír inna n-Óc. Then, they would face the even bigger problem of how to find and rescue Tally. How were two relatively unskilled and inexperienced kids going to go up against a force as malevolent as Zavior and succeed? They had to try. Tally was not only their teacher, he was the closest thing they had to a father. They could not turn their backs on him now.

"Embarr!" Thane burst out.

"Shhh…what?" Orphan whispered.

"Embarr! He can get us out. He's a magical horse. He can walk on water!" Thane said excitedly. "You saw him…when we rode him across the sea, out of the waterfall, and over the pool."

"I thought it was Muirghein who made him walk across the water," she exclaimed excitedly.

"No. It was all Embarr. Do you remember that day when you first put on a dress?" he coughed uncomfortably at the memory. "Well, I had been riding him on the beach that day. I looked down and realized that he was running on top of the waves not through them. I was going to tell you but…uh…I forgot."

"Remember, that Tally said the woman who brought you to Anne rode a white horse 'out of the ocean.' He didn't say, 'along the beach.' I should have put it together before…I mean, how many white magical walk-on-water horses can there be?"

Thane paused for a moment as he tried to get his jumbled thoughts in order. He looked at Orphan.

"What?" Orphan said, confused.

He was not sure he wanted to share his next thought. She might be upset if he talked about her mother, but he continued because she needed to understand.

"Tally said the old woman told him that your mother rode a white horse across the water and she recognized Embarr as the same horse, right? So, he should be able to get us out of here just like he was able to get you and your mother across the sea."

Thane regretted mentioning her mother, because Orphan looked like she was going to cry. He quickly changed the subject and hopped off of the bed.

"Anyway, Tally said he's mine now. So I can take him wherever and whenever I want. I am sure he'll know how to get us out of here!" Thane picked up his belongings. "We should leave as soon as possible. Let's go find him," he said.

He headed to the door as Orphan slid off of the bed, and slowly picked up her bag. When she joined him at the door, he snuck a quick peek at her from under his eyelashes and was relieved to see she had pulled herself together. After first looking out to make sure that there was no one in the hall, they slid out of the room. Their boots made little noise on the thick rug in the hall but they had to tiptoe their way down the stone spiral staircase.

When they reached the main entryway, they paused. The Fæ guards were still at the end of the hallway in front of the Throne Room.

"What are we going to do?" she whispered in his ear.

Thane looked at Orphan and winked. "We walk out of here like we have every right to leave. My grandfather is the King, and he did say to treat this as our home, so we should be able to come and go as we please."

He pulled his shoulders back, lifted his chin and sauntered into the hall like he owned it; his cape billowed out behind him like a royal mantle. Orphan shrugged then followed suit. The guards didn't even glance their way. They walked right through the heavy front doors. No one tried to stop them.

Sentries were also still posted outside the entry doors. They tipped their standards to acknowledge Thane but didn't attempt to stop him or say anything to him, so Orphan and Thane continued on down the stairs without pause.

At the bottom of the stairs, Thane pulled Orphan to the side of the courtyard. Thane pointed to a narrow stone road and said, "I saw Embarr take that path when we first arrived. He galloped away like he knew exactly where he was going. Let's follow it."

The castle walls rose sharply up to their right as the cliff dropped steeply down to their left and disappeared into the river below. Thane walked as far from the edge as possible and tried to stay in the shadow of the castle wall hoping to remain unseen. They followed the path as it wound along the side of the castle as quickly as they dared.

Thane stopped abruptly as he rounded the corner of the path. Orphan plowed right into his back with a whoosh. "What's wrong?" she hissed.

"Look," he said and turned sideways so she could peer around him. "I think that's the stables."

"Whoa, I wouldn't have minded spending my winters sleeping in there!" she whispered in awe.

The long low structure was carved out of the cliff wall. Great stone pillars and arches marked the wide entrance to the stables. Here again, two Fæ sentries stood guard. Rows of shuttered windows suggested dozens of stalls lined both sides of the entrance.

"I bet he's in there. Come on," Thane said.

No one stopped them as they walked boldly up to the immense silver doors. As before, the sentries tipped their standards to acknowledge Thane's presence. A sentry opened one of the doors and Thane and Orphan stepped boldly through the doorway. The sentry closed the door firmly behind them.

Thane breathed in the familiar stable scents. He closed his eyes. He could easily imagine that he was back in the loft at the inn. He smiled to himself as he thought, "No matter how fancy a place may look, horses smelled like horses."

Silver gate posts held chest high doors of whitewashed carved wood. Lanterns topped the posts, glowing with the same strange white light they had seen in the castle. It was just enough light to see by without disturbing the sleeping horses. Orphan nudged Thane and pointed to the right. Embarr was in the last stall. He was standing at the gate watching them. Standing beside him was the older man from dinner.

Thane stopped, unsure of what to do next. Would this stranger prevent them from leaving? Would he alert the King?

"Nathaniel," the man greeted him with a nod then turned to Orphan, "Ceara."

He waved his hand and indicated that they should join him. Up close, Thane could see that he was older than Thane initially thought.

Fine lines fanned out from the corners of his blue eyes and his dark brown hair was sprinkled liberally with gray. He knew this man's face but he still couldn't place it.

"Who are you?" Orphan demanded from behind Thane.

"That is irrelevant. Right now, what is important is getting to Taliesin. I had a feeling you two were not going to let things lie as the King decreed. You are right in your belief that Taliesin will not last long in the hands of Zavior. I know he will be tortured for information about you and your whereabouts. I believe Taliesin will hold fast but he cannot last long against such determined evil. He is no longer a young man and is, after all, only a mortal."

"Thane, he is at the castle of your youth. Embarr will take you to him if you request it of him." The man put his large hand on Thane's shoulder. "He can find him."

"I have packed food, water, and extra arrows for your quest," he turned to Orphan and said, "Are you sure I cannot persuade you to remain behind?"

She frowned up at him and shook her head.

"I thought not. I have placed a vile of elixir and a spare poultice for your wound in one of the side bags. Use them sparingly. I understand they are quite strong. They should help you mend."

Thane looked at Embarr and realized that he had been saddled and there were bulging bags hanging over his sides. Thane was confused but grateful. "Thank you," he said hesitantly. "Why are you helping us?"

"One more thing..." the stranger continued as if Thane hadn't spoken, "...you will not be able to defeat Zavior in a face to face confrontation. You would most certainly lose. You must find your way into the castle unobserved. Stealth will give you your sole chance for success. I am confident you will know what to do when you get there."

"I believe that the Fæ vulnerability to iron does not effect you?" The stranger reached behind him to grab something that was leaning against the wall in the shadows. "Take this. I have no use for it here and you will need more protection than that small dagger at your side." In his large hands he held a scabbard wrapped with a thick leather belt that held a long steel sword.

Thane was dumbfounded. "You're giving this to me?" he stuttered. "Why? Why not just come with us?" His eyes lifted from the sheathed blade to the man's blue eyes.

"I cannot leave here. You must do this on your own." He thrust the sword into Thane's hands and turned him toward Embarr. "Hurry, it will not be long before you are missed and your intentions discovered."

Thane thanked him. Without examining the sword, he secured it and his bow to the saddle, and shoved their bags into the large leather packs hanging from Embarr's side. He hoisted himself up on the horse's sturdy back and waited nervously while Orphan was helped up behind him. He turned around and saw her breathing through clenched teeth. Her face was pale again and little beads of sweat dotted her forehead.

"What are you looking at?" she grumbled in his ear.

"You! You look awful. Are you going to be all right?" he asked.

"I'm just fine!" she said as she gripped the wool of his cape to hold on. He just hoped that whatever medicine they gave her had healed her enough for this. He was afraid she was still too weak.

The man led them out of the stables. With one last stroke of Embarr's neck, he handed the reigns to Thane and said, "Good luck." He gently slapped Embarr's flank.

Embarr galloped along the path that led around the castle. Thane looked back as they rounded the last corner. The stranger was silhouetted against the light from the stables, standing where they had left him with his arms folded across his chest, watching them go.

Embarr headed noisily over the bridge and into the dense pine forest. He followed the same path they had traveled earlier that morning. Thane and Orphan both breathed a little easier once they were out of sight of the castle.

"Who do you suppose he is?' Orphan asked over Thane's shoulder.

"Who? The stranger in the stables? I don't know. He looks really familiar though. I think I have seen him somewhere before... maybe he stayed at the inn? Did you recognize him?"

"No. I don't think so," Orphan rested her head on his back and mumbled into the wool, "I wonder why he helped us?"

Thane shrugged. Embarr was trotting briskly through the pine forest. He seemed to be as eager to leave the castle behind as they were. He moved confidently through the woods despite the darkness.

The pale flowers brushed across their faces as they entered the grove of ancient trees. Thane could hear the roar of falling water as they neared the pool. They had finally arrived at the waterfall. Thane pulled Embarr to a halt for a moment as they gazed at the beauty of the scene before them.

Silver moonlight glistened off of the surface of the water transforming the pool into a mirror that reflected the pale blossoms and sky above. Orphan's arms tightened around his waist as he led Embarr slowly across the surface of the water to stand on the stone platform before the falls.

Thane turned around in the saddle and looked into Orphan's eyes.

"Are you sure you're up to this?" he asked her one last time.

She took a deep breath and nodded, "Let's go."

Thane turned back to face the waterfall.

"Embarr, take us to Tally!" Thane commanded the horse. Orphan buried her face in his back with a groan. He laughed out loud as Embarr lifted his head and whinnied. They charged forward through the waterfall and disappeared…

ACKNOWLEDGEMENTS

Writing is a solitary endeavor, but as John Donne wrote in 1624: "...No man is an island...." As cliché as the quote sounds, it has proven to be true. I could not have written this book and prepared it for publishing if not for my family and friends.

I can't thank my wonderful husband, Joel, enough for his love and support. He is the other half of my heart, my mind, and my soul.

My four children, Alex, Chris, Jon, and Katie, are my inspiration. Thanks for all the nights you made dinner and for your unending enthusiasm. My Mom and my Aunt Adla have always been there to love and encourage me.

Thanks to my wonderful friends who have spent the better part of the last two years reading my manuscript. A huge thanks to Kimberlie Fair for late nights, lots of giggles, and for making sure I said what I thought I was saying. Yep, Yep, Yep...

Made in the USA
San Bernardino, CA
17 December 2013